The Bridge Between

Mamommy~

An Edisto Novel

Enjoy Edisto!

Lindsey P. Brackett

by

LINDSEY P. BRACKETT

FIREFLY
SOUTHERN FICTION
LIGHTHOUSE PUBLISHING OF THE CAROLINAS

THE BRIDGE BETWEEN BY LINDSEY P. BRACKETT
Published by Firefly Southern Fiction
an imprint of Lighthouse Publishing of the Carolinas
2333 Barton Oaks Dr., Raleigh, NC 27614

ISBN: 978-1-64526-076-9
Copyright © 2019 by Lindsey Brackett
Cover design by Elaina Lee
Interior design by Karthick Srinivasan

Available in print from your local bookstore, online, or from the publisher at:
ShopLPC.com

For more information on this book and the author visit: LindseyPBrackett.com

Brought to you by the creative team at Lighthouse Publishing of the Carolinas:
Eva Marie Everson, Jennifer Slattery

Library of Congress Cataloging-in-Publication Data
Brackett, Lindsey P.
The Bridge Between / Lindsey P. Brackett 1st ed.

Printed in the United States of America

PRAISE FOR *THE BRIDGE BETWEEN*

Lindsey Brackett, once again, brings Edisto to life in her second novel *The Bridge Between*. Her descriptions of the island were so real and stirring, I needed to step out of my office located on Edisto, and go take it in for myself! Her characters capture interest right away and her ability to project their emotions and empathy is a rare talent.

~**Julie Gyselinck**
Editor *Explore Edisto* Magazine

In *The Bridge Between*, Lindsey Brackett has penned a story that will hit you in the heart, in that sacred place between the sweet and the bitter. Reminding us that forgiveness is the only way to truly heal tangled thens and broken nows, she weaves a beautiful, sometimes heart-aching, tapestry of two families who stand at the cusp of what was always meant to be. A must-read!

~**Carrie Schmidt**
ReadingIsMySuperPower.org

A delightful story, rich in detail and nuance in both setting and character. *The Bridge Between* is insightful as to the heart's motivation and celebrates Southern culture as focused on South Carolina's wind-swept Edisto Island. This is a wonderfully entwined story that examines inter-personal relationships, the meaning of family ties, life's choices and far-reaching repercussions. Relatable, engaging, and full of well-drawn personality, *The Bridge Between* is an absorbing, satisfying read.

~**Claire Fullerton**
Author of *Mourning Dove*

Lindsey Brackett can weave a story that leaves you waiting for the next one. I loved her debut novel and her sophomore one, *The Bridge Between,* doesn't disappoint. Realistic characters, a great plotline, sigh-worthy romance, plot twists and surprises ... what more can you want?

~**Ane Mulligan**
Bestselling author of the *Chapel Springs* series

ACKNOWLEDGMENTS

If writing a first book is a dream, writing a second is when dreams become reality and reality becomes work. Which makes this by far my favorite job.

Once the words are on the page (this involves copious amounts of tears, coffee, and peanut M&Ms), there are many hands creating the book you now hold. I owe so much gratitude to the following people for their patience—and their ability to read between the lines of a text message or an email:

Eva Marie Everson who has believed in my words from the beginning and gave me the gracious gift, not only of her wisdom, but her friendship as well.

Jennifer Slattery, my wonderful editor, who unknowingly helped me find my niche when she sent back the first draft with instructions to rewrite as dual timeline.

Kimberly Duffy, Leslie DeVooght, and Hope Welborn—our friendship and partnership is a blessing. Here's to many more books—and Voxer messages—together.

Taryn Souders, Sarah Bulls, and Heather Iseminger, aka the Party House Girls, for keeping me up too late drinking peppermint tea and writing rough drafts.

Leslie Terrell who asked me to please write this story, Melissa Wood who read it long before it was ready, and Salena McKay who found mistakes I missed.

Nurse Grace Holt and her father, Dr. Gordon Weigle, who answered my medical related questions and helped me figure out the best plan of care for Cole's injury. Any mistakes are mine (and probably influenced by my watching of *Grey's Anatomy*).

Every reader who took a chance on a debut author. You have given me the courage to persevere. I'm so glad to return to Edisto with you!

My Payne-ful siblings and Ashworth-Beeson cousins, who let me pull from our childhood to tell these stories. Remember Bo in the bathtub at Grandmommy's?

The wonderful people of Edisto who helped make sure I got it right: John Girault of the Edisto Island Open Land Trust, Gretchen Smith of the Edisto Island Museum, and the lovely ladies of Explore Edisto, Julie Gyselinck and Caroline Matheny.

I could never live this dream if it wasn't for the support of my husband, Joshua. Thank you for never letting me walk away from an argument—especially the ones about how I should just give up and go back to a regular job.

To my children, Madelynne, Annabelle, Amelia, and Gus who never fail to remind me that being Mom is my first and most important job, thank you for letting me use up all your sticky notes and sharpies plotting this book on the back porch last summer.

As always, to the One who seeks our reconciliation—thank you Jesus for putting words into my fingertips and allowing me to share them with the world as you show me your good, perfect, and pleasing will (Romans 12: 1-2).

DEDICATION

For Mama who makes the best biscuits and Daddy who sits on the porch with the whippoorwills.

Chapter 1

She still had trouble sleeping.

Standing back from the porch eaves, so the rain wouldn't dampen her flannel pajamas, Lou warmed her hands around her coffee. She'd switched to decaf in the last year—and limited herself to only one cup after dinner—but nearly every night she found herself right here.

Wasn't just Lowcountry storms or her uncertain future keeping her awake. More often than not it was the creaking of those old rockers on the front porch.

Memories rolled over her, keeping time with thunder and flashes of lightning. During storms, Daddy had always sat on the back porch, watching. Clouds, the color of the steel wool Mama used on the cast iron skillet, would bank low over the tidal creek then move across the pastures and pines.

"A storm can scrape land the way wool scrapes rust," her daddy would say, the rocker creaking in tempo with his worry.

Her childhood had been a mix of faith—and superstition. Before she and the boys moved into the Edisto farmhouse, she'd had Tennessee Watson repaint the porch ceiling with a fresh coat of haint blue paint.

Yet those rockers still swayed, even when the wind wasn't whipping a frenzy like now.

Storm debris whirled around the yard. The leaves of the weeping willow, of course—and tiny branches from that big old live oak with the tire swing. Pine needles, because what Edisto Island lacked in sophistication, it made up for with pine trees.

"These trees are our bread and butter," Daddy had told her time and again. Then he'd hold up hands sticky with sap remnants, red and chapped from bundling pine straw into bales for hauling and selling to the landscape designers of Charleston. "Even if they don't taste as good."

Lou stepped back inside, fingering the greenery looped over the back porch door. At Christmas, she and Carolina had strung pinecones and magnolia into garland. Just like Mama always did.

She turned a slow circle until she faced the closed door of the little room where her mother had drawn her last breath. Cora Anne was after her to clean it out, set it up as a little office. After only a semester at Tulane University, her daughter had come back to Edisto. Said she'd found where she belonged.

Time for Lou to do the same.

She pushed at the door. It swung easily. Winter's cool had drawn back the wood's summer swelling. Probably why she kept finding it creaked open an inch or two.

Inside, the spindle bed sat neatly made, but the rocker in the corner swayed with the breeze through the now open door.

She shivered, though despite being shut up, the room's air wasn't cold. This house was simply old—her grandfather had built it, after all—and settling with its memories. Swallowing past the lump gathering in her throat, Lou edged her way inside.

Things were left just as they had been when Mama passed. Pictures and afghans warming the new paint and refinished floor. Lou spied a green shoebox on the side table.

Her own cache of secrets.

She'd left it there the day after Mama's funeral and hadn't opened it since. Too many other things to worry about besides old letters and mementos from her college days. Now she strode across the room and flicked off the box lid. Ran her fingertip across the neat filing of correspondence.

If technology kept advancing the way it had in the last decade, her children wouldn't have boxes like this.

Her hand paused over the envelopes—and a whelk shell that had just fit the palm of her hand. She drew away. May be better if some things remained hidden.

But words her mother had once written Cora Anne came to mind. *We can't carry past despair into the future.*

Lou whipped out the letter.

October 1, 1974

Dear Mama,

Patrick Watson has been writing me. I know you disapprove, even though you say you don't. The way you press your lips together in a thin line when I mention his name—that's your tell. Maybe we'll just be friends. Maybe we'll be more. I don't know. It was one dance at the Pavilion on the last night of summer vacation.

But he makes my heart skip a little.

Her fingers trembled. Once, Pat had made her heart skip. Then David made it gallop like the horses of old, racing down the Botany Bay road. Now he and she both lived with broken hearts.

But at least they lived.

~ ~ ~

David didn't know how else to prove he wanted to be here.

Bumping his newish four-wheel drive Jeep into Lou's yard, derelict leaves and sticks ground beneath his tires. A vehicle meant for this rural community, not the suburb they'd left behind.

The boys' duffels were in a heap at the bottom of the porch steps. Between great arching runs on the tire swing, his triplet sons tossed treats to the barn cats. They were in the gangly-ness of adolescence, all arms and legs—and mouths to feed.

David loped across the dead grass, ducked as he got too close to the swing, and met his ex-wife at the kitchen door. "Since that tree survived their Uncle Jimmy, I guess it'll hold our boys."

"Lord, I hope so." Lou shaded her eyes. The morning sun trekked across the sky. Tonight it would set in one year, and in the morning, rise with another.

David scrubbed a hand through his cropped hair. He'd buzzed the sides extra short yesterday when he noticed gray at his temples. What a thing for a man to realize, that at nearly fifty, he was vainer than he'd ever thought. "You sure you're okay with me having them?"

She crossed her arms. "It's your weekend, David."

"I just meant, because it's New Year's Eve—"

"And I'll be all alone?"

"No one should be alone on New Year's."

She lowered her chin, eyes raking over his old sweats emblazoned with the logo of the high school where they'd taught together for twenty years. "I'll be fine. Cora Anne's coming back."

Huffing, he rolled his eyes like the teenagers in his classroom. "She'll have that boy with her."

"That boy is a man."

"Yeah, that's what I don't like."

Now she smiled. "Yes, you do. He grounds her in a way we never could."

David flinched. "It's coming, isn't it?" He could feel it every time Tennessee Watson spoke to him. As if the young man were biding his time until he was sure David wouldn't protest his daughter was far too young to get married.

Of course, she was nearly the same age he and Lou had been. Then again, look how that worked out.

"No doubt." Lou tugged at her sleeves, drawing them down over her fingers.

"You look good."

She shook her head, but he caught the slight upturn at the corner of her lips. He wasn't kidding. Lou in a ratty long-sleeved tee, and jeans that hugged her in all the right places, had always been his favorite. But mostly, he meant the lines of her face. The furrow between her eyes—the one he had caused—had lessened in the last few months.

"Why are you so chipper today?"

"Got good news. Colleton High hired me to finish out the year. History teacher had to take an extended leave of absence."

She held his gaze without blinking, unfurling something he thought he'd long ago put to rest. "That is good news."

He stepped closer, heard her breath catch. "What about your job hunt?"

To his disappointment, Lou opened the screen door, putting space back between them. "Interview with Dr. Whiting next week. Let's get those bags loaded so you can be on your way."

He followed her inside anyway. "College of Charleston doesn't know what they're missing. You'll be a full-time professor before long, I'm sure."

"Are you?" Her tone turned icy. The triplets' whoops from the yard pierced the heavy silence falling between them.

"What you got going on today?" David changed the subject by perusing the house. All her mother's antique canisters were in the same spots on the worn countertop, though she'd added a basket of grab-and-go snacks for the boys. One of the few changes she'd made since moving in.

And why should he care? She was the one living here with the ghosts of her parents in every knickknack and basic necessity. Like that box of old letters sitting on the kitchen table.

"Thought I'd take down the decorations. Bad luck to leave the tree up past New Year's, you know." How much she sounded like her mother.

"Hey, Dad!" Cole hit the door first, Mac and J.D. panting behind. "Got sparklers for tonight?"

"You know it. And some frozen pizzas too."

They groaned as a unit.

J.D. sidled up to Lou. "You know, Mom, you could come over for dinner…"

"And bring that lasagna you already have made…" Mac wagged eyebrows under his fringe of dark curls.

David grabbed their sons in a headlock, one under each arm, except for Cole, who used his smaller size to his advantage and dodged away. "Are you saying my culinary skills are no match for Mom's?"

"Definitely." That was Mac, ever truthful.

"Boys, go get your duffels in the car." They swarmed through the door. David reached out, crossing the line Lou and he kept with one another. Touched her shoulder, gently, as he would a friend. "Come on over if you get lonely."

She jerked away. "I'll be fine."

He wanted to pull her into an embrace, hold her tight, and let her break the dam holding back all those memories, though Lou had never been one for emotional displays.

But he hadn't followed her all the way to her childhood home to keep letting her weep alone.

Chapter 2

"Found you a conch." Patrick Watson passed the treasure to Lou while they squinted in the white sun bearing down on a strip of quiet beach. They'd left his car at the Edisto State Park and traipsed the low tide land bridge down the shore to Botany Bay, with its bare bones of trees. Haunting and romantic.

Where they'd shared their first kiss.

Lou ran her thumb over the points of the large shell, curve intact and streaked with hues of orange. "Whelk," she corrected, her scientific mind always searching for precision.

Patrick nudged closer along the driftwood log on which they'd perched, sliding his arm around her waist. "Well, Lula May was always calling 'em conch fritters when she'd fry up a batch in the kitchen."

One didn't question Lula May, the Watsons' housemaid, as native an islander as they came.

"Go ahead, see if there's a critter still inside." Patrick's voice teased in her ear.

Lou turned the shell into her palm—and paused. Suddenly her head knew what her gut had been trying to tell her all day. "I have news."

Patrick dug his heels into the sand. But still, he cocked his head to listen.

"The research study at Emory—I got in."

He pulled his arm from her waist and bent forward, hands clasped over his knees. "Oh." He pushed himself up and faced the waves that eroded this shore a bit at a time until someday it would be no more.

"How long does that mean you'll be in Atlanta?"

The man who looked back at her wasn't the impish boy she'd fallen in love with—he was rock steady and knew what he wanted. So did she.

"Two years, at least." When his eyes narrowed, she added, "But we can trade weekends, maybe?" She knew the offer was feeble. Neither of them could afford that kind of constant travel. Not when she would be neck-deep in graduate work and research, while he tried to build a business—literally with his own two hands. His parents had flat out said no, they wouldn't invest in construction on Edisto Beach.

He nodded at the shell. "Told you there's something inside."

She tapped it against her palm and the ring landed softly against her skin. Plain gold, simple solitaire. Exactly what she'd want.

If she wanted this.

"Patrick, I…" She looked at him, silhouetted against the sun.

He dropped to his knees in the sand and took her hands. "Don't do this. We can be happy here, I promise. You can research here—study the beach and the creeks and help me keep them safe."

"I'm a chemist, Pat. Not an ecologist." She worked the ring from her palm to his. "We've been fooling ourselves a long time."

Defeated, he stayed on his knees. "You mean you've been making a fool of me."

The tears burning her throat rushed to the surface, stinging the corners of her eyes like the salt spray beating the shore. "That's not true and you know it. I love you."

"But not enough to marry me."

"Do you love me enough to leave?"

There, she'd done it. Said the words that hovered between them always, since the first time they'd shared each other's dreams. She wanted nothing less than to leave. He wanted nothing more than to stay.

They had reached an impasse, like the rising tide that could trap them here, with their sorrow and regret, on a beach made of bones. She stumbled away, promising herself she'd perfect the talent of leaving. He stayed behind, letting the bridge between them close.

Chapter 3

A kick sounded on his door. When David jerked it open, expecting one of his boys, the reprimand died on his lips. There stood Lou, a casserole tote swinging from one arm, plate of brownies balanced on her hand.

"There's a doorbell, you know," he drawled, reaching for the salad bowl under her other arm.

"Ha ha." She shifted the brownies. "You really don't mind me crashing your time?"

"Do we look like we mind?" He gave her a tour of his new townhome, custom built by the man who might become their son-in-law. From the narrow front porch, one could hear the ocean crashing only a few blocks away. But the small balcony off the second story overlooked the marsh. "Just the right amount of yard work for me."

She laughed, a rusty sound he'd like to coax out more. "As in none, you mean."

"I do like to let nature do her thing." He led her back downstairs, through a hall that emptied into the main living space, a kitchen-living-dining combo. Open floor plan, like he'd always wanted.

Lou liked her spaces sectioned off, orderly. Each thing where it belonged.

For dinner, they settled around the table, like the family they used to be. Lou still made lasagna with layers of heavy sauce sweetened by Italian sausage, but David resisted the urge to moan in homage to her cooking. Instead he refilled her wine without asking.

To a new year—and a new beginning.

After dinner, he made a pot of coffee, surprised when she asked for decaf.

She nestled in a corner of his leather sofa without remarking on its stiffness, an age-old argument they'd had when choosing furniture. The boys tried to get her to play their game, and she only raised one brow at him when she saw the rating on the cover.

He sweetened her coffee with cream and sugar and brought it over.

"Thank you." She smiled up at him, and he saw their daughter and sons in the curve of her jaw. But in her eyes, she still carried the anguish that had been there when she kicked on his door that afternoon.

Biting off more questions, he nodded and brought his own mug over to settle in his old wingback, the only piece he'd claimed from the house during the divorce. Lou and he could enjoy tonight, the façade of family pleasing their boys, but they needed to talk and soon. He didn't like her holing up in that house, dredging up past regrets that ought to lie buried in the Presbyterian Church cemetery.

He propped his feet on the coffee table, blocking the boys' view.

"No fair, Dad!" Cole leapt up and delivered a final blow. "Ha! You're done, J.D."

"You're all done." David crossed his ankles. "Get the cards out of the cabinet, Mac, and let's see if we can take your mom at hearts."

Mac dealt, and David led with the two of clubs. "You know, boys, I taught your mom to play this."

"That's not true. You taught me to play gin because it's easier for two."

He tapped the cards against his palm, eyes on hers. She hid a grin behind the fan of her own cards.

J.D. played and won the trick. "Looks like we're going to take you both."

The boys did win the first three rounds, but on the fourth, Lou laid down a six of hearts. Mac collapsed against the sofa back, hand to his chest. "Mom did it. She broke our hearts."

But from that moment, Lou won trick after trick, chortling at the boys' demise—and blushing when her eyes met his. He turned on Dick Clark around eleven and they got a crash course in popular music from the boys.

J.D. picked along with Rascal Flatts. "Tennessee's teaching me, you know." The pride reverberated in his voice the way the strings sent music all around the little room.

His brothers started a game of Slap Jack. Reluctantly, J.D. laid the instrument aside. David glanced at Lou, wondering if she thought what he did. They'd never discouraged the triplets' individuality—but they hadn't encouraged it either.

Lou stood and gathered the empty mugs. She jerked her head toward the kitchen. He followed.

"He's borrowing one right now, but Tennessee can get us a deal on a used guitar if we want it for his birthday," she whispered, rinsing mugs in his sink. "But I don't have any ideas for the others."

He grabbed a towel and began to dry, noticing they'd slipped back into this habit with ease. "Do the other two have an obsession beyond baseball yet?"

"You mean besides gory video games?"

The lilt in her voice chided him, so he bumped her hip with his. "Or running your daddy's old boat up and down the creek?"

"Fair enough."

"Ball's dropping!" Mac shouted.

The boys chanted with the screen, "Ten-nine-eight-seven-six-five-four-three-two-one!" They catapulted around the room blowing the noisemakers he'd picked up at the Piggly Wiggly and causing the general ruckus they were known for.

"Sparkler time." Cole grabbed the package and headed out the door, his brothers on his heels.

Outside was clear—a sailor's dream sky. The boys set off the sparklers against the midnight black and whooped when someone a few streets over sent up a spray of light.

Lou stamped her feet and rubbed her arms. "I'm going to freeze to death." She'd traded her earlier t-shirt for a sweater, and David could tell it was thin by the way the fabric skimmed her body.

"Here." He slid his coat around her shoulders, pulling the collar close under her chin and brushing aside her chestnut hair. She'd let it grow beyond her jaw for the first time in at least a decade.

"Thank you." They stood that way for only a moment—but in the freshness of the new year under skies beaded with light—eternity could have come and he would've died a happy man.

"Can I ask you something?"

Her eyes shifted from his. "Of course."

"Why'd you really come over?"

Lou shrugged. His coat slipped from her shoulder. He reached to fix it, but she stepped away, tugging its folds back around her slender frame. She'd lost weight since her mother died. She might not think he noticed those things anymore. But he did.

Arms pulled tight across her middle again when she said, "You invited me."

David tipped back his chin. He might never get tired of that clear Edisto night sky. "So I did."

"Cora Anne went to Charleston with Tennessee, and I was—" Her teeth clicked as she bit off her words.

"Overcome with worry for the boys' stomachs." He gave her the out he knew she wanted, and she rewarded him with a crooked smile.

"Besides, I figured if I brought dinner my chances were three times better for a New Year's kiss." Her eyes widened with the implication of what she'd said.

The first time he'd kissed her had been on New Year's Eve, so many years and ideals go. He'd have kissed her the day they'd met, if he'd thought he could get away with it. Getting this woman to bend her rules had always been one of his favorite pastimes.

On that New Year's Eve, she'd been wearing a long dress—with a deep V of a neckline that made him catch his breath when he picked her up for the party. "Thought I'd try something different tonight," she'd said.

Maybe tonight she'd want to be different again. He put his lips to her ear, testing. Murmured, "You never know. Might just be four times better."

But Lou pressed her hand to his chest. "We've had a good night."

David dropped his arms to his sides and stepped back from her touch. "Yes, we have."

"I'm going to head home, let you wrangle the three mischief-teers."

"You're sure?" *Stay*, he wanted to whisper.

But emotion-laden impulses had never served them well.

"We both made choices, David." Her eyes shone in the moonlight for a moment, then she blinked and any sheen of tears disappeared. "But I'm glad you're here."

She walked away from him and called goodnight to the boys. Leaving, a tactic she'd long ago perfected.

Chapter 4

Atlanta, Georgia, October 1975

The Emory green space on a sweaty October afternoon demanded pick-up games. Of course, touch football, as interpreted by David and his fraternity brothers, meant full body contact. Sorority girls lined the field's edges and cheered for the makeshift teams.

Winner got first pick for that night's parties. This was no collegiate World Series, but he felt good.

Almost strong again.

The pass went long, and he took off, side-stepping the other team. He ignored the pop in his knee—it would just have to keep up— and stretched his arms. Fingertips grazed—then gripped—the ball. Momentum stumbled him past the designated end zone. His knee buckled and he fell.

Into someone.

His shoulder caught her squarely in the chest, and they tumbled down together. Her books and his legs sprawled across the sidewalk. Gasps and laughter, catcalls and whistles, pounded behind the sharp edged ache no longer confined to his knee.

David tried sitting up, hoping that would make the green space stop spinning.

"Get off me." The girl's voice shook. She shoved him aside. He nearly fell back again but braced himself, the football still cradled in his arm.

"Sorry about that." His tongue struggled with the words.

"You frat boys have no manners."

Now the girl loomed over him, dark ponytail, eyes like blue flames.

He blinked. Tried to clear the stars from his vision.

She knelt. "You're on my book."

He shifted, and she retrieved a thick textbook. The movement made him woozy. Such a good word for this feeling.

"Hey, are you all right?" She touched his face, turned his chin, and clicked her tongue against her teeth. "You're bleeding, but there's a big goose egg, so at least you didn't smash your brains in." She pulled a handkerchief from her pocket and pressed it against his temple.

He squinted at this girl who was straightforward—but with an ounce of compassion. She looked past him. "Aren't your friends going to hold the game for you?"

"I think I just made the winning touchdown."

She huffed. "Hope it was worth it."

"You know." He focused his eyes on hers and the spinning eased. "I think it was."

"Let's get you to the infirmary, frat boy." She pulled him to his feet, and he slung an arm around her shoulders—for balance, of course.

This girl could fit right under his chin, so he stooped a little and tried not to put too much weight on his bum knee. She smelled good, despite the stack of chemistry books in her hand. Nothing antiseptic, which was the first scent that hit him when she pushed open the infirmary door. He turned his nose to her dark hair instead.

Lavender.

"Are you sniffing my head?" She ducked away and waved him to a chair.

"Sure. You smell clean."

"It's called showering." Her eyes went to the sweat stains on his t-shirt. "You should try it."

"Hey, David Halloway." The nurse behind the desk came over with a clipboard. "What did you do now?"

"Well…" He tipped a smile at the nurse—old enough to be his mother. "I got knocked down by this pretty lady. You better check her out too."

She crossed her arms. "You ran into me." To the nurse, she said,

"Better check his head. Took a hard hit to the concrete. Clearly he's a little mixed up." The nurse made a note, and the girl added, "And his knee. He's limping."

David stretched his leg. "Nope, knee's fine."

"We'll get you back in a minute."

When the nurse walked away, the girl put her hands on her hips. "Your knee is not fine."

He shrugged. "Yeah, I busted it back in March playing baseball. You might have heard of my team—the Emory Eagles?"

Arms back to crossed. Not impressed. "So now you're a semi-professional clumsy athlete?"

Ouch. Time to give some of that coldness back to her. "Nope. Just a college recruit who can't play anymore and might lose his scholarship."

Her mouth rounded. Then her lips—which he'd already noticed bore only the faintest sheen of gloss—pressed together. "I'm sorry."

"Me, too." He held out a hand. "David, by the way."

She shook—no surprise about that firm grip—and sat down beside him. "Louisa Coultrie."

"Well, Louisa Coultrie …" What a lot of vowels. But he liked the way her name made his mouth stretch. He shifted and leaned into her. "Want to grab some dinner with me after this?"

Her palms rubbed the knees of her bell-bottom jeans. "I … actually have plans." He raised his brows, and she shrugged. "To get Chinese takeout and watch the World Series."

"You know … " He feigned interest in his fingernails. "I might like baseball a little bit."

"Just a little bit?"

Peeking at her, he saw the smirk. How it brought out a faint dimple in her left cheek. "Cincinnati's going to take it all."

"No way. Boston's got this."

"Want to bet on it?"

The eye roll put her gaze squarely back on his. He liked her eyes, blue as a summer sky. "Sure, frat boy."

"Loser buys second dinner."

Laughter came from someplace deep, and David figured she didn't let loose like this often. If ever. "Did you just trick me into a second date before we've had a first?"

"I might not be able to play the game anymore." He brushed a hand over her ponytail. "But that doesn't mean I don't know how to win."

Chapter 5

The next afternoon, Lou set a pot of collard greens and another of black-eyed peas on the stove to simmer. She'd wait to make cornbread when David brought the boys home. Maybe she'd invite him to stay.

After all, those black-eyed peas were supposed to bring luck for a new year.

Though they probably both needed to eat a double dose of collards since early retirement salaries weren't going to raise—or feed—three teenage boys for very long.

Feeling nostalgic, or maybe just masochistic, Lou retrieved the box of letters.

She lifted the shell from the box and held it to her ear the way children do, listening for the sound of the ocean. After Patrick's proposal, she had walked all the way back into town and called her daddy from the Whaley's payphone, before realizing she'd kept the shell. Into the box it had gone, memories sealed with tears and dust, while she forged a new life away from this place that once held her captive.

"Captivity's a mind game, Louisa." Her mother's voice echoed in her thoughts. "We're only imprisoned by what we let hold us."

But the Edisto of her youth had been a yoke around her neck. Too plebian and too isolated for her mind caught up in the progressive movement of the seventies. She'd wanted the freedom to make her own choices and forge her own way.

Fearing if she didn't leave then, she'd spend the rest of her life following the boot prints of her daddy through a muddy field.

~~~

If only Grace had learned to keep her mouth shut. Or hardened her heart. One would think a lifetime of abandonment would do that.

But nope, she'd always bled wide and open, arteries pumping compassion for all to see. Which is how she wound up in charge of the January food drive. Not only that, but canvassing the island for folks to personally hand over their leftover canned goods and extra bags of holiday baking flour.

She bumped over the ruts in the old dirt road leading to the Coultrie homestead. There she'd be forced to have a conversation with Louisa Halloway without the buffer of their children between them.

They weren't friends or enemies or hardly even acquaintances, but soon, if the look in her son's eyes stayed true, they'd be family.

Grace slowed the car with a mile to go.

She'd never been jealous of Louisa. Not even when Patrick first shared their story. To her mind, Lou had done the leaving, and he'd picked up the pieces, fitting his heart neatly back together and giving it to her full and whole and ready for something new. She'd never doubted his love for her, and until the night he died, she'd never thought Louisa Coultrie had really cared.

Grace pressed a little harder on the pedal now as the white house came into sight at the end of a dirt lane, bordered with pecan trees. In the distance, Russell Creek glinted in the afternoon sun. She remembered the stream of visitors pouring in for Annie's funeral, parking all over the one field Thornton Coultrie hadn't sown with pine trees.

"Lou sees difficulties instead of opportunities is all. You can help her, Grace." Mrs. Annie's words echoed in her head. She'd promised.

Cora Anne's worn Civic was in the drive, and Grace didn't even try to control her relief. But when she knocked on the back porch screen, Louisa, wariness in the edges of her blue eyes, came to the door.

"Hey, there." Grace's Tennessee twang crept in under the Lowcountry rounding of vowels she'd learned to emulate. But she could never possess the accent—especially when nervous. "Happy New Year."

"Same to you." Louisa's voice sounded raspy, as though she'd been crying. "Would you like to come in?" But she didn't push open the screen.

The formality of the invitation—and Lou's ramrod-straight stance—would've quelled someone raised with these genteel rules.

Yet Grace nodded and pulled the door. "Sure is cold out here today."

Lou tightened a cardigan across her chest. "It's that wind off the Atlantic, my father used to always say."

The kitchen was impeccable, except for a worn box of letters on the table, though without the warmth Annie had always given it. By now Lou's mother would've had the teakettle going, the breadbox open, and her chatter filling the space. As it was, Lou merely shifted foot to foot and looked at Grace.

Well, small talk never had been one of the woman's attributes.

"The church has me collecting for the food pantry, so I'm doing some old-fashioned canvassing. Figure now that the holidays are behind us, most people have a little extra taking up room."

"Doesn't hurt that most probably made the obligatory 'eat healthier' resolution yesterday." Lou crooked her fingers around the words, and actually grinned.

Grace laughed. "Made that one myself. Course Tennessee will undo it by bringing home a key lime pie before long."

"Oh, let's break it now." Lou jammed the lid with its busted corners back on the shoebox, and Grace wondered for a moment what reverie she'd interrupted. But Louisa was suddenly her mother's daughter, as though she'd remembered what it meant to invite another woman into her kitchen. "Coffee or tea?"

"Tea, please."

"You and Cora Anne." Lou filled the kettle, her back turned. "She's off with him, you know."

If Grace knew Lou better, she could tell if that tone was flippant—or wistful. "No, I didn't know. I thought he'd be getting back to a job today."

Lou brought two mugs and a canister of teabags to the table. "Help yourself." Grace flicked through the choices while Lou unwrapped an Earl Gray packet. "Does he confide in you?"

Her hand stilled opening the paper from a bag of peppermint. She met Lou's eyes and saw how they were rimmed in red, the lashes still matted, and she knew it wasn't just the weather that had her down. "Yes, he does now."

Lou's eyes lowered. "So you'd know if he, if they—"

"If they had concrete plans and not just castles in the sky?"

The kettle whistled, and Lou jumped. Her hands shook as she poured, and Grace grabbed a dishcloth hanging over the stove to wipe the spill. Louisa Halloway didn't make messes, that she knew, and she wondered again what she'd interrupted that had her skittish as a hermit crab scooting back into its shell.

"Patrick used to say that." Lou jerked the string on her teabag.

Grace brought the sugar bowl, still exactly where Annie had kept it, to the table without asking and fetched her own spoon. "Yes, he did."

"His mother said it first, you know." The words were a challenge.

No, she didn't know. Patrick's mother had collectively had no more than a dozen conversations with Grace the entire thirty years she'd known her.

"When she was trying to shame him into doing things her way." Lou continued. "*You can build all the castles in the sky you want, young man, but the real stronghold will always be right here.*" She got the inflection just right because, Grace supposed, Louisa herself had grown up with a Charleston-bred mother.

"She was wrong."

"Yes." Lou lifted her mug and drank the tea she'd now probably steeped too bitter. "Charlotte often was. But I suppose she loved him, in her way."

"In her way." Grace sipped her tea, eager to change the subject. "But Tennessee and Cora Anne, they'll be happy, don't you think?"

Lou pushed away her cup and folded her hands. "I hope so."

The unspoken lay between them—the idea that maybe their children were righting a wrong—but how could that be? Grace knew she and Patrick had been meant for one another, knit together in soul as well as flesh, and she'd often thought, if Louisa hadn't done the leaving, he would have. Eventually.

Eyeing those old letters she'd shoved aside, Lou added, "But they want different things."

"No," Grace countered. "They want each other's happiness. That's the same thing."

"Not always."

Grace bit her tongue before she said more. What did this woman know of sacrifice? Grace would be amiable because she loved Cora Anne and had loved Mrs. Annie, but Louisa's prickly self would have to find a friend somewhere else.

Lou rose. They were done, no doubt. "I'll get you some canned goods. I'm sure there's a box around here somewhere."

And that, Grace thought, was that.

~~~

Once Grace Watson had taken her canned goods and judgments back down the drive, Lou dumped the teacups' contents. She wanted to dash the porcelain against the sink just to hear the smash. See if breaking something would relieve the tension tightening her lungs.

But she knew it wouldn't. She'd broken many a dish in the months after David left. That tension hadn't dissipated until she hit her knees more often and learned contentment looked less like perfection and more like soldiering through a broken mess.

Gripping the sink's edge, Lou leaned over, resting her forehead on her white knuckles.

She needed a distraction beyond those old letters and breakables. A plan that would solve the looming financial hole she'd dig living off her retirement salary. Retrieving her file from upstairs and a thick afghan from the den, she settled on the porch in a rocker. The winter sky shone deep blue, and clouds scuttled across like snow flurries—a rare sight for the Lowcountry.

Creaking the rocker into a steady tempo, Lou flipped open her notes and shut herself off to the memories. Like the one of her daddy scraping thin powdery snow together to make a pitiful snowman while Mama rocked and laughed right here on this porch.

Her father had always been content. She knew he'd wanted that for her, too. Why he'd always encouraged her to study the ecology surrounding this place, even as she argued the better jobs were elsewhere.

Technically on paper, the farm now belonged to Lou, her sister Carolina, and their brother, Jimmy. But Jimmy preferred Walterboro where he'd made his own name running their daddy's landscape supply business, and Carolina thrived outside Charleston as an event planner. In one of life's ironic twists, Lou had been the one to come home.

Jimmy and his crew would continue to tend Daddy's rows of trees. Eventually, she and Carolina would clean out the house. By then their brother may want it, and if not, there were options that didn't bind her to this place.

But if she was going to make a living here, work until she was accepted into a PhD program, she needed a job. Preferably, conducting research would suit her best. Unlike her fellow teachers, Lou enjoyed analysis. She thrived on data maps. Each statistic was like a road map telling her exactly where to go.

She chewed her lip over the College of Charleston job description her father's old friend, Liam Whiting, had sent her. The degree requirements might be a problem. Her specialist was in educational leadership, and her master's was biochemistry, not environmental science.

Another engine rumbled down the drive. Lou pulled a lip balm out of her pocket and rubbed it across the sore spot she'd created. A moment later, composure intact, she waved to her daughter as Cora Anne bounced from Tennessee's truck. He stuck a hand out the window as he turned around and left.

Cora Anne jogged up the porch steps. "Hey, Mama. Why are you out here?"

"Vitamin D." But Lou tucked the afghan more snugly over her legs. "How was the beach?"

Her daughter shivered. "Cold. But Still Waters was good." The sale of the family cottage would have been heartbreaking if anyone but Tennessee Watson had bought it. Now, it seemed destined to stay in the family.

"So I was thinking …" Cora Anne dropped into the other rocker. "What if I stayed in the cottage for the rest of winter?"

Lou raised her brows. "I thought you were staying here to save your spare change? Working at a non-profit historical museum will barely pay a power bill."

She should know. Opening the latest one for the farmhouse had made her want something stronger than coffee.

Cora Anne called the museum job her "in-between." She'd already negotiated a transfer from Tulane University to the College of Charleston, starting in the fall. For once, the gap between plans hadn't bothered her daughter who usually lived by a calendar and to-do lists.

"I still have Nan's money." Cora Anne pushed her rocker, slow and steady.

Lou brought her own to a halt. "She intended that for school, for whatever you need."

Cora Anne stretched out her arms, wide. "Whatever else could I need, Mama?"

Lou closed her notes, lips pressed together. Her child had fallen in love, deep and strong, certain she desired nothing else.

She'd been that way too, once.

Chapter 6

Nashville, Tennessee, Spring 1976

Dad had left nearly three years ago, and now, Grace counted the days until graduation, so she could leave too.

Nearly midnight, and she should be studying for final exams—but her mother had been in a frenzy when Grace came home. At least the meal had been good— golden brown gravy drizzled over cubed steak and potatoes, green beans simmered in ham hock, biscuits light as air. But more than her mother's sudden hunger alerted Grace's senses.

When she'd gone outside to water her plants, she caught the sweet-over-putrid smell that still lingered on the porch swing cushions.

But the high wore off and Mom fell asleep on the couch, and Grace now scrubbed burned potatoes from the pot. The roller coaster of up and down had worsened after Dad left, and her mother found another way to cope. For that alone, Grace despised him. But she hadn't stopped wishing he'd come back.

She gave up and left the pot to soak. Soap bubbles floated up from the sink, popping before they went too far.

Mom wasn't on the couch, and Grace frowned. The drugs weren't the only demons eating her mind, and for long years now, she'd worried her mother would find another route out of her depression.

A lamp glowed on her mother's bedside table. She sprawled across the bed, the angle unnatural but not unusual. Grinding her teeth against her frustration, Grace pulled the blanket up over her mother's bare legs.

Something seemed wrong.

Mom often slept deeply but she didn't stir at all, and when Grace leaned over, she could barely feel her breath against her cheek. She glanced around—and saw it.

An empty pill bottle tipped on its side. Grace snatched it up. Her mother's sleeping pills. Empty though the prescription had been filled only two days before.

She fumbled through the yellow pages for poison control, all while trying to shake Mom awake. "You need to call for an ambulance," the blunt voice on the phone line instructed.

An ambulance.

Grace swallowed and dialed their neighbors—her mother's only friends. Patsy and Robert came at once. While he made the emergency call, Patsy led Grace to the couch in the living room and sat with her, arm around her shoulders. "She's not in her right mind, sweetie."

"She never has been."

The older woman brushed her fingers through Grace's curls, smoothing them into place. "Robert thinks she's a manic depressive. Your father's leaving has made it harder for her to cope."

"I don't want to do this anymore." Grace heard the smallness in her voice, the near whine, like a child. She was all her mother had—how selfish of her to think this. But how unfair of the world to ask it of her.

Patsy hugged her tighter as the siren's wail approached. "That's all right, hon. You don't have to anymore."

Two days later, after her mother's stomach had been pumped and she was stable, the state of Tennessee committed her to a psychiatric ward—and Grace to the temporary care of Robert and Patsy Bell.

Chapter 7

David would never have called himself a jealous man, but the green edge of envy crept up in his periphery anytime he drove out to the Watson property. Patrick had chosen well when he bought this little bit of land with Steamboat Creek cutting across its corner. Over the fall, when he'd visited, Tennessee had put the boys and him up in the little bungalow down by the creek. There one could swing on the porch and smell the tides coming in. They'd sat for hours on the dock, watching the dolphins feed and languish against muddy banks.

His townhouse made a good investment—even if it had sucked his savings dry—but David figured if they all stayed around here, eventually he'd want something like this. The Coultrie farm met the requirements. He nudged those thoughts back in the box they belonged—with the lid shut tight.

First things first. Home. Job. Which had brought him to Grace's door with a laundry basket of canned goods and non-perishables.

When he rang the bell, he heard a quick bark and a scuffling of nails on hardwood floors. She pulled open the door but left the screen closed. Seeing the size of the dog whose collar she kept in a firm grip, David was absurdly grateful.

"Hey, there." Grace's blond curls were tamed behind a scarf of bright colors that spilled over one shoulder. She'd exchanged her typical skirt for wide pants that puddled at her socked feet. "What brings you over?"

How the woman planned to cross her muddy yard while wearing those pants mystified David. But then, Grace had often been a conundrum. He offered the basket. "Heard you're a collection agent."

"That I am." Tugging at the beast, she pushed open the screen.

"Come on in. I promise he won't bite, but I can't promise he won't lunge."

The dog was nearly half her size, and although Grace was not a large woman, this made for a large enough dog. He had a head the size of a football. Floppy ears belied the massive teeth. But his eyes were, no other word for it, soulful. Soon as David stepped over Grace's threshold, the giant leapt.

"Hank!" She protested as his wet nose inspected David's collar and deemed him friend.

Laughing, David set down the basket so he could scrub Hank's neck with both hands. Had to be a mix of boxer and something else bigger—maybe even some greyhound the way those legs went on and on. "So you're not really a big scary watchdog, huh, boy?" He'd dreamed of a dog scuffing up their floors. Lou always said she had enough messes to handle already.

Grace huffed. "More like a giant, sloppy toddler. Come on into the kitchen, David, and I'll get you some tea and a towel for the slobber."

"When did y'all get a dog? Tennessee never mentioned him."

"Hank bears mentioning, for sure." Grace filled two glasses with ice and tea. "I'm fostering him for a little while. Apparently a family brought him on vacation and decided that was the last straw for the mongrel. Isn't that right?" She cooed at the puppy-beast nuzzling her leg and handed David his glass across the granite island.

"So they left him?"

"They at least called the rental company and asked for a shelter recommendation first." Grace shrugged. "Sometimes that's me."

"Ah, food distribution and local humane society. That's quite a reputation, Mrs. Watson."

Her eyes sparkled. "Don't forget I've been voted 'Edisto's Favorite Hairdresser' for at least five years running."

"I suppose it helps when you're the only one."

"Oh"—she lay a hand on her heart—"that was cold, David. And after I served you my special peppermint tea."

He grinned. Grace made everything—even their entwined lives—

30

seem simple. Though her tea could do without being that hippie green stuff.

"Well, we all have our own pet projects. Pun intended." She laughed and leaned on the counter. "Heard you're taking on Colleton High."

"That's the plan. Wanted to ask you about it, actually."

She arched one brow. "Looking for the local gossip?"

"Just want to know what I need to do so this can become a more permanent position."

"Aha." She straightened and crossed her arms. "I do the assistant principal's hair you know."

He did know, but he sipped his tea in innocence.

"People around here are proud. Don't go in there thinking you've got a better way of doing things."

Well, he knew better than that. Though, his ex-wife may beg to differ.

Grace continued. "But volunteer. Pick up the slack. There's never enough parent help for anything and those teachers get run ragged."

Typical of every high school where he'd worked. He could do that, though. Be the default. Long as he didn't let it interfere with helping Lou. He hoped not to repeat that particular issue. "Think I got it. Thanks, Grace."

"Anytime. Boys are at the middle school, right?"

"Indeed. Taking them to baseball tryouts next week."

"Glad you aren't holding with some high-falutin' private education for them. Patrick's mother, bless her cold heart, has never let it go we sent Tennessee to public school. But Pat believed if we were going to live in this world, he better learn it, and sooner rather than later."

"I'll remember to tell Lou that."

Grace winced. "Well, don't tell her it came from me."

He shook the ice in his drink. "Y'all okay?"

"We're fine as two people can be with all that water under the bridge."

A truck rumbled over the gravel drive and Hank rushed the door, knocking aside a potted plant in his descent, barking like an army was coming.

"Oh, you." Grace strode the short distance between kitchen and front door. "That's just Tennessee and Cora Anne." She opened the screen, letting Hank bound across to the truck like a literal welcome wagon.

David helped her right the potted succulents that had spilled dirt all over her clean pine floors.

"Thank you." Her gray-green eyes met his, over those plants that thrived no matter how dry the soil.

"Mom! Call off this yacht, please."

Together, they chuckled, and David felt a stab of guilt. He hadn't laughed easily with a woman in a long time. Lou had tried on New Year's Eve, but there had been stiffness as they stumbled through once familiar banter.

"Hey, Dad." Cora Anne came up on the porch with Hank at her side.

"That dog is the size of my boat and still growing. Hey, Mr. Halloway." Tennessee stuck out his hand for a shake.

David grasped it, putting all his strength behind the clasp. But his middle-age history teacher's grip was never a match for Tennessee's. Like his mother, Tennessee bore simple strength, coming from more than his physically demanding job as the island's top contractor.

"Are y'all here for supper?" Grace eyed the bucket in her son's hand. "I hope you brought a contribution."

"Flounder so fresh it was swimming 'til half an hour ago when Cora Anne made her first catch."

"Supper-sized too." She beamed and David felt envy nudge back. He and Lou should have given her that confidence, but she'd found it for herself in the company of this young man. Cora Anne flung an arm around his waist. "Why don't you stay and be impressed, Dad?"

She didn't even glance at Grace when she issued the invitation, but he did. Grace's grin was directed at their children, and he figured she'd worked hard to make his daughter feel at home here.

"I'd love to stay." He wanted to get to know these people who made his daughter happy. Looking to Tennessee, he said, "Give you a hand with those fish?"

"Never turn down an offer to help, so my mama always said." Tennessee winked at his mother and led David out the back door.

Over the porch utility sink, he and Tennessee gutted and skinned fish. The winter sun sank low over the creek, bathing the yard in its auburn glow. Tennessee worked swiftly, and David struggled to mimic the man's movements that seemed as natural to him as breathing.

"You fish much?" Tennessee dropped a fillet into a stainless bowl.

"Used to, as a kid. My dad loved a good trophy trout stream." David's chest pinged, remembering. Even now his heart ricocheted with grief at unexpected moments. "Taught me to cast a fly same weekend he taught me to throw a curveball." Mostly because he'd been a lonely eight-year-old kid in another new town.

Tennessee paused, the flurry of his hands ceasing. "Sounds like a guy I'd have liked."

"He was ..." David slit the belly of a flounder and spread it. "Memorable."

"Cor's never really mentioned her grandparents." Tennessee fished for information like he did dinner. Subtly and with good bait.

David finished the flounder and flipped it in the bowl. "They died long before she was born. Car accident. Lou and I were barely engaged." The fish all done, he reached for the soap and let the bite of the cold water wash over his hands. "You know this family. We avoid talking through sadness like the plague."

Tennessee rinsed his hands. "Yeah, but no one should carry grief alone."

David rolled his shoulders, like he did when planning a game's defense. But Tennessee was right. Which only made his chest twinge again, remembering the haunted look in Lou's blue eyes.

Chapter 8

Edisto Island, February 1976

"You should tell them." Carolina, Lou's nosy younger sister, lined a basket with a linen napkin and filled it with neat rows of saltine crackers. "They might like him."

"Might like who?" Their mother sailed into the farmhouse kitchen. "Carolina, where are my knives?"

"I put them right there, Mama." She pointed to another sweetgrass basket. "Lou met someone."

"Thanks a lot." Lou snatched the crackers. Her parents always had an opinion, and while she respected them, she wasn't ready for one formed about David. Mama and Daddy had enough thoughts already about what she should do with her fancy education. "I'm going out to the fire."

Her mother's hand on her arm stopped her at the door. "You met someone?"

She shrugged off Mama's touch. "Just an undergrad student. We're friends."

"Friends who talked on the phone all night."

Lou wheeled around. "You're one to talk. John Calhoun kept you out so late Daddy locked the door."

Carolina grinned. "But not the window." Her sister never had been a stickler for rules.

"Girls." Their mother rarely raised her voice. She didn't need to. "Louisa, if you have a friend, we'd enjoy hearing about him. Especially since your father invited someone else tonight."

Lou swallowed hard. "Not Patrick."

"No, not him." Mama's smile faded as she nudged Lou out the door.

Outside, dusk settled over the farm. The guests for the oyster roast gathered around the fire where the hissing steam and the popping of oyster shells harmonized with conversation.

Lou went to her father, tall and sturdy in his canvas overcoat and work boots. "Sounds about ready."

"Nearly there."

Beside him stood a young man she didn't know. Daddy tipped his head. "Lou, this is Liam Whiting. He's going to intern with me."

"You're interested in growing trees?"

The man laughed. "Well, yes, but in a broader sense, I'm interested in conservation. Specifically of our waterways."

"Lou wrote a big paper one time about our little creek and how far-reaching its impact is. Impressed her professor so much he had to come see it for himself."

Four years since she'd fulfilled an extra science credit with an ecology course, and her daddy still bragged.

"You get it, then?" Liam moved around her father to stand beside Lou. His eyes widened with excitement, and his voice thickened with passion. "We have to start taking action now because everything won't be like this forever."

"I get it, sure." She'd heard that her whole life from her father. "But I'm planning to work in medical research at the Center for Disease Control. Then get my doctorate in biochemistry." She eyed her father. No reaction. "That's why I'm at Emory right now."

Liam shook his head. "Everyone wants to cure cancer. But this—" He waved his arm at the creek glimmering under the winter moon. "You grew up here, so you'd be an ideal candidate for teaching conservation."

"Exactly. I grew up here." Lou closed her eyes for a moment, blotting out the images she loved. Her family, her home, and her father's pride.

He'd taught her to love those creeks, but she'd also seen him work sixteen-hour days his entire life. One storm, one dry summer, one late frost—there were a thousand factors outside his control that could destroy his work.

And Lou preferred to be the one who had control.

Chapter 9

Letting David take the boys for their first day back to school was no doubt a concession—and necessity. Only taken her the last five years to realize, punishing him by refusing his help really only hurt the boys—and made her life that much more difficult.

Having him here was an opportunity to start over. Like this interview could be for her career.

Would be.

She had to think positively. Otherwise, she'd wind up substitute teaching like David because bills had to be paid.

Lou smoothed her hair in the rearview mirror. Lipstick—too bright? Makeup had always given her qualms, so she kept it clean and simple.

David told her once he liked that.

But of course, he'd spent his whole life surrounded by perky cheerleaders, classy baseball moms, and flirty first-year teachers, so the novelty of her bare face had surely worn off by now.

She'd worn her only pantsuit, navy blue with a cream shell underneath, low heeled pumps, and pearls of course. Because every good Southern woman understood the power of accessories. She could practically hear her sister's voice in her head.

Professional. That's all she wanted. Put together enough to be a professor at the College of Charleston.

The icy wind blew off the Atlantic and through Charleston's harbor as she walked. Lou wished she hadn't left her fleece in the backseat out of dignity. By the time she pushed through the heavy doors of the science building, she had decided Southern propriety had nothing on practicality. She should have worn the fleece.

She blew on her hands to warm them and stomped her heels waiting for the elevator. Ought to take the stairs and warm up.

"Louisa, you made it." Liam Whiting greeted her when the doors slid open. With his tousled brown hair, barely showing its silver, and perfectly balanced smile capping off khaki cargos and a flannel shirt, he could have been mistaken for an angler's magazine model. Perfect polished casual.

As usual, she'd tried too hard.

When he took her stiff hand, he gasped. "You're freezing. Cold outside?"

"Just a bit with the wind is all." She drew back. This made twice in the last week there'd been concern about her wellbeing. Remembering the weight of David's coat on her shoulders still unsettled her.

"Let me get you some coffee, and we can talk." He turned down the hall. "You're awfully spiffed up today. Meeting with more than just me?" In his office, he went straight to the coffeepot under the window.

Lou took a deep breath. "No, only you, Dr. Whiting. I'm very serious—"

"I've told you for years, call me Liam." He handed her a hot mug of black coffee. "Need anything in it?"

She shook her head. "This will be fine." But the first sip made her eyes widen.

Liam grinned. "I like it strong. Too much?"

"No." The cup had already warmed her hands, and his informality thawed her nerves. "No one ever makes it as strong as I like." An indulgence she'd regret tonight.

He raised his brows. "How'd I do?"

"Quite well."

"Excellent." He indicated the leather chair in front of his desk. "Have a seat. We'll talk roasting our own beans—because that's how you get the best flavor—and credentials."

She perched on the edge of the chair, one leg tucked neatly behind the other as she'd learned long ago in debutante class. They chatted nonsense about the weather and holidays, and then switched to Edisto.

He'd built a small house on Steamboat Creek, not far from the Watsons.

Once Lou had drained her coffee, she pressed her hands to her knees to keep from shaking out caffeine and impatience.

"Louisa, here's the deal." The professor had leaned back in his chair and steepled his fingers, studying her. Lou felt like a specimen in one of the college's labs. "I can't bring you on full-time. I tried, but it all comes down to the college's accreditation. You'll need a doctorate to teach."

She kept her face polite, though inside frustration built like a storm. "I thought I could work in one of your labs."

"I already have grad students filling those positions, so I can't use you there, either. Unless you want to finally pursue environmental studies?"

She tossed her head. "You know that's what my father wanted. Not me."

He cocked a brow. "You promised him if things didn't work out—"

"Things have worked out just fine. Only slower than I expected."

He sat forward. "I did speak on your behalf to the head of the Education Department. They have an adjunct opening and would like to speak with you." He waved a hand at her. "I thought maybe they'd already called you for an interview."

All dressed up and nowhere to go. The old cliché rumbled through Lou's mind. "Dr. Whiting—"

"Liam."

"I really have no desire to teach others how to teach. My first passion has always been science—research, actually."

He leaned back. "Then I'm not sure I can help you. You'll have to get your doctorate to be a viable candidate."

She bit her tongue before the gale of emotions swirled out. It wasn't his fault those plans had derailed long ago.

He stood. "I'd like to have you here. You'd be an excellent asset to the education and science programs, but my hands are tied."

She nodded, standing as well. "Thank you for your time."

"Are you sure you don't want me to call Dr. Pierce and see if she can meet with you?"

She ought to say yes. The paycheck would cover so many extra expenses headed her way, and she desperately needed a focus before the ebbing waves of grief broke. But she couldn't see herself with idealistic students, fiery and ready to change the world one classroom at a time. She fell into teaching out of necessity, not calling. "No, thank you. I'm ready for a bit of a break from that right now." She forced a smile. "Time to try something new."

"Consider a doctoral program, then. I recommend Clemson, of course." He waved at the large framed diploma behind his desk. "And study this." He handed her a graduate catalog from the stack on his desk. "My Environmental Studies program could use someone with a unique understanding of this area."

She took the small book, felt the weight of it shift in her hand from a mere collection of class offerings and degree programs into a time capsule of all the plans she'd once had.

Clenching the book to her chest, Lou offered her hand. "Come by the house next time you're on Edisto."

His eyes brightened, and his grip was strong, secure. "Thank you. I just might. Your father was a viable asset as we built this program."

Lou nodded. "He knew his creek." Though he'd never really understood her.

Liam came around his desk. "Let me see you out."

He guided her down the hall, and she barely registered the light touch on her elbow. Numb beyond any cold, Lou even allowed him to push the elevator's buttons. When the doors cranked open, she pressed her lips into a thin smile. Best she could do. "Thank you again, Dr. Whiting."

The doors jerked to close as soon as she stepped in, but he stuck his foot and then his head between holding them open. "Liam, please, Louisa. I'd like you to call me Liam."

She tipped up her chin, and all the anger swirling beneath her surface stilled for a moment when she noticed two things. One, his tone held a slight plea, and two—he wasn't wearing a ring.

Chapter 10

Lou hadn't asked for his help in a long time, and David didn't figure she'd change now. But she had invited him to the boys' birthday dinner, and anyone cooking three different meals on one Saturday afternoon deserved support. He hadn't moved to Edisto so they could keep operating like a Venn diagram in his classroom—only overlapping what they had in common.

Once, more than their children had filled that space.

At the farmhouse, he knocked and pushed open the screen door. "Guess locking's only for the city."

In her mother's kitchen—he would think of it as Annie's until Lou put some of herself into this place—counters overflowed with groceries and serving dishes. Lou hefted a large bowl of chicken pieces and buttermilk and nodded at the fridge. "You're early. Now make yourself useful."

"Exactly why I'm here."

Lou's cheeks lifted like the notion made her want to smile. But the look faded quickly. "Where are the boys?"

He took the bowl and slid it onto a shelf she'd cleared. "Tennessee and Ben whisked them away for a ride on Lenny's shrimp boat." He passed a glance over her plaid button-down and old jeans. For too long she'd kept herself swathed in khakis and cardigan sets. "They told me about the menu."

She pursed her lips. "I never indulge them like this."

"I didn't say anything."

"You thought it."

He pulled his lower lip beneath his teeth—and Lou pointed her finger. "That's your tell, David. Never play poker."

After all these years and all the angry words they'd flung at each other, she still knew him. Better than he knew himself sometimes.

Turning her back, she reached for an apron draped over a kitchen chair. "I'm quite capable of cooking three meals. It's all about the timing."

"I know that." David shrugged off his coat.

"I don't need help, but ..." Lou cinched the apron at her waist, fumbling a bit with the strings. "Since you're here, I appreciate the extra hands."

Whistling, he went to the sink and washed his hands. Poured a cup of coffee and made himself at home.

Lou grabbed a package of Italian sausage from the fridge. J.D., who appreciated simplicity, had requested spaghetti. The tortillas on the counter must be for Mac's extra-spicy enchiladas. That chicken he'd put in the fridge would be fried, with mashed potatoes and green beans on the side, because Cole loved tradition. Lou's fault for naming that boy after her father.

He figured she'd be moving through her list, one thing at a time. How she'd keep from becoming overwhelmed—

She dropped the sausage on the counter and gripped it, knuckles whitening.

"What?" For a half-second he thought she was having a panic attack, and it had been years since he'd seen that.

"I forgot a cake." She straightened, raking her hair behind her ears. He could practically see her mind whirring through possibilities. "Maybe I can call cousin Rose and see if she can make one real quick?" David nodded as she rambled. "Or does the Piggly Wiggly bakery do cakes? They don't, do they?"

He shook his head. The Pig was too small for a bakery.

She threw her hands in the air. "One of us will have to drive to Charleston and find a Publix, I guess." Breathing heavily—he might have been right about the panic—Lou dumped the sausage in a pan to brown.

He reached around her and snagged a spatula. "I got this."

"No, you don't." She snatched the utensil. "You've got to get a cake."

"So you need my help after all?"

"David ..."

"What if I told you I knew where you could get a cake, and all it requires is a simple phone call and maybe set an extra place at dinner?"

She didn't bother to look at him as she stirred the meat. "Who?"

"Grace makes cakes on the side for The Hideaway sometimes."

Her shoulders jerked. "How do you know that?"

"She told me."

Lou stabbed the simmering meat.

"So, anyway ..." He closed his hand over hers. "Before you take your frustration out on dinner, maybe you should try asking your neighbor—and friend—for a favor." He worked the spatula from her grasp.

This time she wheeled a glare he knew well. "If y'all are such good friends, why don't you?"

Grinning at her, because he really couldn't resist antagonizing the moments Lou wasn't perfect, he said, "Because I'm not the one who forgot."

~~~

Grace knocked on the screen, chocolate cake in one hand, stomach knotted.

David swung the door open. "Thanks for saving the day." Behind him, Lou drizzled butter over mashed potatoes. If she didn't know the history, Grace might've sworn she'd walked into a Norman Rockwell painting.

"Based on how good this house smells, I'd say no one would've missed this." She passed over her Tupperware container without passing over the threshold. "You've outdone yourself, Lou. That chicken looks good as your mama's."

Lou took the cake from David. "Thank you."

"No problem. My pleasure." Between them, politeness was chilly as the January air, but Lou had sounded sincere.

"Hey, Mom." Tennessee came in the kitchen and lifted the platter of chicken. "I hope you brought that cake for me because those crazy hooligans don't need any more sugar."

"Perhaps someone shouldn't have let them drink a six-pack of Mountain Dew on the boat." Cora Anne trailed him. "Is that one of Grace's chocolate cakes?"

"Yes, she was kind enough to help me out today. No time to make a cake with these three dinners." Lou met Grace's gaze then, as if entreating her to play along.

Grace blinked, recognizing the chink in this woman's armor. Lou couldn't abide failure—even over something as minor as forgetting a birthday cake.

"I'll set an extra place, then. You'll stay, right? Half the fun of feeding people is watching them enjoy it, right, Mama?" Cora Anne breezed out of the kitchen without giving her mother—or Grace— time to respond.

David cleared his throat, and Lou cast him a desperate glance. Grace bit back a chuckle. Cora Anne had learned quite a bit during this past summer about how to handle tension—and her mother.

"Grace." David pushed the screen wider. "Would you like to stay for dinner?"

"Well, I did always like Annie's fried chicken."

The compliment nudged a smile out of Lou. "Supper's the least we can do for your help."

As Grace hung up her coat, David leaned over to whisper in his ex-wife's ear. Whatever he said made a blush sweep her cheeks. Tears pricked the corner of Grace's eyes. How she missed having someone to share little moments with.

"David, take that cake and put it on the sideboard. Set out Mama's china dessert plates, too, please." Lou gave him a shove—almost playful.

"We can't just use paper Happy Birthday plates?"

"David, Mrs. Annie would never have approved." She spoke before she thought.

Lou stepped back. "Of course. Grace would know." The jesting had gone from her tone.

Grace escaped, following David to the dining room where she set out the delicate plates from their customary place in the left cabinet of the sideboard.

He arched a brow. "You know this house well."

She shrugged. "Might be the problem." Nearly everything she knew about cooking and entertaining, she owed to Lou's mother.

At dinner, she sat between Tennessee and Cole, who gave her a rundown of their fishing trip in between three pieces of chicken and mounds of vegetables.

"I bet you never had a birthday dinner as good as this one," Mac challenged Tennessee. To Grace, he added, "He told us you don't like to cook."

She laughed. "I like to cook. Just seems tedious when it's only the two of us, and most of the time, it's only me."

"Back home—" Cole darted a glance at his mom. "Back in Marietta, if Mom was too tired, we'd get KFC. But she told us not to tell Nan because she'd think it sacrifice."

"Sacrilegious." Lou and Grace spoke at the same time and then stared at one another a moment too long across the table.

Grace dropped her eyes to her plate. "You know, y'all were really blessed to have a grandmother like Mrs. Annie. Tennessee's grandmother is not nearly as …"

"Easygoing," Tennessee supplied.

"Exactly."

"Why?" How Cole managed to speak around that bite Grace didn't know.

"Well, for starters, at Mrs. Charlotte Ravenel Cooper Watson's you'd be dismissed from the table for talking with your mouth full." Lou leveled a look at her son.

"You know, I think it's high time you took me to meet this infamous grandmother of yours." Cora Anne tipped her glass at Tennessee. "Before I get too scared."

"Aw, she's not that bad. Just stiff."

"Charlotte is simply old Charleston society at its prime. She doesn't embrace change very well." Grace patted her son's arm. "But she's definitely developed a fondness for this one, so I'm sure she'll extend that to you, especially given the family history." At least, she hoped Charlotte would extend to Cora Anne the acceptance she'd always kept from Grace.

"I wouldn't be so sure." Lou's tone hardened, and David laid his hand over hers. She pulled away, lifting her tea glass with a sniff. Grace frowned. Charlotte hadn't cared for Louisa either?

"What history?" Cora Anne furrowed her brow and looked between the adults. Tennessee shook his head.

Lou's face tightened, and Grace sighed. They might as well know. It wasn't a secret. "Charlotte and Annie were best friends but Annie's first engagement was to Charlotte's brother—"

"And she broke it to marry my grandfather." Cora Anne sat back. "She told Hannah and me a story once, about her and Granddaddy's first kiss and how she couldn't share it with her best friend."

"That would have been Charlotte, yes. And the woman's blood must really run blue, because she's cold and unyielding as ice." Lou's statement struck Grace as ironic, and based on the way David coughed, she probably wasn't the only one.

"Well, maybe," and she aimed her words at her son and the girl he loved. This might be the triplets' birthday, but Cora Anne and Tennessee were the reason they could all come together. "It's time for a thaw."

Chapter 11

As the service at the historic Presbyterian Church began, Lou and the boys slipped into the pew that would always be her parents'. Across the aisle, Grace caught her eye. Last night, when the dishes had piled in the sink and the boys challenged Cora Anne and Tennessee to Monopoly, Grace had apologized for mentioning Charlotte.

Lou shook her head over the running water and pretended it didn't matter. But it did. Even as she'd encouraged her daughter to seize her own happiness, she'd pushed away the thought she would be back in Charlotte Watson's jurisdiction.

The January service was sparse, as were most things on the island this time of year, but Lou saw Liam Whiting cross the lot after it was over. Probably spending the weekend at his cabin on the creek.

At home, the boys dove into leftovers, but she went upstairs to the writing desk in her bedroom. The walls were stacked with boxes. Clothes and books she had nowhere to put until she came to terms with removing some of her parents' goods. The desk, however, was impeccably organized. She had no trouble finding the course catalog Liam had given her, right beneath her doctorate application for Clemson University.

The environmental science classes intrigued. Reading these course descriptions was like hearing her daddy talk about their creek and land, how he hoped it would be sustainable for generations. But she didn't need another master's degree. She already had one and intended to build upon it for her new career. Putting the catalog aside, she looked at her application.

"Hey, Mom." J.D. stood in the doorway. "Can we finish the cake, too?"

"If you spend the next three hours outside burning it off." Lou started a list. Clemson would require letters of recommendation, and her best bets were those who'd worked chemistry labs with her during her teaching career.

"Are you mad?"

She raised her head and took in that boy-turning-man she was trying to raise to be ... who? Her father? His father? Himself?

"Why would I be mad?"

"Cole says all that stuff about Tennessee's grandma, the mean one, that she didn't like you or Nan and something about how you and Tennessee's dad dated, like, a million years ago—"

Now she laughed. A deep chuckle that came from her belly. Not for the first time, she thanked the Lord for giving her these boys who kept her life from any measure of seriousness.

"It's all water flowing out of the creek now." She pulled out one of her daddy's old sayings as she crossed to him and ruffled his hair. He ducked away, of course. Thirteen was too old for that affection. "But it does make me sad to remember."

He wrinkled his brow like he couldn't understand, and Lou figured that was true. After all, in looking at him, with her mother's blue eyes and David's sunny smile, how could she be sad about a history that never needed to play out?

~~~

The phone rang twice before he answered. Lou almost hung up, sure he was out. David always made friends more easily than she—and he enjoyed parties and gatherings and impromptu pick-up games. They'd argued more than once about his open-door policy versus her desire for planning ahead.

"Hello?" Weariness tinged his voice.

Lou bit her lip. "Hey, sorry. Did I catch you at a bad time?"

"No, not at all." His old inflection—which he was good at faking—came back. "I've just been grading these essays. High school diatribes on the causes of World War I will put any old man to sleep."

He used to read her those essays aloud, punctuated by funny voices and exaggerated mispronunciations of his students' weak spelling. But only in jest, and then he would turn serious and find the one strong point he could praise. David, always seeing the good.

"Lou, you okay?"

She blew at a strand of hair that always stuck to her cheek these days. "Yes, I'm fine. I called to say—" Now her throat went dry as Sea Island cotton. This shouldn't be so hard. She swallowed. "Thank you."

"Well, you're welcome, though I'm not sure for what."

"Thank you for helping me yesterday." Now she could exhale again.

"Thanks for letting me ... I enjoyed it." She heard wistfulness—and the once before haunting them both.

"Guess I owe you a favor now." Keep it business. The raising of kids together. That's what they still had.

"Well, I can think of a few things."

"Really?" He hadn't asked her for anything, except the shared custody, since the day she'd told him to please leave. She'd really said *please*. Only later did that strike her as ironic.

"Sure. For instance, I've been thinking about lasagna since New Year's and Stouffers just doesn't taste the same."

"Oh ..." She twisted the phone cord around her wrist and settled against the down pillows on her bed. "I could make you some. I've got leftover sauce from J.D.'s spaghetti."

"But then I'd be dependent on you anytime the craving strikes."

Her stomach quivered. A crazy idea, of course. They hadn't depended on one another in years.

"Anyway," David continued. "What about you teach me the trick? Think I can finally learn to cook?"

Yesterday while helping, he'd found an excuse to touch her, a hand at her back or lingering on her shoulder. He'd never been that interested in cooking before. "I have been told I'm a pretty good teacher."

"True, and I don't think we should waste that sauce. Want me to swing by tomorrow after school? I can bring the boys, so you don't have to make the trip."

There and back and there and back again—her life had become a taxi service with the boys in school and no other concrete commitments. David's offer was welcome. She might consider his original suggestion they always go and come with him. Would free her up to work on the house—and her applications.

"Thank you. I appreciate it." Maybe they could make this work, though Clemson—with its three-hour commute—would make her the weekend parent, a role he'd always played.

"All you ever have to do is ask, Lou. See how well it's worked for me?"

Except ... her hand trailed over the paperwork spread across the bed. One time she had asked ... and he'd said no.

Chapter 12

Edisto Island, April 1976

She brought David home over spring break.

"Guess that fling with Patrick Watson really is just water gone to the sea," her daddy said, as they sat outside one morning. "Heard he's working construction over at the new Fairfield Resort."

Lou concentrated on a knot in the shrimp net she wanted to untangle. David had never caught shrimp before. "That's good for him. Hope he's well."

"Funny." Her father took the net from her and in one swift move freed the knots. "He always tells me the same for you."

"Did you enjoy talking to David last night?"

Daddy had taken him out on the porch and kept him there until the shadows were long across the pastures. Mama made her stay in the kitchen and help Jimmy with his math homework. But she'd heard them laugh a time or two, and David hadn't seemed any worse for wear.

"I reckon I like him all right." Daddy handed the net back. "Boy doesn't know his way around a farm or a tidal creek, though."

"Everyone doesn't have to."

He shrugged. "No, so long as he knows how to take care of you, don't guess it matters."

She rolled her eyes. "I can take care of myself, Daddy."

"You keep believing that, baby girl. But one of these days, you'll find out it's not true."

Her father's ideas were as outdated as these shrimp nets. Lou stood on the steps and dusted dried mud off her jeans. "I'll teach him to shrimp at least. So when we come here you'll have something to do with him besides play chess."

Daddy kicked back in the rocker. "He beat me."

Lou grinned. "I know."

"Promise me something, baby girl." He tipped forward again, tone serious. Lou sat back down. She knew this face. "If things don't work out, you'll come home."

"Daddy …"

"You'll come home and give my ideas a try, all right? That's all I'm asking. You'll know when it's time."

She twisted her fingers in the net, wondering if she'd misread him. Was he talking about David—or her career?

In the kitchen, she found David drinking coffee with her mother. "Let's make dinner."

He pinched his brows together. "It's not even noon yet."

"This might take awhile." She held out her hand and he took it, following her down to the creek bank. They waded in.

Beside her in the creek, David's vibrancy waned, conquered by a simple net. "I'm gonna get this all tangled up."

"It's not hard." She chuckled at the look he gave her. Like a pouty student. She'd been helping him tutor at an after-school program, and that was the face of every one of those junior-high boys.

"All in the wrist." She flicked her net, aware she was trying to appear graceful.

He pitched his. She laughed. "It's not a baseball."

"But baseball is what I know." He furrowed his brow as he drew the net back out of the water. "Tell you what, if I learn to do this, you have to learn to throw a curve."

She moved behind him and slid her arm down his to hold his wrist. Her heart beat under her jacket, against his back, ricocheting up a notch with the idea that if her father saw her, it wouldn't matter that she was twenty-three years old and could be as close to a man as she liked. "Deal."

Chapter 13

Her son had made sure she had the kitchen of her dreams, and Grace was always most grateful on the days her anxiety rose like a king tide and manifested itself in the form of shortbread. She thought she'd baked herself out at Christmas, and then Louisa called requesting that cake last week. Now her counters were covered in no less than six-dozen cookies, the pecans finely chopped, the butter excessive.

"Whoa, Mom, did you discover a stockpile of flour or something and decide to whittle it down?" Tennessee came through the back door stomping his muddy boots in the laundry room and shaking the late January rain out of his blond hair.

She poured the coffee she knew he'd come for. "No, simply felt the urge."

His eyes probed hers over the cup's rim. She turned to the sink and began rinsing stainless mixing bowls. "Nothing's wrong, if that's what you're wondering."

"I never wonder." He handed her a towel to dry her hands. "I know."

She followed him to the table where they always sat when he wanted to talk. Here she'd counseled him through grief and rebellion. Helping him work through the torments of the past, so he could find the man God called him to be. These days he was strong and purposed, no longer defined as a fatherless son.

She'd never been more proud. Or felt less needed.

"So what's wrong?"

Grace sighed and hooked her arm over the back of the chair. Closed-off had never been her style. "Little restless is all. Probably winter slump. Everything is slow right now."

"But the salon's doing okay, right?"

He worried far too much about her financial stability. "Typical off-season, but it's fine. Making desserts at The Hideaway helps keep me busy at least."

"Ben better be paying you what you're worth."

She shook her finger at him. "You better quit worrying. I'm fine."

"You know, Cora Anne's mother could use a friend."

"Louisa and I have never had an easy time being friends."

"I figure give it time, Mom. Isn't that what you always say?"

It was. Somehow as the days turned to months and years, the sting of grief lessened and the sweet remained. She knew that to be true. But Louisa seemed to have let resentment burrow so deep in her, it had become like a splinter she'd have to soak a long time in Epsom salt before she could pull it out.

"Cor says her mom really is different, now. Not nearly as cold and unyielding."

Grace chuckled. "Sounds like Charlotte."

"Ironically, yes." Tennessee leaned into her, his gaze intense. "But the difference is, Grandmother doesn't want to change. I think Lou does."

A knock sounded on her front door. Tennessee swiveled in his chair. "That'd be David. Told him I'd help him strengthen that tire swing out at the farmhouse before the triplets wear it out completely."

"Might as well ask him in." Grace waved at her countertops. "Somebody's got to eat all these cookies."

~ ~ ~

"Eight schools in twelve years? Really?" Grace broke her shortbread in half. Last piece. She'd told herself that three times already.

David's foot bounced. She might need to stop refilling his coffee. "Really. One reason I worked so hard at baseball. If I could walk into a new school and make the team, I was instantly in a group."

She played with her cookie pieces. That feeling of being on the outside as familiar now as it had been in high school. Hard to make friends when no one could come over for study sessions or slumber parties.

"That why you became a coach?"

David's laugh was brittle, like the remnants of shells beneath her feet when she walked the shore. "No. I wanted to go professional, but I blew my knee out freshman year at Emory. Could still hit, though, so I didn't lose my scholarship. Just every athlete's big dream."

"You met Lou there? Emory?" A story she'd heard.

"Knocked her down with my charm." His eyes twinkled. "Literally."

In the kitchen where he'd busied his hands loading her dishwasher, Tennessee said, "Speaking of Lou, you about ready to head over there?"

"Let me finish this coffee, and we can." David smiled at her, and Grace could see the easygoing charm that had swept away even Louisa Coultrie's resistance. "What about you? How'd you wind up on Edisto?"

"A story best told over something stronger than coffee and cookies." Grace twisted her curls over her shoulder. "Basically, I was visiting a friend and working at Dockside. Met Patrick. The rest is history."

He nodded. "You know, history is my thing."

But she didn't tell him anymore, even as they cleared the table. He and Tennessee headed over to fix the swing, and Grace put on her rubber boots, walking Hank down to the creek's muddy banks. The tide was out, so the dog chased crabs skittering across the muck. Grace picked blades of spartina grass and wove them into a chain, the links looping into one another. Intertwined, like the lives of everyone she knew.

Chapter 14

Edisto Island, Summer 1976

Grace balanced the tray of tea glasses, praying she could navigate the small dining room without spilling. Her table was in the far corner, where men sweaty with work sat shoulder-to-shoulder, eager for their dinner.

She made it across the room, knuckles white on the tray's edge. Somehow she should use one hand for delivery? The other girls did. Her heartbeat skidded, and her own sweat stains probably blossomed on her new uniform.

"Let me help." The man at the end jumped up and grabbed the tray. She didn't move. "You can let go." He seemed sturdy, dependable. Even his fingernails were clean.

Grace released her grip and passed out the glasses, but not without sloshing. She apologized, even though the spill happened because some men couldn't keep their hands to themselves.

Her first day waitressing at the Dockside, and if the restaurant hadn't been so new, she was certain they'd never have hired her, a girl whose syllables twanged rather than rounded off her tongue. When she said her thanks to her helper, she knew he heard the difference.

The corner of his mouth quirked up. He said, all drawl, "You're not from around here, are you?"

Her cheeks heated. "My friends have a house here."

"Who's that?"

"The Bells."

The man nodded. "Robert and Patsy. They know my parents." He held out his hand. "Patrick Watson." His grip was warm. Secure.

"They know mine too." Or they had. Grace hadn't figured out a story yet. She'd come home from the hospital with Patsy and Robert, and they offered the first stability she'd known in years. Her mother had been placed in a psychiatric ward, but then released. Grace didn't know where she'd gone. She wasn't sure she cared.

A week at the Bells' Edisto house had turned into longer when she found the job. The manager had winked at her during the interview and said the boys building the new Fairfield resort would probably enjoy having a face prettier than his bringing their shrimp.

"Stop fooling around with the help, Pat." One of the men—his hand had grazed her thigh when she passed over his drink—waved Patrick back to the table.

"Thank you again." She fled and waylaid Ginger, who'd trained her the day before. "Want to swap tables?"

The older woman snapped her gum and eyed the construction workers. "Why? They tip good, so long as you put up with their mess."

"Please."

"Fine, new girl. But you're gonna have to learn."

As the last of the sun faded from the sky, the men left to smoke on the dock. She could see them, as she refilled cocktail sauce bottles. Pinpricks of fire in the dusk.

"So you're around for awhile?" Patrick Watson stood before her, hands shoved in his pockets.

"I'm around." She glanced over her shoulder at Mr. Flowers, who frowned. No fraternization with the customers. At least not on the clock.

"Maybe you'd like to get a bite to eat sometime—one you don't have to serve?"

Nice boys never had the time of day for her before. But this was a new place, a new life. "Maybe." She let his kindness edge out her smile.

He leaned over, only a breath between them. "I'll be looking forward to it, Miss Grace."

Then he strode, so tall and strong and confident, out the door, and she pressed a hand to her chest, unable to calm her quickening heart.

Chapter 15

Lou's coffee grew cold while she read letters she'd written Mama and Daddy during her Emory years. Riding memories like a johnboat on the creek. Falling in love with David and his eternal optimism. Bringing him home for the first time and then again, for his first oyster roast.

She dumped the cup in the sink and stared out the window, over the pasture to where the land dipped down and the banks of the tidal creek rose.

Her daddy never cut those banks, but he'd trim them out occasionally when her mama got worried about snakes. Vegetation keeps the creek fertile, he'd say. Helps give us what we need. Then he'd go down and haul in a net of the tiny creek shrimp, and Mama'd make chowder or shrimp and grits.

Lou rolled that thought over her tongue. She could almost taste the cream—as surely as she could remember the way her heart raced when she tucked herself against David. Stuffing her feet into a pair of old galoshes from the hall closet, she pulled on a warm coat and gloves. Found Daddy's old net in the barn.

There are many ways to cast a shrimper's net, but Lou had only learned the one. She waded into ebbing tide and flailed the net in a wide arc. It landed in a perfect circle on the water and sank. She pulled the line.

Like riding a bicycle.

Her muscles remembered what her mind had pushed aside. The wind whispered over the water and she heard her father's and mother's voices arguing over the prices of tomatoes versus trees. The wind shifted and grazed her cold cheeks, Patrick telling her they could have a good life here. She pushed the sulfur smell into her lungs, letting the breeze lift her hair and the memories lose their tang.

David's old challenge meant she did learn to throw a spiral. A trick that now came in handy with the boys.

She emptied her net over the cooler. A few small flounder—easily tossed back—but only a handful of brown shrimp. Lou frowned.

"Looks like somebody forgot it's not shrimping season." Liam Whiting's voice echoed across the water.

Behind him, the sun dipped low. Lou shaded her eyes. "What are you doing here?" Apparently her manners had gone out with the tide.

"You said stop by anytime." He strode down the bank, with wide, confident steps. No worry with the sticky pluff mud beginning to ooze as the sifted water flowed back toward the sea. "Seriously, you got a license?"

"Are you here to arrest me for fishing my own creek?"

His eyes twinkled. "Nope. But I do have a proposition for you."

"I'm listening."

"I've been awarded a research grant."

Her brows shot up. He held up his hands. "I didn't say anything the other day, because I wasn't sure yet. We'll be studying estuaries of the ACE Basin." He waved at the creek. "Exhibit A."

She nodded. Their creek qualified. The ACE Basin referred to the Ashepoo, Combahee, and Edisto rivers. They combined together here in this triangle of the Lowcountry to make one of the largest undeveloped estuaries along the Atlantic coast. An area teeming with life and mystery for scientists and conservationists. Like her father had been.

Like he'd wanted her to be.

"There's been a lot of discussion about an onsite lab of sorts—really more of a place to store equipment, serve as a home base, so to speak."

She glanced toward the old barn.

Liam nodded. "The barn could work. And I could give you access to be the onsite facilitator. Make sure samples are being handled correctly, kids aren't poaching flounder for their dinner, and so on."

This time her smile came easily. "I could do that."

"Excellent. Want to have dinner with me later and talk it over? I'll pick up oysters from Flowers because they're in season."

Lou rolled her eyes and hefted one end of the cooler. He took the other, and they tossed back her meager catch. "I forgot about winter."

"Really?" Liam eyed her galoshes and coat.

She shrugged. She had forgotten. How the wind bit through layers but the sun blistered her cheeks, how the ocean churned under a slate-colored sky and lay subdued as a lamb under the china blue. How the creeks rose with rains and swelling tides, protecting the sleeping life within.

The Lowcountry might make an environmental researcher of her after all. The thought tiptoed around her mind. But to Liam she only said, "They're regrouping in the winter. The shrimp."

He laughed. "Yes, and all us novice catchers are grateful."

"Want some coffee?"

"Always."

He followed her up the bank and over the pastures to the back door. She held open the screen, and he stepped around her.

"You haven't changed a thing."

Passing judgment or observation? Standing in her mama's dated kitchen, in an old sweater and socked feet, she couldn't have felt more vulnerable if they'd been on a date and he'd asked her back to his place.

Why, for her, dating had never worked. She hadn't realized divorce meant she was expected to find someone else. Why bother? Now this man was in her kitchen, smiling at her, and he knew the past and the present but not the mess in-between.

Lou reached for the coffee grinder. "We're still settling in."

"I'm guessing the boys aren't here?"

"The quiet tip you off?" She whirred beans over the rattling of her thoughts.

His laugh had a nice, uncomplicated sound. "I'm sure they are not as wild as you paint them to be."

She filled the carafe with water and kept her back to him. "Have you spent much time with middle school boys?"

"No, but I was one."

Looking at him then, she found herself blushing, imagining him as a gangly teenager. "Did you have those glasses then?"

He tapped the thin wire rims. "Nope. Big, thick ones so I could see through the microscopes better."

Now she laughed, and the sound seemed to fracture the cold air that always seeped in through the cracks of this old farmhouse. She'd filled the place with a whirl of gaiety at Christmas, and then let January shroud her with its silence.

"Louisa? You all right?"

Her full name sounded sweet on his lips. Bracing her back against the counter, she turned and forced a narrow smile. "I'm fine. Just feeling a little lost these days. I'm sure the study will help."

He knit his brows together, clinical now, instead of friendly. "Did you consider a doctorate program?"

She took down mugs to avoid his gaze. "I've looked into it. But that's still a semester away at the earliest."

When she sat, he tapped the table between them, grazing her knuckles—surely in accident. "What about—"

A car door slammed and shouts filled the quiet.

She arched an eyebrow. "You wanted to meet the boys?"

The door burst open before she could get up. Cole gasped, "Hey, Mom, Dad says—" He stopped at the sight of Liam. "Who are you?"

J.D. and Mac were on his heels. David paused in the doorway. The cold crept back into the kitchen.

In Marietta, he'd drop the boys in the drive and maybe wave as he backed out. But on Edisto, he'd taken to coming inside and lingering.

And now Liam sat in David's chair.

Not that it should matter. "Y'all, this is Dr. Liam Whiting. He's a professor at the college and was a friend of your granddaddy's." Liam stood as David edged into the kitchen. "He came by to tell me about a research project the college is starting. See if I wanted to help."

Her rambling didn't seem to fool either man.

David held out his hand. "David Halloway." His tone held the same edge as the night she'd first introduced him to Patrick.

I got this, it seemed to say.

But this time Lou wasn't so sure.

Chapter 16

If he could sit in Grace's kitchen and eat cookies, Louisa could have any man she wanted over for coffee in hers.

David shoved the vacuum across his tiny living room. After the boys left, he always found a bountiful supply of potato chip crumbs and popcorn in his carpet. He knew their mother never had this issue. They'd argued about Lou's strict "eat only at the table" rule for years. Mostly because nobody watched Saturday afternoon football from the table.

The phone rang over the vacuum's whine, and he snapped it off. An afternoon of basketball would have done more for his irritation than housecleaning. He snatched the phone. Thornton Coultrie showed on the ID. Yet another thing Lou needed to change. "Yeah?"

"I hope you're teaching the boys better manners than that."

"I figured you had that covered."

"Clearly I caught you at a bad time."

"Clearly."

"In that case, you can call back when you're in a better mood." She hung up.

David tossed the phone on the couch. He rubbed his temples and fought feelings of—jealousy?

"We're divorced. She left you, remember?" Talking to himself was healthy, right? Might should have gone to see a therapist after all.

A run. Cora Anne swore by those. He'd do that instead of washing the dirty towels he was sure the boys had piled on the bathroom floor.

The phone rang again when he opened the door. He paused. Could let the machine get it. He still had one of those, even though his students said cell phones would soon usurp the house phone.

"David?" Lou's voice, clear and sharp, came over the line again. "I'm not sure what your issue is today, but I need to ask if you'd like to trade weekends. Dr. Whiting is coming out with students on Friday afternoon and setting up the lab. I'd rather the boys weren't underfoot."

As if they were still toddlers. He rolled his eyes. Ought to tell her no and make her deal with reality. But she so rarely asked for help—

"Please call me back when you'd like to have an adult conversation."

Ah, the last jab. Lou was good at those.

~ ~ ~

The run cooled his head enough that when he found Mac's math book under the couch—he was good about making them do homework at least—he tossed it in the Jeep and drove over to the farm.

Lou met him at the screen, arms crossed. "Can I help you?"

He held up the book.

She raised her brows. "Is your phone broken?"

"No."

"It's common courtesy to call before you visit someone."

"It's impolite to let someone stand out in the cold."

She huffed and shoved the door open. "What's the matter, David? Finally get tired of the slow life?"

He'd memorized the dance steps of this argument long ago. But might be time to make her lead. "Nope, just got in a mood earlier. I guess you've been entertaining?" He nodded at the coffee cups on the table alongside paperwork and maps detailing rivers. He knew enough South Carolina geography to recognize the Edisto River. It cut like a lifeline through the lower part of the state until it split and surrounded this island. Separating its inhabitants into another way of life.

Lou lifted one shoulder in her familiar noncommittal shrug. "Liam and I had to work out a few things."

"Aha."

"What's that supposed to mean?"

She moved next to him, anger heating her cheeks. He smelled the freshness of the soap she must have recently used. Lavender. Desire rose in him and he stepped back. How he could still want her after—

"You sure you're all right?" Her hand slid under his elbow.

She hadn't shown concern like this in quite awhile.

He laid his hand over hers, fingers brushing together, and watched as her cheeks flushed again. This time, he was sure, not from anger. "I'm fine. Sorry to take my bad mood out on you."

She pulled her hand away. "I guess I deserve it sometimes."

As close as she'd ever come to saying she was sorry. He slid an arm around her waist and pulled her in. An embrace of friendship, yes that's all he needed. She circled her arms around his neck and let him hug her. They'd fought about this too—his need for contact versus her need for space.

"Whoa, you guys are being weird." Mac came in the kitchen, and the moment shifted from David's grasp. His son raised his brows in an expression exactly like his mother's. "I left my math book at your house, Dad."

"Yeah, I brought it over." David nodded at the table. Lou had moved back to the sink and turned on the water for dishes, the expanse between them wide as ever.

"Thanks." Mac took his book and backpedaled out, still looking at them both with a furrowed brow.

"Did you get my message?" She held out a dishtowel. A wordless offering, but he took it.

"Sure, they can come over."

"I know they're not toddlers—"

He hid his smile, concentrating on drying a glass as she continued.

"—but I'm already having a hard time focusing and I know they'll get me distracted and flustered."

Lou hated being flustered, how well he knew. "Not a problem."

"I thought, maybe ..." She plunged her hands in the soapy water. "Liam suggested an oyster roast at the end of the month. Said it was one of his fondest memories when he worked here with Daddy."

David twisted the cloth inside a cup already dry. An oyster roast. Her parents used to give one every February, and when she finally invited him to one, he knew they'd turned the tide. From her silence to the way she continued swishing flatware in the water, David figured Lou hadn't forgotten quite as much as she pretended.

"Sure." He set down the glass. Reached for another. Kept his tone light. "Sounds fun. Guess you're asking for some help?"

"I'll have to haul tables out of the barn, clean out the fire pit …" She glanced over her shoulder at the closed door of what had once been the maid's room off the kitchen. "And I guess I need to set myself up an office of sorts so the kitchen table's not always so messy."

"My services might cost you." He enjoyed the way her lips pursed as if trying to decide if he was joking or serious.

"What's your price?"

"Enchiladas. Mac says the Taco Bell doesn't cut it."

"I should think not." She tugged the dishtowel from his hand. "Let's switch. My hands about can't take another round."

"Let me see." He cupped her hand in his and ran his thumb over her reddened knuckles. She let him trace the lifeline of her palm, before curling her fingers and pulling away, as if she was afraid of what he'd seen.

Chapter 17

Edisto Island, Summer—Christmas 1976

For their first date, Patrick took Grace for an upscale dinner in Charleston. She wore a pink dress and rolled her hair. On the way home he put the top down on his fancy convertible. Curls streaming, Grace imagined all her worries being carried off with the wind.

Because one date changed everything.

The next afternoon he appeared at the Dockside soon as her shift ended. He took her out to the family plantation at Cooper Creek—this time in his work truck—and fetched a picnic supper Lula May had packed. The housekeeper stood on the back porch clucking her tongue at Pat, telling him in a mix of Gullah and drawl that his "mama weren't gonna like 'is."

Patrick smacked her cheek with his lips. "Aw, Lula May, you worry too much."

She crossed thick arms, dark and shiny against the starched white of her apron. "Somebody's gotta worry about you."

They motored down the creek in a little johnboat barely big enough for two and the basket. She sat with her back against his knees. When the rocking tide made her queasy, he hooked his arm around her shoulders and held her still.

Three days ago she only knew his name. Now she figured Patrick Ravenel Cooper Watson was the type of steady man she could fall in love with.

So she did.

One Saturday night he took her dancing at the Pavilion. When the air inside became close and stale, they wandered down the boardwalk stretching over the water. A ribbon of moonlight sparkled on the waves. She leaned over the railing, quoting "The Highwayman" while Patrick held her waist. His soft chuckles tickled her ears.

"Pat?" A woman's voice said his name with a familiarity that made Grace's spine tingle.

They turned, but he kept his arm around her. "Hello, Lou."

She wasn't short, but next to a man whose elbow crooked around her neck and kept her tucked beneath his chin, she appeared so. Dark hair, wide eyes. Grace saw no threat, except in the way Patrick's jaw tightened.

"This is David." Lou gestured between the men. "Patrick Watson."

David loosed his arm and held out his hand. Pat grasped it. The other man smiled, as if he knew a secret. "Nice to meet you."

The current between them pulled, like a riptide. Pat broke free first. "Likewise." He took Grace's hand. "Grace, this is Louisa Coultrie."

Lou acknowledged her with a nod and lifted her fingers in farewell. "Have a good evening."

Patrick slid his arms around Grace again, propelling her around. "We are, indeed, having a good evening."

She wanted to ask him about Louisa, but she already knew the answer. And right then, she didn't want to know more.

~ ~ ~

By Christmas, Grace had met Patrick's parents, Charlotte and Temple Watson, a handful of times, each colder than the last. Frostbite, explained Patrick, was his mother's preferred expression of disapproval.

She knew they didn't want him working construction on Edisto, dreaming of environmentally sustainable building practices and his own company. Made sense they wouldn't care for her—a nobody girl without a lineage of pride. Grace thought she had stumbled into a feud between parents and son, but she hoped to shift Charlotte's opinion about her at least.

Until Christmas when she realized why she couldn't.

Over a simple family dinner at the plantation—only Patrick's mother could call standing rib roast simple—Charlotte said, "Is Louisa home for the holiday season yet?"

Pat's cheeks colored, but his voice remained smooth. "I don't know, Mother."

"One would think," Charlotte's eyes grazed over Grace who sat to Pat's left and longed for invisibility, "you would keep up with a woman you tried to marry."

Grace heard Lula May's breathing—as if she was the only one in the room not holding her breath to see what would happen next.

Patrick laid down his fork and placed his napkin on the table. His plate was full and his eyes furious. "That was not necessary, Mother."

"Oh?" Charlotte lifted her wine glass and nodded down the table to Pat's father. "We assumed you told Grace about her. After all, the Coultries are old family friends."

When Pat stood, he towered over his parents, Charlotte cool and calm, Temple placidly eating, letting her run the show, as he always did. His face contorted into a man she almost didn't recognize. "I hope then, Mother, I treat my friends with more respect than you do yours." He put a hand on Grace's shoulder. "Let's go."

She took his hand, ice in the pit of her stomach that for once had nothing to do with Charlotte.

They drove back to the beach in silence, the December night so mild he left the top down again. This time Grace wrapped her hair in a scarf and covered her legs with an afghan. She kept her face tilted up against the wind so she could see the stars.

They were close enough to smell the pluff mud of low tide before Pat spoke.

"I guess you want to know."

"Not if you don't want me to." She meant that. If he couldn't tell her this time, that would be all the answer she needed.

His hand found hers and clasped it. "Louisa Coultrie's mother and mine were old friends. They had a falling out years ago—before we were born. But that didn't stop me when I met her at a Pavilion dance. She was in college, had big dreams of graduate school and medical research, but mostly she wanted off this island. Her parents raised her here, and you know…" He pressed her fingers. "We don't always see the beauty that's right in front of us."

"So she left?"

"We dated that summer. Wrote letters when she went back to school. And if you think my mother doesn't like you, you should've seen her with Lou." He chuckled a bit, and Grace's heart quivered. She wanted that laugh to belong to her, to be a memory of moments only they spent together. "We fed each other's rebellion until the day I asked her to marry me."

"She said no?" Grace wondered about his words—what if she was only another pawn in this game he played with his parents?

"Lou wanted to leave. I wanted to stay. It really was that simple of an impasse." He pulled into the dark drive of Patsy's family home where Grace stayed as housekeeper, keeping the place ready for weekend getaways. Someday, she wanted a home of her own.

Pat turned to her, moved his hands to her shoulders, and pulled her close. "But Grace, I've never been so glad she left as I was that day you smiled at me at Dockside."

Leaning into his kiss, she faded into him, her choice made.

And one by one, the stars winked out of the sky.

Chapter 18

"David, I already told you, I understand." Lou shifted the phone to her other ear, so the cord would stretch the extra few inches she needed to peer out the kitchen window. In the yard, tables and chairs stacked askew. She was nowhere near ready for this event.

"We're short two teachers and an administrator. Can't leave the basketball tournament in the hands of a first-year coach." David's voice strained with frustration.

"I know. You're the best choice." She'd perfected this speech when they were married. Except this time, she was trying to mean it, and recognize it wasn't always his fault when he got called in to cover a duty. Though she didn't have to like it. "Go do your job, and I'll figure this out."

"It's just setting up the tables and chairs, right? I can come over in the morning and finish it."

By now her mama would have had everything arranged just in case a guest dropped by for a cocktail the evening before. She might strain her back hauling that heavy table into its correct place, but morning wasn't good enough. "I said I got it, David. Just feed the boys a decent supper, at least."

"I'm sorry, Lou."

She'd heard that before too.

Hanging up the old phone, Lou shrugged into her fleece. She could do this. Strategy was all she needed. And muscles. Maybe she could call Tennessee and ask for help—

A vehicle rumbled down the drive. Liam Whiting's Land Rover, which he exited easily, boots crunching on the gravel. "Evening, Louisa. Thought I'd come by and see if you needed an extra hand."

Embrace opportunity. Yes, indeed. She put on her best hostess face. "You are always welcome—and just in time for set up." She pulled on a pair of gloves that would protect her hands from cold and splinters. "My mama wouldn't approve of me accepting help before offering you a drink, but daylight's fading fast."

"I remember these." He hefted one end of the plywood table and helped her reposition it parallel to the side porch. "Eaten many a good oyster right here." Liam grinned at her.

The knot of tension in her neck eased as she returned his smile. Tonight he wore faded dungarees and a flannel work shirt. His dark hair needed a cut and curled just over the collar. For no explicable reason, Lou thought of David and his clean-cut blond trim. Hopefully he wasn't letting the boys eat too much junk at that ballgame.

They unfolded chairs into a semicircle around the fire pit. "How many shucking knives do you think we'll need?" Lou had counted a dozen in the kitchen drawer that morning.

"Hopefully someone told my students it's good etiquette to bring your own." He'd invited his class, and she'd extended invitations to what felt like half the Presbyterian Church as well as her family—and Grace. All in all, there would be at least thirty people.

"There's plenty of gloves." She'd found a trunkful cleaning out the barn so Liam could use it as the lab.

"Stop fretting." Liam laid a hand on her shoulder and she stilled, the easygoing contact raising goose bumps on her arms. He squeezed her shoulder. "You don't have to do this the way your mother did. I'd say, given your last six months, it's a wonder you're doing it at all."

"You want to stay for supper?" The question burst from her.

Liam's eyes sparkled like the lights overhead. "I thought you'd never ask."

Chapter 19

Edisto Island, February 1977

Lou had explained the science behind when oysters were best. But David preferred her father's everyday knowledge.

One didn't eat oysters in months without an r.

Mr. Coultrie had a lot of practical know-how David appreciated. His own father could catch trout by the stringerful and rebuild an engine, but his applicable skills ended there. Of course, based on his turbulent job history, Dad's skills were no match for his temper.

They'd lasted only one season in Boy Scouts. His father could build a fire just fine in a metal garbage can with plenty of lighter fluid, and David never learned another way.

Until now.

"You lay the sticks over one another like this." Mr. Coultrie crossed the narrow branches in the fire pit. "The air's got to circulate. Fire's got to have oxygen to breathe."

David, squatting in the dirt beside him, grinned. "Like us."

T.C. Coultrie cut his eyes sideways. "You don't want to be like a fire, son."

Despite the forty-degree weather, he started to sweat. Lou's daddy evidently wasn't much on metaphors. "No, sir, I—"

Mr. Coultrie pulled a matchbook from his shirt pocket. "You know what happens when I light this?"

David licked his lips. "Yes." The narrowed eyes again. "Sir."

"What then?"

"The fire starts."

"Nope." Mr. Coultrie flicked his wrist and the flame sprung to life.

"Looks hearty right now, but when I put this little heat right here on this kindling …" He poked the match down into the teepee of sticks. Smoke curled up. "It takes work to make that spark into a fire."

He might have been wrong about T.C. Coultrie and the metaphors.

"Sometimes the wood's not too good. It's been scarred." Mr. Coultrie hefted one of the logs still lying in the grass. "See here? This piece'll burn right up, but it ain't gonna make me a fire worth cooking on." He tossed the piece aside. "You get what I'm telling you, son?"

David held out his hand. "I believe so, sir."

Mr. Coultrie handed him a bundle of twigs. "Then show me."

David tended the fire all afternoon and into the evening as Lou bustled around with her mother and sister. More than once, he looked up and locked eyes with her father, rocking on the porch.

At sundown, Mr. Coultrie moved back to the yard. "Stir up those coals. Let me see how you did."

David dug a thick stick into the embers, glowing red-hot and orange, streaks of blue in their depths.

Mr. Coultrie clapped him on the shoulder. "Well done. Guess you can be counted on to stick with something stubborn—even if in the end you might get burned."

Lou crossed the yard, lugging a bucket of oysters. No doubt what this was really about.

"I can, sir." He held out his hand.

Mr. Coultrie grasped it. "Good then. Let's get to the real purpose of this fire."

They laid a piece of sheet metal over the fire. When drops of water on it sizzled, David took Lou's bucket and followed her father's directions for spreading the oysters evenly. Once popping commenced, like tiny sparklers on the Fourth of July, he helped rake the opened shells into clean metal tubs that were upended over the tables.

Most folks had eaten by the time David joined Lou. "This is amazing."

She passed him a shucking knife and a set of gloves. "It's one-of-a-kind, for sure. Not something you'd see in the city."

"That's what makes it special." He kissed her—a quick brush of his lips against her cheekbone.

Lou looked down. "Want me to show you how to open a shell?"

"Sure." He copied her movements, but bore down too hard and in an instant his hand welled blood, red as the coals.

"David!" She grasped his arm and pressed a napkin against the gash. "You're supposed to wear the gloves."

"Next time I'll listen."

The corner of her mouth twitched. She lifted the napkin, and pushed it back down. "You need stitches."

No doubt. He could now feel every beat of his pulse pushing blood out that cut. But he'd had worse. "Just tie it up good, and I'll drive over. No reason we should both miss the party."

Lou leaned into him like she had that day in the creek when she'd taught him to shrimp. "I don't care if I miss the party."

They drove to the Medical University of South Carolina in downtown Charleston. More than once, Lou's hands slipped from the wheel. Much as his hand hurt, it was worth it to see her worry.

At the hospital, she sat beside him jiggling her leg, which made his cut throb all the more. "Hey." He put his good hand on her knee. "Why don't you go find us some coffee?"

"You sure you'll be all right?"

"There are a dozen medical professionals within shouting distance. I'll be fine."

She bolted from the chair, and he waited until she was gone before dropping his chin to his chest in quiet laughter. That woman. Good thing she wanted to do medical research and not actual practice.

"David?"

A tall man loomed over him, and he took a moment to place the face. Patrick Watson.

"Hope you're here for a better reason than me." David extended his other hand before realizing it was streaked with blood from holding the napkin.

Patrick eyed the bloody palm. "Buddy of mine had an accident on the Ocean Ridge site. What in the world did you do?"

"First oyster roast."

"Ah." Patrick grinned. "You're supposed to wear a glove."

"Lou pointed that out."

Patrick chuckled. "I'll bet she did." He held David's eyes for a moment too long for comfort, but David clenched his jaw and refused to look away. "Y'all serious?"

He lifted one shoulder and then refused to wince. The pain had spread. "I hope so."

Patrick's ghost of a smile hinted at something deep and sad. "She wouldn't have brought you here if she wasn't."

Chapter 20

"Y'all ready to get dirty?" Lou addressed the students away from the heat of the roaring fire. David had tried to redeem himself for last night by being overly helpful today.

"Tonight?" One of the girls asked, wide-eyed.

"Well, shucking oysters isn't exactly pristine." Lou eyed the girl's white fleece. "I've got some old coats hanging inside if you need."

"Professor Halloway's mother had to loan me a jacket at my first roast, too." Liam winked at her.

"I'll go get them." She fled, away from the students' curious stares, to the safety of her kitchen.

David was there, washing his hands. "You get too close to the fire, Lou? Your face is awfully red."

"I'm fine."

He patted her shoulder as he went back out the door. "If you say so."

Long as she stayed in here until her cheeks—and now butterflies—subsided, she would be fine. Sometimes even her mama had hidden in the kitchen from awkward situations.

By the time Lou gathered an armful of outerwear and came out again, David stood beside Grace at the fire pit. She said something, he threw back his head and laughed, and she pressed a gloved hand on his forearm. Lou felt a sudden sour taste in her mouth. So, David and Grace weren't just friends.

They were *friendly*.

"Mama, look out!"

A huge beast of a dog leapt at her. Lou careened backwards, lost her footing, and landed in a heap while the dog licked at her face.

"We got him, Mom!" J.D. yelled. Her boys pulled at the leash someone had obviously let go.

"Here, I got you." Liam put a hand under her and helped her to her feet while David and Grace rushed over.

"Lou, I'm so, so sorry." Grace grabbed the beast's leash. "I thought surely he wouldn't get loose from three boys."

"He's yours?"

"Why, yes. This is Hank." She swung her head back to David. "You didn't ask her?"

He gave the sheepish grin Lou had come to know too well during their marriage. He'd always been unselfish to a fault, but he also often forgot anything he didn't think a big deal. Like getting milk on the way home or switching the laundry before it soured in the machine. Little things that had become hurdles to Lou's system.

"Sorry, ladies. I forgot. Lou, is it all right if Grace brings the dog? He's a foster, you know. And he gets awfully nervous when he's left alone."

"Pees on everything," Tennessee confirmed from over David's left shoulder.

Lou dusted at her jeans in avoidance of David's pleading gaze— and Grace's wide-eyed innocence. "Well, since he's already here, it's not like I'll send him back."

"Really, I'm so sorry." Grace rubbed under the beast's chin. "I'd make him apologize if I was capable of such a thing."

"Just keep him away from the fire." Lou's hip ached when she turned.

Liam took her arm again. "Why don't you sit down for a minute?" He'd gathered up the scattered coats under one arm, and with the other, led her over to a lawn chair.

She sat, frowning. Her mother never had a rest when hosting.

Once the boys had taken half the college kids and Hank off to romp at the creek bank, David appeared at her side holding a red Solo cup. "Figured you might need this."

"Thanks." This time the graze of his fingers against hers didn't make her stomach quiver. Seeing how Grace had angled her body toward his, hearing the familiar tone in which she'd said his name, Lou no longer felt any guilt about supper with Dr. Liam Whiting. Clearly, David had been having suppers of his own.

"The boys like that dog."

One of them had found a thick piece of driftwood to hurtle back and forth and make Hank fetch. The dog trotted back gleefully, the wood dangling from his giant jaws, and Cole playfully wrestled it free and flung it again, this time toward Mac.

"Boy's got an arm." Liam said from the chair beside hers.

David grunted, though Lou didn't know how he could resent the observation. He'd taught Cole to throw.

"They love baseball." She tilted her head toward David. "But this one thinks they're big enough for football now."

"She wouldn't let me sign them up until they got some height and weight." David rubbed the back of his neck. "Said we spent too long praying over them in the NICU to let them get concussions on a football field."

"Sounds wise."

Liam's words were met with another grunt from David. "Want me to wet down that burlap and get a bushel going?"

She almost choked on her sip of wine. "You sure you remember how?"

"I remember." David's eyes narrowed, and Lou wondered what else he remembered. Her parents' oyster roasts had bound their courtship from beginning to end. Lately, he'd been open and unguarded, but tonight—with her at least—he closed off tight as one of those shells.

"I'll help." Liam stood.

Her sister and brother-in-law arrived while David and Liam were hosing down burlap sacks. Hank, who must have lost interest in the driftwood, bounded over to greet new guests. He knocked Carolina's picnic basket right out of her arms and a bottle of hot sauce shattered against the cement blocks ringing the fire.

Grace, her face the color of the Tabasco, dragged him away and shut him in the cab of Tennessee's truck while order was restored. In the end, John was elected grill master, and Grace caved to Hank's whining and the boys' promises to keep him on his leash. Several of Liam's students, also enamored with the behemoth, stood guard around him and the triplets as they tried teaching Hank simple commands.

"Lou, doesn't Hank remind you of that dog your parents had back when the kids were young?" Grace took the platter of raw vegetables Lou had fetched. She set it on the table, almost exactly where Mama always had. Lou resisted the urge to adjust it.

"Beau?"

Grace snapped her fingers. "Yes, Beau."

Her mama's basset hound hadn't exhibited a fourth of Hank's energy. For heaven's sake, the dog would hide in the bathtub if it thundered or a crowd of people gathered.

The next driftwood toss landed at Grace's feet and when Hank retrieved it, she grabbed his collar and turned his face to Lou. "They have the same eyes, don't you think?"

Lou thought a lot of things that didn't have to do with either dog.

"Hey, Mom, don't you think we need a dog? I bet Grace would let us have Hank." Cole pulled on the leash. "C'mon, boy, let's play."

"I don't think so, boys." Lou looked through the steam rising off the metal and met Grace's gaze. "Dogs require a lot of attention."

"Your mother's right." Grace tipped up her chin. "Hank would be a lot to take on. He needs constant affection."

Had Grace meant to change her word? Lou turned away and focused on the popping of the oysters.

She tightened her hold on her emotions. Even though she knew—a little steam was all it took to crack the tightest shell.

Chapter 21

"Heard that dog of yours caused quite the ruckus over at Lou's Saturday night." Gloria Jenkins settled her wide seat into the chair at Grace's sink, all ready for her wash and set—and a dose of good gossip.

"I got him under control." Grace turned on the water and aimed the nozzle at Gloria's steel-colored head. Usually she considered tolerating Gloria one of her acts of service, but not today. Maybe with water running in her ears, the woman would keep quiet.

"I told you before, Gracie—"

Grace ground her teeth. She'd told Gloria for the last twenty years she hated being called that.

"—ain't no reason you can't take those critters up to the shelter in Charleston. Nobody says you have to take in every stray left behind by good-for-nothing tourists." The fact the tourists' presence kept life stable on the island meant nothing to Gloria. She'd been born here, and she'd die here, regardless of how many people rented beach houses and booked fishing tours.

Maybe Grace could hush the woman with a scalp massage.

"I also heard Lou's ex-husband and you are getting pretty chummy. You been seen walking together on the beach." Gloria raised her brows with a scalp full of suds. The effect reminded Grace of Munch's *The Scream.* Fitting, of course.

"David and I are just friends." She didn't owe this woman an explanation, but anything she said would be repeated over hot toddies that afternoon at Gloria's Garden Club meeting. Might as well set the record straight while she had the chance. "Sometimes I bring Hank over to run around with the boys when he has them. Wears everyone out."

"They're giving those boys whiplash raising them like that. Back and forth, one weekend here, one weekend there. At least they both bring 'em to church." Gloria held the towel around her head as Grace helped her to her feet. "Now I know you did a fine job with Tennessee— eventually."

Grace cast her eyes to the salon's drop ceiling. "Yes, ma'am."

"But you know firsthand a boy needs a daddy all the time. What Lou was thinking letting that man walk away, I'll never figure."

"You know, Ms. Gloria, it's really none of my business." *Or yours either.*

"Sure it is. You're keeping company with him, and your son has his sights set on Cora Anne."

"That he does."

"So you may want to cool things down with his father-in-law to-be until all that's settled." Gloria leaned her head back and sighed. "I do like it when you do that massage thing, Gracie."

"Let me get the comb through it first." Like pulling through steel wool, and Grace didn't try to be gentle. Gloria must've got the message because she stayed quiet for the rest of her cut and style.

While Grace cleaned her combs, Gloria wrote out her check in broad strokes. The woman was going to live to be a hundred and never show a sign of frailty. "You give David my best next time y'all are together, all right?"

Grace whipped around. "David Halloway and I are not together, Ms. Gloria. And I'd appreciate it if everyone wouldn't make assumptions. He's here for his wife, for goodness' sake."

The moment the words were out, she clapped her hand over her mouth. "Oh, gracious. Please don't repeat that."

Gloria's eyes twinkled. "Repeat what, dear? After all, anything I say is merely gossip."

~~~

"Aw, Mom. Really? Gloria Jenkins?" Tennessee dropped to his seat at her dining table, looking bone weary but clean, at least. A day spent working with drywall left him covered in a fine film of white. When he showed up at her door asking to join her for supper, she'd sent him over to his little A-frame to shower and change. While the beef stew kept warm, she went back on her resolution to eat less carbs and made a batch of biscuits.

"She gets me all riled up and I can't think straight." Grace set down his bowl. "Makes me actually feel bad for Louisa, having to call that woman family."

"How's she related anyhow?"

"Third cousin on Annie's father's side."

He grinned at her. "How do you keep up with these things?"

"People talk when they're getting their hair done."

They ate for a few moments until she could stand the suspense no longer. "You got something to tell me?"

"Sure. These are great biscuits." He pushed back from the table. "But I'd like a little of those peach preserves to go with 'em, so why don't you look this over while I get it."

He set a small velvet box on the table. A box the color of the ocean in summer. Grace grabbed it. Inside, nestled a ring of fine simplicity. Gold band, solitaire diamond, studded on the side with sapphires.

She met her son's eyes with tears in hers. "It's breathtaking."

"It's an antique, of course. Hannah helped me out in a shop downtown."

So he'd been shopping on King Street. She felt a pang he hadn't asked her to come along, but he was a grown man now, who didn't need his mama to pick out the ring he wanted to give the woman he loved.

"Cora Anne will love it."

He grinned. "I'm going to talk to David first. And Lou. Think I should ask them together or separate?"

Grace fingered the stones and thought of the words she'd hurled at Gloria that afternoon. "Together. That's what David wants, and truthfully, I think Lou probably does too."

Tennessee covered her hand with his work-callused one. She closed her eyes, and for a moment she could feel Patrick, as palpable in the room as the smells of beef stew and fresh biscuits.

"Someday, Mom, if you want it, I think God will send you someone."

Grace repeated the words she needed to be true. "You and your dad are all I've ever needed."

Too bad no one needed her. Not anymore.

Chapter 22

Friday afternoon, Lou stood knee-deep in the creek. High tide and the water rushed in gentle swirls around her father's old galoshes. She kept the wind from her face with her mama's straw gardening hat tied beneath her chin.

She took samples from different areas and marked each cup with block letters with a black Sharpie. The time, date, location—more specific than Russell Creek at the Coultrie farm. She listed "old oyster bed" and "small tributary app. 25 feet" and "strong flow". Each sample would be sent back to the college lab for further study, then to the research hub at Clemson. Probably over to the Army Corps of Engineers too. There were so many fingers stirring this pot of Liam's, she couldn't keep up.

She knew one thing for sure. This wasn't the same creek she'd been raised on. Since moving home, she'd heard the locals murmuring. How Big Bay Creek behind The Hideaway was now useless for gathering. How they didn't dare eat anything pulled from the ponds and estuaries of South Edisto. The Edisto River split in two and rimmed the island. The north remained, for the most part, fertile. But the south suffered the pollution of overpopulation.

The Coultrie farm occupied a sliver of the island's north side, so Lou had no qualms fishing and eating from her own creek. But the vibrancy of life she remembered seemed subdued, even here. Once, her parents had culled all the oysters they'd need for a roast right from their own backyard.

Her roast had been supplemented with bushels from Charleston.

Interesting the two rivers could now be so different, having run the same course for so long.

Lou heaved herself up on the dock and sat for a moment, watching an egret take flight. No different, perhaps, than herself and her siblings. Carolina had carried on their mother's love for hospitality, and Jimmy developed Daddy's business far beyond what he had ever dreamed. They'd come from the same womb, and yet, she struggled to believe this may be her place.

Her father had wanted her to use her gift—her love of science and structure to see their world. To protect it.

Lou ran her thumb across her carefully documented samples, smearing one a bit. She might be able to help revitalize this creek more effectively than she could reinvent her own life.

These samples measured the water's turbidity—its cloudiness due to particles—as well as pH levels and conductivity. Probes, now mounted on tall poles in varying locations along the creek as it ran the length of her father's land, measured the water in real time. She and the students helped monitor the data, looking for triggers that indicated ecosystem stress.

If only she'd monitored the stress in her marriage with the same attention to detail.

Back in the kitchen, Lou made a pot of coffee and frowned at the chuck roast she'd bought on sale. This was David's weekend and while she'd never disdained leftovers, the idea of three days of the same meal held little appeal.

She had David's number half-dialed when she heard tires crunching on the gravel outside. Liam knocked a moment later.

"Hey, there." She pushed open the screen. "Come on in out of the cold."

He inhaled deeply. "I could smell those Charleston beans soon as I pulled in."

She chuckled, appreciating his appreciation for her coffee. "Sure you could."

"Thought I'd come check out the week's work and take you to dinner. I heard The Hideaway has an oyster casserole on the menu this week."

Liam presumed and she liked that. David had always waited on her to decide, and sometimes, the thousand decisions of motherhood couldn't stretch to include whether or not they should eat Chinese or order pizza.

"Tennessee says it's delicious, and he should know." She pulled her coat around her shoulders. "Work first?"

"Like you read my mind."

Liam made this easy. Yet, somehow, she wished mind-reading had worked for her and David.

~ ~ ~

Lou let Christy Townsend, The Hideaway's resident hostess, hug her and lead them to a table with a water view. "Expect Ben to send over an appetizer. He likes to take care of family, you know." The young woman winked and sailed off to greet another couple entering the cozy establishment on this chilly night.

"They're turning quite a business here for the off-season." Liam observed.

He seemed so poised, pursing his lips as he perused the wine list, totally at ease with the surroundings of white linen and votive candles. On her first official date with David, they'd gone to Captain D's because he knew she liked seafood.

She folded her hands under her chin and gazed around the now-familiar restaurant that Tennessee and Ben Townsend had made into one of the most up and coming destination eats on the coast. "They are smart young men. Hoping some of it will rub off on mine."

"Keep them surrounded by good influences, and surely something will stick." Liam set down the menu as a server approached. He ordered a bottle of Chardonnay, and Lou asked for water. Moody as she'd been lately, she didn't need more than one glass of wine.

"Speaking of influences, they're enjoying your students' company."

"That goes both ways."

"They want me to get a dog."

He raised his brows. "You didn't seem too taken with that beast last weekend."

"Well, definitely not one like him." Transparency didn't need to include her lingering envy of Hank's owner. She shook her head, tossing off the unwelcome thought. "What?"

His eyes—dark as the coffee beans they both loved—narrowed. "You have an ulterior motive."

She gaped. "I do not."

He pressed his lips together again—she had a wildly fleeting thought she shouldn't be noticing his mouth so much—but the moment broke when Jeanna Townsend set a bottle of wine on the table.

"Hey there, Lou. They're short-staffed tonight since that terrible flu is taking everyone out like a tidal wave." Jeanna, Ben's mother and Grace's best friend, twisted the corkscrew deftly. "So what's a mother to do but come to her son's rescue? He's even got Hannah back there in the kitchen."

This was a bad idea, coming to a place where everyone knew her and would speculate. David was sure to hear—

"Oyster casserole's the special, as I'm sure y'all heard. It's what's bringing everyone in here this week, but personally," Jeanna leaned in again, "I'd get the flounder. Ben and his chef have been perfecting it since Christmas and it will melt in your mouth." She tossed her sunny smile to Liam.

An introduction might be needed. "Jeanna, this is my colleague, Dr. Liam Whiting. Liam, Jeanna Townsend."

"We didn't get to meet officially at Lou's oyster roast. I was on grandmother duty, you know."

"Lovely to meet you." Liam extended his hand. "Your son has quite a place here."

"He does, and thanks to Lou's niece, that darling Hannah," Jeanna clasped her hands together in giddiness, "it's getting even better. Now can I bring y'all the flounder?"

"How about one flounder and one oyster special?" Liam met Lou's eyes over his glass.

"Sounds perfect."

"All right then." Jeanna sashayed off, still working the room as both a proud mother and an eloquent hostess. Hannah stuck her head out the swinging kitchen door and beckoned her back, but she caught sight of Lou in the process and waved.

"Is there anyone left on Edisto you won't be related to before long?" Liam chuckled. "And people around here make jokes about Alabama cousins."

"Oh, hush." Lou twisted the stem of her glass. "It's a small community is all."

"One your family has made quite an impression upon."

"I suppose."

He reached across the table and caught her wrist. "Be proud of your heritage, Louisa."

She pulled away, but still felt his heat on her skin. "I am."

"But you're still pursuing a doctorate in chemistry."

"I thought you said we weren't going to talk business."

"And I thought you said teaching at Charleston would be an honor. Ecology's a more likely position."

"I told you almost thirty years ago why I didn't want to do that."

"Guess I hoped you'd change your mind."

She crossed her arms, drawing her thin cardigan close around her body. "It's cool in here."

"I'll see if we can't get the heater going." He rose and crossed to the corner where a tall silver heater promised warmth for her skin but not her memories.

Chapter 23

Edisto Island, February 1978

On the back roads from Atlanta, the drive to Edisto pushed seven or eight hours with stops. Lou reveled as the highway's pine-rimmed fields, ripe with soybeans, tobacco, or summertime rows of cattle-feed corn eased into narrow roads shadowed by old forest growth. Then the vista broke open, revealing thin ribbons of tidal creeks.

The long drive always gave her the right amount of time to steady her heart and remind herself, one couldn't live off nature's raw beauty. Especially when one strong storm could bring it all down.

For David, however, the drive's novelty had worn off.

As she coasted down Highway 174, Jimmy Buffet on the radio, she forgave him his antsy behavior. Reminded herself he'd been raised among traffic that snarled like the branches of the live oaks over their heads.

Driving home through this tunnel felt like a baptism sometimes, anointing a welcome return. On others, she only remembered the sense of captivity. Lovely as these old trees were, they held her to this place, rooted her here in this soil born of pluff mud and blood.

Much as she longed for a taste of her mother's table and a gruff embrace from her father, today's drive felt like a cage. The realization this remote farm may be the only place she'd ever belong weighed heavy.

Beside her David shifted, trying to fit his long legs into the little VW Bug's space. "You want to talk about what you've been chewing on this whole drive or should I just keep pretending I don't notice?"

She cut her eyes from the road over to his. Usually that dimple in his left cheek was deep in a smile, his easygoing, loping grin his most prominent feature. She was a sucker for a man with a lazy smile, no doubt.

David scrubbed his hand through his blond hair, now cropped short to match his teaching persona. Likely this would be his last trip to Edisto for a while. Baseball season would start soon as they returned from this year's oyster roast.

When she still said nothing, he held up his palm so she could see the scar. "C'mon, Lou. I took a knife for you."

"Trust you'll put on a glove this time."

"Only if you tell me what's wrong."

"I'm not sure that's an even trade." She slowed the car into the line of traffic waiting on the Dawhoo Bridge to close itself back down. Along the Edisto River a shrimp boat chugged beneath the bridge, nets raised high.

In the small confines of the car, he leaned over, his face next to hers, his aftershave tickling her nose. She leaned her head back and let him nuzzle her neck. He didn't stop there, feathering small kisses up her jaw line to her ear. "David … we're in the car in the middle of the day…"

Even Patrick Watson hadn't undone her composure like David Halloway could with nothing but a simple kiss.

"Guess if you don't want to do this while we wait half our lives for that bridge to close, you'll just have to talk." David sat back, arm still slung behind her shoulder, smugness tipping his chin.

Lou groaned and laid her forehead against the steering wheel. "You're a horrible person."

"Frankly, my dear, you're no picnic yourself, even if you were raised a stone's throw from the ocean." David held a persistent belief about her longevity in decision-making and her slow response to even the most mundane of questions. When it takes an hour to get to civilization, he'd say, you can take an hour to choose.

She scrunched her nose at him now, irritated and aroused, annoyed and relaxed. He wanted her to be more than this sleepy island, and she liked that. Had believed in herself until yesterday.

"I didn't get the job."

"At the CDC?"

"No, at the high school." She rolled her eyes. "Of course at the CDC."

"There's other jobs."

"No, there's really not. Know why I didn't get it?"

He arched a brow and slid his fingers under her ponytail to knead the tension in her neck. "Why?"

"Because I'm a woman, and while there are a limited number of opportunities available for women in the medical research field, they have already decided to fill this position with one who is less qualified—but prettier—than me."

David's hand stilled. "They said that?"

"In not so many words." She sucked in her lower lip. The committee of doctors who interviewed her had all been men about her father's age, pompous and arrogant with wing-tipped loafers and pressed collars. One of them had crossed his arms and sniffed her direction. As she gathered her things to leave, she heard him tell his colleague a box of KFC had bigger breasts than her.

She shook off David's touch. He withdrew his hand and placed it over hers. "Lou, they're all fools. I'm sorry."

"So am I." She sniffed, willing the tears back. "There aren't many other options in Atlanta right now."

"So do something else."

He didn't get it. She didn't want to do anything else. A lab ensured a controlled, safe environment. Quiet and methodical, research wasn't a job that could be rushed. It required thoroughness and attention to detail. She bore those traits well. Something else would mean she'd have to cultivate different tendencies.

Traffic lurched forward, the bridge having smoothly and slowly lowered back into place.

"What about teaching?"

She tapped the break—hard. At David's suggestion, the VW had surged forward too quickly for the car in front. "I'm not a teacher."

"But you could be." Excitement mounted in his voice, the timbre of it rising as it did anytime he hit on what he thought was the best idea. "Lou, there are never enough science teachers. You could run a department someday—teach upper-level classes, maybe even college."

"I don't want to teach. I want to research."

"Then teach until you find a research gig. At least then"—he slipped his fingers into hers—"we can be on the same schedule. Think about it—summers off to travel, always plenty of time at the holidays to visit family…"

His voice tripped only the tiniest bit on the word, and she knew what he was thinking. Her family would always be in the same place. Who knew where his parents would land next?

"Especially since it takes half a day to drive out here." Voice steadied again, he waved his hand at the river sparkling in the setting evening sun.

The offer tempted, no doubt. But she couldn't commit to that kind of decision, staying on with him in Atlanta, unless—

"By the way, I asked your dad if I could take him out to lunch tomorrow."

Her hand slipped on the wheel.

"Since I know you take forever to make decisions, that's all I'm going to tell you, all right?" David squeezed her fingers, his teasing smile returning, his eyes alight with hope.

She blinked to clear her vision and nodded, wondering how long was too long when it came to making a decision meant to last a lifetime.

Chapter 24

First thing Saturday morning Tennessee called. David fumbled the phone when the young man asked if he and Lou might join him for brunch after church tomorrow.

"Cora Anne will be tied up with the museum all day, you know."

David did know.

A moment later, the doorbell rang. "Dad, Mom's here." J.D. and his brothers thundered up the stairs, then back down again.

He met Lou in the hall and took the grocery sack out of her arms.

"Morning." Under the sunglasses on her head, strands of her dark hair billowed, reminding him of the way she'd looked at Emory. "I think I've got everything we need so you can learn to make an actual Sunday dinner."

He began unloading contents. "Let's make it Saturday supper since we have a brunch invitation tomorrow."

"I know. He called before I left." She smirked. "Told you this was coming."

"Doesn't mean I have to like it." What he did like, however, was the idea of spending the afternoon with her. "Amazing how some things work themselves out, huh?"

Lou creased her brows, studying him as though his words carried a heavier implication. Maybe they did. He held his breath. Did she feel the tension that hovered around? The kind that didn't spark anger—but possibility.

Her face smoothed back out and she rolled her shoulders, easing into the distance between them. "Yes. Amazing." She reached for a bag of carrots. "Let's get this meal going."

Washing potatoes and carrots put them hip-to-hip in his small kitchen. She seemed right at home as she searched his drawers for a knife she liked. "I might get a dog."

"You hate dogs."

"I do not." She snapped the narrow end of a carrot, and he raised his brows. She shrugged. "Bad spot."

"You don't like dogs." He wasn't going to be distracted by wilting carrots or the fact that this close, he could tell she'd switched back to her old standby Dove soap.

"I don't like messes," Lou clarified. "Dogs, in and of themselves, are not the problem."

"Dogs make messes."

"So do boys. And boys like dogs."

Ah, now they were coming to it. "Are you jealous of Hank?"

"David James Halloway." She pressed the knife against the pockmarked skin of an innocent potato. "I am not jealous of some animal."

He thought maybe it was the dog's owner she envied, but didn't think that statement would be safe in the vicinity of the knife and all. "So you want to get a dog?"

"I'm not sure why you aren't following this conversation."

Because it made no sense. He tried a new strategy. "What kind?"

"Mama always liked goldens. Beau was the exception."

A golden retriever. He could see that actually. "Would be good company for you when the boys are over here."

She dropped the knife and wheeled on him—or into him, rather. The kitchen was very small and he'd had to stand nearly on top of her to share the cutting board. "You are not listening. A dog for the boys. So they'd bring it when they come over. Because it would be their dog."

"Our dog."

"Excuse me?" She picked up the knife again and the carrots were on the receiving end of frustration he truly couldn't follow.

He stepped back. "*Our* dog. If it travels with the boys, it would be *our* dog. Just like they're *our* kids."

She'd narrowed her eyes each time with his emphasis. Slicing the last carrot, she banged the knife on the counter. "Fine. *Our* dog for *our* kids. And you remember you said that, not me."

He felt safe enough now to retrieve a Pepsi from the fridge and pass one to her. The boys banged back in the front door. "So, when are we doing this?"

"Doing what?" J.D. rounded the corner first, followed by Mac and Cole who pushed their way into the small space to open the refrigerator. He and Lou were hip-to-hip again.

"Your father," she slid her eyes over to his, "thinks we should get a dog."

"Really?"

"Oh, awesome!"

"Can we go today? After we finish our game?" Mac led the charge back out the door.

Lou kept her eyes on his, their blue depths unreadable, but a smile twitched her lips. He almost bent his head to hers, wanting to see if he could tease out more than a smile. But instead, with great effort, he reached around her and plugged in the Crockpot. "What do we do now?"

"Come over here and we'll do a little research. Daddy used to have a friend in Charleston who bred goldens."

He joined her at the computer set up on his tiny work desk. She sat in his swivel chair and twisted like an impatient child. When he pulled another chair over from the table, her spinning made their legs collide.

His hands stilled her knees. "Calm down. We'll find what you want."

Beneath his hands, her legs jerked. Her blue eyes had gone dark, pupils widening as she stared at him. He lifted one hand and cupped under her chin, passing his thumb over her lips—

"Dad! Where'd you put the football?"

She pulled back, the wheels on the chair pushing her beyond his grasp. He dropped his hand, but kept his eyes fixed on hers.

"In the front closet, Cole. With all the other equipment."

The door slammed again, and he reached forward and drew her

chair back beside his.

"What are we doing, David?"

He heard the tremble in her voice, the worry and fear so like his own. With great effort, he tucked a lock of her hair behind her ear. The stubby ponytail she could now wear made her girlish again, and he remembered how skittish she'd been when they first met.

"We're getting a dog," he told her, smiling. "That's all for now."

~ ~ ~

When David had asked Lou's father if he could marry his daughter, they'd had to drive all the way into Walterboro, and even then, there'd been no fancy restaurant. Just the soda fountain on the square. He could still remember dripping burger grease all over his dress slacks.

But T.C. had been gracious—even as he gruffly informed David he'd only ask him to do one thing. "Take care of my daughter. I don't want her to keep thinking she can only count on herself."

Lou's father died before they divorced, but David always figured he knew it was coming. Like he also believed T.C. and Annie never stopped praying Lou and he would work everything out.

As he pulled into The Hideaway's drive, David hoped there was no statute of limitations on when God answered prayers.

With the perk of business owner, Tennessee commandeered the best table, in the corner of the screen porch. The February day had turned mild enough that Lou, who'd complained incessantly about the cold all winter, actually removed her jacket.

She'd worn slacks to church, as was her habit, but chosen a demure blue sweater studded with tiny pearls along the collar for her top. David had given it to her one Christmas, and he'd felt a rush of hope when he saw her come in the church doors that morning.

The shoulder of her coat slid from the chair and dragged on the floor. As he leaned over to retrieve it, he whispered, "You look nice today."

The flush barely touched her cheeks, but he sensed the glow. Satisfied, he shifted his seat a bit closer to hers, making sure Tennessee understood, for today at least, Cora Anne's parents were a united front.

The young man he'd come to admire over the last nine months rarely lacked poise. But today, Tennessee fidgeted with his fork, raked fingers through his blond hair, and tugged constantly at his tie. Only at Annie's funeral had David ever seen the man in a tie.

Lou read over the brunch menu. "Their ham biscuits are almost as good as my mother's. We might have to get some extras for the boys."

"Ben's been listening to his chef—and Hannah." Tennessee's bold grin seemed to drain the tension from his face. Once the server had filled waters and coffees, he settled his elbows on the table. "I'd bet my stake in this business, you know why I've asked you here."

David glanced at Lou. "I'm sure we do."

"It's simple as this." Tennessee spread his hands wide. "I love Cora Anne, and I have for a long time. I think even when we were kids, there was a …"

He faltered and Lou picked up softly. "A connection. Yes, we saw it."

David covered the hands she was twisting in her lap with one of his. Their daughter and this man moved like two pieces of a whole, in sync with one another's thoughts and plans.

Maybe, for them, that had always been the problem. Despite the advice her father had given him, Lou and he had operated in their own spaces, rather than fusing their lives into one.

"I bought a ring." The words came from Tennessee with great pride and equal fear. "And I'm going to ask her to marry me if—" He sat straighter and his jaw squared. "If you'll give us your blessing."

If. David doubted there was any power on earth that would keep this man from his daughter. Before he spoke, he looked to Lou for confirmation, as perhaps he always should have. She turned her hand beneath his, and their fingers slipped together. Sharing this moment.

"Our blessing is yours." David's voice trembled. "Welcome to our family."

Now he only needed to put that family back together again.

Chapter 25

On the first Thursday afternoon in March, Lou needed to be in three different places, one right after the other. Since cloning hadn't worked yet, she jotted down a plausible schedule and ignored the warning light on her van's dash. She didn't have time to deal with an oil change today.

At home, the ecology students required her to sign off on water and soil samples. At the college, Liam wanted her to present with him during a lecture. Soon as she finished the students' reports, she hightailed it to the Charleston campus. Her interjections as Liam taught—mostly she repeated what he said using her father's everyday vernacular—drew laughter and questions from his students.

With her schedule already fifteen minutes behind, she had no time for pride.

"You're in a rush," Liam observed as she swung her laptop bag over her shoulder and gathered her coat.

"Boys' first game. Got to make it to Colleton High by five." She wound a scarf around her neck, waved, and dashed out of the lab.

But this time, when she turned the ignition of her faithful minivan, the engine made no sound. Lou furrowed her brow and stared at the dash. Blank. And dark. Even the digital clock showed no numbers. Lou groaned and dropped her head on the steering wheel. A new battery at the very least. But likely, something more complicated.

And expensive.

She fumbled in her purse for her cell, though calling David would do no good. Even if he answered—which was rare when getting ready for a game—he was nearly an hour away.

A light rap on her window made her squint against the low-hanging sun. Liam. Relief coursed through her, and she pushed open the door.

"I wouldn't call this running." His easy grin made her smile in return—despite the frustration.

"It's dead."

"Need a jump?"

"Not sure that will even work. Nothing's on at all, see? And it's clicking when I turn the key." She caught a whiff of his cologne as he peered in and pulled back. No inexpensive Old Spice for him.

"Guess I'll have to drive you. Good thing I like baseball." He leaned in again, his face close to hers. "And you."

~ ~ ~

Liam let her navigate and kept the conversation light as they plowed down the highway in his Land Rover. They pulled in the full lot at the high school baseball fields just as the boys' team took the field.

"Did I miss anything?" Lou rushed to David who leaned against the fence, rather than sitting in the stands.

"Nope." He looked at her and then over her shoulder. "Liam."

The men shook hands without any camaraderie.

"Van wouldn't crank." Her words came out in a rush, like her day. "Had to leave it in Charleston, so Liam drove me."

"I told you to let me look at it last week." David crossed his arms.

"Why?" Frustration threatened to erupt. "So you could look under the hood and say, yeah, you should take it to the shop?"

"Well clearly you should."

"And obviously you don't understand what all I've been dealing with lately."

A crack of the bat pulled their attention. The ball sailed high and landed neatly in J.D.'s outstretched glove in center field.

"That'll get it done!" David pumped his fist in the air, Lou clapped, and their son threw the ball to the pitcher.

She gasped. "Cole's starting?"

"Yeah." David's shoulders relaxed. "Made the eighth graders mad, but he's better."

She moved next to him, twisting her fingers through the chain link beside his. The cold metal cooled her anger. She wasn't the only one who'd been busy. "You've been coaching him."

"A little."

"He mentioned something the other night, but I was working on my application and forgot." She hadn't even looked up when Cole came in before bed. He'd dropped a kiss on her head, telling her she'd be surprised soon.

"I was a pitcher myself, back in the day." Liam's voice reminded Lou she owed him some gratitude—or at least a cup of coffee.

David arched a brow. "You played ball?"

"How I put myself through school. You?"

"Catcher. Shortstop sometimes." David turned his attention back to the game as a ground ball skidded across the infield. "Like Mac."

"He's being modest." The words popped out, and so did David's eyes. She'd argued plenty, but praise had been less frequent. Maybe it wasn't too late to rectify that mistake. "David was a star for Emory until he hurt his knee. Then he became the most-winning coach in North Georgia."

Liam rocked back on his heels, hands in his pockets. "Why'd you quit coaching?"

David's gaze swept over hers. "Life changed."

Cole struck out the last batter, and David jogged down the fence line as the boys came in, talking smack with the team.

"Your kids just made those guys go three up, three down." Liam shook his head. "That's pretty impressive." He strolled beside her in search of coffee at the concession stand.

"David bought them their first gloves for their first birthday." She glanced over at his tall form, now assuming a stance beside the dugout. "I was afraid he'd push too hard, but they've always loved it."

"Can I ask you something personal?"

She tugged at her scarf and shrugged. "Sure."

"What happened between you two?"

"I don't know what you mean."

Liam stooped and tilted his head, forcing her eyes to meet his. "I mean, you seem to get along, you obviously love raising your kids together … he watches you. Especially if I'm around."

Heat crept under her scarf. David's eyes were, in fact, on them now. He'd turned from J.D. warming up his swing, and looked, she knew, for her. She held up one finger and tipped her chin toward the concession stand. He shook his head in return and rotated again, his back telling her he didn't like seeing her with Liam. A sense she'd felt from the moment the two men had met.

But what did it mean?

"Lou?" Liam touched her elbow. "I didn't mean to offend you."

She startled. "Oh, no. I'm fine. David and I … we just …" She blinked against the tears gathering in the corners of her eyes. "We fell apart is all. And I never figured out how to put us back together."

Liam lifted the collar of his coat as he nodded. "I never figured out how to put my marriage back together either." At the counter, he ordered coffees and wouldn't let her pay. Heading back to the stands, he added, "But you know, I never tried."

"Do you wish you had?" Why was she asking him this—as though she had time to think about anything besides her kids and bills and career?

"Sometimes. But then—" he lifted one shoulder and offered her a sheepish grin—"I met you, and I've hoped, maybe I might get a fresh start."

A fresh start. Like the way coaches pulled pitchers when they got too tired, so they could keep the game in their favor. On the field, J.D. had gotten a single, the second batter popped out, the third advanced, and now Mac batted cleanup. He swung hard and the contact sent the ball soaring over the heads of the outfielders. J.D. slid around the bases for home.

"Go, go, go!" David jumped along the fence.

Lou would have joined him if not for the hot coffee and the conversation she'd rather not be having at her sons' ballgame. She cupped her hand around her mouth. "Way to go, boys."

David faced her again, arms thrown up in a what-did-I-tell-you gesture, and she found herself, despite Liam's admission, laughing. Those were her boys dominating this game, and her heart swelled with David's jubilance and maternal pride.

And she knew what she needed to do. "Liam, right now, my whole life is a fresh start. And I honestly don't know what's happening."

He nodded. "In that case, I think I'll keep on keeping on, and we'll see."

"All right."

"But for right now—" He glanced at his watch. "If David can get you home, there's a lecture I need to facilitate."

He had driven her all the way here at the cost of his own time crunch. His kindness warmed her as much as his words had a moment ago. "Of course. I'm so sorry to inconvenience you—"

He put his hand on her arm. "Lou, time with you is never an inconvenience. But I am in the way here. This is a moment y'all should have." He squeezed her elbow and strode away.

"What was that about?" David didn't take his eyes from the game when she came to stand beside him.

"He needed to leave. All right if I hitch a ride with you? I'm going to call a tow truck about the van, I guess."

The batter in the box swung and then beat on the dirt when the umpire called third strike. On the mound, Cole grinned wide, and David swung an arm around her shoulders. "I guess we could let you hitch a ride home with the best middle school players in the Lowcountry. Since you birthed them and all."

And Lou leaned into his side, thinking about that fresh start.

Chapter 26

They went out for pizza after the game, and David figured his prayers were working awfully fast, though perhaps he should be a little more specific. Lou's wince when the tow-truck company quoted her the cost chastised him. But he'd wanted to jump for joy—like he had over Mac's homerun—when he saw Liam Whiting's retreating back.

At a Pizza Hut off the highway, they ordered pan pies loaded with meat and cheese, and Lou didn't even bother advocating for vegetables. She fixed herself a salad but praised the boys for their game—and to David's surprise, him for his efforts helping them learn.

"Maybe you're all headed for scholarships to fancy colleges like your dad." Lou ruffled Mac's hair and pulled back, grimacing. "But first showers. How anyone can sweat that much in forty degrees is impressive."

"It's the price of victory, Mom." Cole flexed his arm. "Ow. So is soreness."

"Take some ibuprofen and get some ice on those muscles when you get home." David helped himself to another slice of pizza and divvied up the rest among the boys. "Pitching an entire game'll take a toll on you."

"And on my washing machine." Lou's eyes roamed over the boys' dirty uniforms.

On the drive home, the boys tried to talk over one another, in competition, David suspected, for his and their mother's attention—though like all young teens they'd never admit it.

At the farmhouse, the porch lights were on, and Cora Anne's car and Tennessee Watson's truck were parked side by side.

"What are they doing here?" Lou climbed out of the Jeep, casting a wary look his way. No doubt they knew why their daughter and her beau were waiting for them at nine o'clock on a Thursday night.

"Cor better be ashamed she missed our game." Mac swung his bat bag over his shoulder. "We're way more fun than an old museum."

"Say hello and then hit the showers, guys, please."

David caught up with her on the bottom step. "It's been a great evening, Lou. Don't rush this moment."

She jerked her arm away. "My whole day has been a rush. Don't you think I'd like to do this when we have time to celebrate?"

David swallowed a retort. Just when he thought they'd taken a leap forward, her need for control snapped like a coach losing in overtime.

Cora Anne and Tennessee were in the living room, books spread on the coffee table. Evidently they'd been killing time studying Edisto history for her upcoming lectures at the museum.

"Don't sit anywhere," Lou admonished the boys when she could get a word in over their din of sharing the game's highlights with their sister.

"Sounds like we're not the only ones who had an incredible night." Cora Anne's smile radiated across the room, and David had to catch his breath at the sight of his daughter's happiness. How long they'd waited to see hope shining again in her eyes. He reached for Lou and slid his arm around her shoulders.

She didn't move away—nor did she soften against him. "I guess you've got some news for us."

Cora Anne crossed the room, Tennessee at her heels, and gave her left hand to her mother. Lou took it, caressing the setting of diamond and sapphires, as a single tear slid down her cheek.

"I hope those are happy tears." Cora Anne pulled her into an embrace and David reluctantly released his own hold to shake Tennessee's hand.

He stayed until the boys had been exiled upstairs and Tennessee had gone home for the night. Cora Anne said she'd drive out to the beach house later, and David knew she wanted her mother alone.

Lou followed him out on the porch as he left. "Thanks again for getting me home, and helping with the van, and dinner ..."

He nodded. "Of course. Almost like old times, huh? Those chaotic t-ball games when they were little." He quirked a smile at her, hoping she'd focus on how they'd always had pizza, rather than how they'd always fought about how much was too much extracurricular when the boys had barely started school.

"Almost." She crossed her arms tight across her chest. "They're going to be happy, right?"

He wanted to step closer to her, take her in his arms and reassure her, of course, Cora Anne and Tennessee would be happy. But they had been young and in love once, too, hadn't they? And their happiness hadn't lasted.

He offered her the only words he knew. "I pray so."

She studied him, as if trying to see the man he'd been before in the man he was now. "Did you pray for us?"

"No." His exhale came out long and slow. "But I wish I had."

"Me too."

Now he eyed her in return, wondering exactly what she meant. Lou released her arms and lifted her hand in a goodbye gesture.

He wanted to shout that they could fix this, right here, right now. But she turned and went inside, shutting the door between them.

Chapter 27

Grace paid for Caller ID but never looked at it. A decision she regretted when her mother-in-law's clipped tone—no soft Southern drawl for Charlotte Ravenel Cooper Watson—came through.

"I trust I've caught you at an appropriate time, Grace." Charlotte never minced words.

Grace cast her eyes toward the big clock over the mantel. No, this wasn't a good time. She was late for work, and Hank had decided the porch pillows tasted delicious. What she got for choosing down-filled. Tiny white feathers littered her porch, and her dog whimpered in his crate. "It's fine, Charlotte. How can I help you?"

"Tennessee came to see me last week, and he called this morning."

Gauging to see if Grace knew what she knew, as usual. "Yes, ma'am. I couldn't be happier for him and Cora Anne."

"I'm sure you can imagine my reservations. They are so young, and of course, were raised so differently."

Grace bit her tongue. Tennessee was twenty-seven years old. Charlotte had been barely twenty-one when she married Patrick's father. As to the being raised …

"However, as he is my only heir—" Charlotte paused for what Grace supposed was dramatic effect. This was an old chide, that she hadn't borne more children. Never mind she'd nearly died having the one.

"I will have to give this event a proper acknowledgement. I'd like you, and her parents, to attend a luncheon next week, so we can discuss the engagement party."

"Well, I'm not sure they want an engagement party." Actually, Grace knew Hannah had already offered to plan one, but Tennessee and Cora Anne didn't see the need. They wanted to get married sooner, rather than later, and saw no reason to put effort into both.

"Nonsense. Tennessee understands social obligation."

Grace curled her fist. Patrick had disdained an engagement party— and a church wedding. Thirty years later, and his mother still hadn't forgiven that misstep.

"We can certainly discuss this over lunch. What day were you thinking?" Better to bite the bullet now than have it fester.

"I am available on Wednesday."

"All right then. I'll put it on my calendar."

"If you'll be so kind as to share with me a contact for her parents, I will call them myself."

"Of course." Grace found David's number quickly in her recent calls list, but had to hunt for Lou's. Charlotte made no comment on the delay, though Grace was sure she could hear the woman's lips purse in displeasure—and disapproval.

"I will see you on Wednesday, then. Please dress accordingly. After all, this is a somewhat formal event."

"Goodbye, Charlotte." Grace hung up and threw the phone at her couch. There was no person in her life she despised—and wanted to please—more than Charlotte Ravenel Cooper Watson.

She only hoped her daughter-in-law-to-be wouldn't feel the same.

~~~

Grace's last client of the day was a sweet member of the Presbyterian choir who had lived on Edisto for five years and still found every moment of it charming. The older woman had almost softened Grace's countenance toward Charlotte's ridiculous social obligations—until Louisa Coultrie came striding across the parking lot.

The bell jingled over her head as Lou held the door open and bid a good afternoon to the exiting customer. To Grace, she extended no such niceties.

"I'd say who spit on Charlotte's grits, but I'm sure she's simply being herself." Lou folded her arms and glared. "I need you to tell her we are not interested in an engagement party."

Grace swept hair and wished Jeanna hadn't already gone for the day. She could use a buffer—and a friend. Lou, of course, was neither. "Charlotte doesn't listen to me. So you might want to have this conversation with Tennessee and Cora Anne."

Lou huffed. Her hair had fallen in her eyes, and as she shoved it back behind her ears, her hands trembled. "Cor says keep the peace. Let's go to lunch and see what she says. Might be small ..."

"Charlotte does nothing small."

"Oh, I know." Lou met her eyes then, and Grace remembered. They had this in common. Charlotte hadn't approved of Patrick's first choice anymore than she had his second.

"You told her y'all would come Wednesday?"

"David did. I missed her call." Lou bit her lip. "I'm not sure I can face her. She didn't even come to my mother's funeral."

Grace looked down at the pile of silver hair she'd swept, giving Lou the chance to collect herself. She filled the dustpan and dumped it. An idea sprang to mind.

"Sit down." She jerked her chin toward the chair.

Lou frowned. "Why?"

"Because if you're going to face my mother-in-law, you need a trim. And because if we're going to be a united front for our children, it's time we got to know each other."

Lou lifted her chin, and Grace figured she might walk right back out the door. Go ahead, she wanted to say. At least she tried.

But Lou dropped her purse on the waiting bench, and giving Grace a nod, sat. "I haven't had my hair cut since we moved."

Grace snapped a drape around Lou's neck. "It looks good this length. Just needs a little shaping to be even more flattering."

"I think David likes it." Lou fidgeted. "Not that I care what he thinks or anything."

Grace paused, her comb and spray bottle suddenly heavy in her hands. "Can I ask you a personal question?"

Lou met her eyes in the mirror. She nodded slightly and set her head straight, chin tipped up, already defiant of what Grace might ask.

"What happened?"

The mist of water enveloped Lou's dark hair and Grace began working the comb through, surprised to discover how thick the woman's hair remained. Her own had begun to thin with age. Lou sat silent, and Grace didn't press. She already knew the answer must be complicated.

"You only see the man he is here, so you must wonder why I let him go."

"Seems to me, he hasn't gone very far."

"Oh, but he did." Lou closed her eyes, and Grace massaged her scalp, as she would for any client in her chair. "He ran all the way down the beach, from Still Waters to the Pavilion, the night I told him to go. I thought, when he came back, he'd refuse ... but he packed his bags and left. Went on home and boxed his things and rented an apartment and fought me on nothing. We were beyond arguing at that point. Everything had turned so cold ..." She shivered.

Grace reached for her scissors. "From what I see, he's warmed back up." She set her hands on Lou's shoulders. "So have you."

"He's different lately. Since Mama died. Since Cora Anne let your and Tennessee's forgiveness wash over her." She met Grace's eyes in the mirror again. "I guess you forgave me, too?"

Unprepared for the question—and all its implications—Grace fumbled her scissors. The polite answer was that there had never been anything to forgive, but they both knew that wasn't true. Lou Coultrie had grieved like a widow herself that awful night on the beach when Patrick drowned. For years, Grace had found comfort with the knowledge that Pat chose her, though the thought wedged in the back of her mind remained. Would he have gone in the water for anyone's child? Or did he go because Cora Anne belonged to Lou?

The answer would always be tangled as an old shrimp net—and never settled. Patrick wasn't here to ask.

And no two ways about it, Lou had borne some of that blame. More so even than the daughter she'd pushed aside and let break.

Grace pulled breath into her lungs and exhaled the words God had given her long ago. "Forgiveness is the only way to heal, Lou."

Lou turned in her chair, no longer letting the mirror be their buffer. "Thank you."

"You're welcome."

Lou turned back. "That night broke us all, Grace, and I'm so sorry. I should have said that to you then instead of losing myself in my own grief."

Grace lifted hair and snipped, the mundane task making this conversation easier. "So you pushed David away?"

"We were already at an impasse. The boys—well, you had one. So can you imagine what three at the same time was like?"

"Somewhat hellish, I'm sure."

"I wanted to escape, and I'd even floated the idea of moving back here, so we could be closer to Mama and Daddy. Get some help."

The loneliness of motherhood. One more thing they had in common.

"But he said we couldn't afford to move. Maybe in a few years. Only I needed help right then. I was drowning trying to work and take care of them, so he suggested I quit my job."

"Guess that flew all over your somewhat feminist nature." Grace grinned at Lou, who actually chuckled.

"Definitely. But it was more. At least when I was teaching, I felt successful—and I wanted to get my doctorate. When I was working, I could finish something. At home, as soon as one was fed, another one had to be. Two would go to sleep and one would wake up." She pursed her lips. "Still how it is, actually. J.D. hates thunder, Cole's secretly still afraid of the dark, and Mac's always hungry."

Grace groaned. "I can only imagine."

"Daycare was eating us alive financially, we were fighting all the time about everything, and then," she fumbled over the words, "the accident happened."

"And he felt betrayed." Grace had read that on David's face more than once when Patrick was mentioned.

"Yes." Lou looked down, so Grace took the opportunity to trim the back. "After … it was like living in a fog. Two people co-existing. No spark … of anything.

"We tried counseling, but I wasn't ready. And Cora Anne drifted further into herself, the boys got bigger, and Daddy died so Mama gave us some money …"

Lou had closed her eyes again, so Grace snipped at the locks around her face.

"Then one day, I decided. I didn't want to do this anymore. He had kept on trying, all those years, and I was tired of feeling selfish that I couldn't reciprocate." She sighed. "Sometimes you have to go, so you know you can come back."

"Cora Anne said that to Tennessee."

"Where do you think she learned it?"

Grace turned on the hair dryer, sensing they both needed a moment. When she finished, she smoothed Lou's hair, marveling again at how the new cut hid much of the gray, making Lou appear younger.

In the mirror, Lou's eyes widened. "You're good." She sounded awed.

Grace smiled. "Was just thinking that myself."

"What do I owe you?"

"On the house."

Lou shook her head, and the softer cut swung gently against her cheeks. "I can't do that, Grace."

"Fine, then." Grace glanced at the clock. "It's dinnertime. You owe me dinner. We still haven't discussed our Charlotte strategy."

Grace expected a rejection. Haircuts and talks were one thing. Breaking bread together would cross another line.

But the crease between Lou's brows smoothed as she nodded. "No doubt we'll need one."

Chapter 28

"If I tell you to leave, please do it."

Grace smoothed her skirt over her belly, still flat as a pancake, though not for long. "You're being awfully dramatic. I think you forget I know about difficult mothers."

Patrick shook his head. For once, his wavy blond locks were perfectly combed. "Your mother has a mental illness. That's different than being cruel."

Patrick hadn't lived through cruelty. But if he wanted to protect her from more ugliness in the form of his mother's snobbery, she'd let him.

At the mansion Charlotte's great-grandfather had built during the height of Charleston opulence, they all sat in the parlor and were served drinks. Grace declined the champagne, whispering to the maid to please bring her water.

"Not celebrating with us? We had assumed that is why Patrick called this conference." Charlotte perched on her chair. Her skirt's folds skimmed her ankles, tucked one behind the other. She twitched one foot, and her heel slipped off.

A small chink in the woman's armor of propriety.

"We're happy to celebrate with you, Mother." Patrick raised his glass. "Father." The three sipped, and Patrick reached for Grace's hand. "We've come with news. We're going to be married. Next week."

Charlotte's expression did not change, but this time her shoe thwacked the floor when it popped off her heel. She recovered quickly, rearranging her ankles, spreading her skirt again, all while corded tendons appeared on her neck.

At least she tried to maintain composure. "Is there a reason you need to marry without any preliminaries? Not even an engagement party? There hasn't even been an announcement, Patrick."

Pat squeezed Grace's fingers. "It's necessary, Mother, and it's what we want anyway."

Spots of color blushed Charlotte's cheeks. "I see."

Grace took a deep breath and straightened her posture. Patrick was their only son, after all. "I'm open to a small wedding, if you'd prefer."

"What's done is done. A white dress won't change it." Charlotte's icy gaze raked over Grace.

"Well, then." Temple Watson poured himself another bourbon. "I suppose you need money?"

Patrick shook his head. "We're not here for that. We wanted you to know, that's all."

"No, let's talk about the money. Such a delicate conversation, but under the circumstances ..." Charlotte waved her hand, as though Grace were nothing more than a fly flittering around her face.

"The offer still stands, son. Full partner in my practice. You only have to pass the bar exam." Temple crossed his knees. "You've had your fun, but now that you're going to be a father yourself, it's time you faced reality."

Patrick pulled Grace to her feet. "Why don't you go wait outside?"

She wouldn't question him, not here. Besides, after this, tolerance was the best she could ever hope for from Charlotte.

In the garden, she boosted herself up among the thick branches of a live oak. The tree cradled her like her womb held this tiny life. Not a mistake. But not how she'd wanted things to happen either.

They'd talked of marriage for well over a year. But Patrick wanted his business stable—and without his parents' investment, the timeline lengthened. Grace offered contributions from her Dockside shifts and her new hours at the beauty parlor, where she learned to style hair and manicure nails.

Neither job a career, but she enjoyed making people happy whether it was with fried shrimp or bleached highlights.

Patrick refused her money. She swung her legs like a child as the shadows lengthened over the garden. His stubbornness matched her own. But they stood united in the most important decision.

Edisto would be their home.

A door slammed, and a moment later Pat strode across the garden, calling her name.

"Over here."

"Time to go." He grasped her waist and boosted her down to the ground as though she weighed no more than the pieces of lumber he'd been hauling all afternoon.

"I'll just run in and say goodbye." She turned to the house, but he wrapped his arms around her. Buried his face in her hair, her neck. When he put his lips on hers, all the passion and turmoil he'd built up cascaded down.

She put her hands on his chest, pushed him gently away. "What's wrong?"

"From here on out, it's just us." He pressed his forehead against hers, stroked her jaw with his thumbs, let no tears slip down his cheeks. But his eyes shimmered as moonlight filtered through the Spanish moss. "They're going to cut me off completely. Either I come back to Charleston and work with my father, or we come to them for nothing."

"They don't even want to know their grandchild?"

He only drew her close again. Grace sucked in a breath, felt the sharp stab of it under her ribs, the swelling of her heart and the breaking of their innocence—all due to one choice.

She may have been wrong about Charlotte and cruelty.

"You're sure?"

"I would rather live in a shack on that island than stay here and be strangled."

Her chin trembled. He'd chosen her. She, who had never been wanted.

Chapter 29

On Wednesday, in the interest of time—and presenting a united front—Lou picked David up at school where he'd secured a half-day substitute. Her van, which hummed nicely thanks to a new alternator and new rotators and something else she couldn't remember but came with a hefty price tag, hardly belonged in Charleston's upscale historic district.

He whistled, low, when he slid in the passenger seat. "Wow, Lou."

She ducked her head, thankful her new haircut hid the pleased purse of her lips. She'd changed outfits three times that morning, a knot in her stomach every time she imagined Charlotte's disapproval. But David's obvious appreciation might make up for that. The day, balmy for early March, meant she'd opted for a black dress with a floral print—acceptable for pre-Easter. With a cardigan, pumps, and pearls. She might prefer wearing waders in the creek with her students, but Lou hadn't forgotten those basic tenets her mother had taught her about dressing like a Southern lady.

"We made a plan." She filled him in on the basics of the engagement party Hannah would execute, with Charlotte's blessing, of course. Based on the tension both Cora Anne and Grace exhibited, Lou knew Charlotte's blessing was really the only thing that mattered.

When she rested her right hand on the console as she drove toward the city, David squeezed her fingers in much the same comforting gesture she had done with their daughter as each detail was decided.

Except his touch made the knot in her stomach dance.

And cinch again the closer she drew to the exclusive South of Broad neighborhood where Charlotte lived in the Georgian-style mansion her great-grandfather had built in the 1820s. The imposing white columns and wrought-iron gates, artistically crawled with ivy and flanked by live oaks dipping their branches over the sidewalk, hadn't changed in the thirty years since Lou last visited. To her then—and now—it was a grand palace.

The kind of place for those considered Lowcountry royalty. The kind of place her mother had lived and disdained for the pluff mud of Edisto.

Beside her, David chuckled. "Guess I see now why all you ladies worked up such a frenzy."

"Impressive, huh?"

"It's gorgeous. I bet Cora Anne wants to write a thesis about it." He couldn't contain the smile he always had that their daughter had followed his footsteps into the realm of history, her love the preservation of historic architecture.

"She probably does." Lou parked on the side street. She unbuckled. Loosing the seatbelt did nothing to relieve the tightness building in her chest. Even though David scooted out first and came around to open her door, she climbed out and stood, heaving.

"You all right?" He slipped a hand under her elbow.

"A little nervous, that's all."

He tipped his head and studied her. "What happened when Patrick brought you here?"

"The same that happened to Grace, I imagine. Charlotte's standards are … rather high."

Rubbing her sternum, she stumbled up the walk. David caught her, his touch once again a comfort. Breathing suddenly required more effort than she had. The fleeting thought she might be having a heart attack South of Broad in Charleston seemed ludicrous and ironic all at the same time.

"Let's sit over here." They'd passed through the gate, which Charlotte must've instructed the groundskeeper to leave open for her visitors, and into the Robert Chesnut-designed garden. She couldn't breathe, but she could remember all the boasts about this garden and its fountains and hedged paths as ornate as the trim on the eleven-foot ceilings of the house. David sat her on a stone bench and knelt in front, his hands on her knees.

"Louisa, listen to me."

She closed her eyes against the assault of so much green, so much light, too much brightness for the task at hand. Seeing this place where she could never have belonged.

Seeing this mother whose son she had taken away.

David put a hand to her cheek. "Open your eyes and look at me."

She did and slowly he, and his face only, came into her focus.

"Breathe, nice and deep, with me."

They lifted breaths together, in that garden of stateliness, until her pulse—he'd set his fingers on her neck, she realized—calmed beneath his touch.

"You haven't had one of those in a good long while." David sat beside her now, and kept his hands in hers. How many years had it been since he had to breathe her through the panic? The attacks stopped when she'd detached herself from feeling—anything.

From believing she could ever be enough for anyone.

David glanced at his watch. "Grace might send out a search party if we're late."

Lou took in another deep breath filled with the early spring garden and willed herself to see only the here and now. David, her support even if no longer her husband, and Cora Anne, her daughter loving Charlotte's grandson enough to let go of her guilt.

Surely she could as well.

"I'm ready now."

They stood together, and she let David keep her hand, a living reminder he'd never intended to let her go.

Chapter 30

The urge to flee with her from this place rose up in David. But he had learned long ago how to hide his feelings until Lou got a handle on hers.

Maybe they'd have survived if he'd been more transparent. Instead, he had set her up to bear all the culpability of both their shortcomings.

He took her hand and they walked to the portico. Charlotte may have the means to give their daughter a glorious wedding, but he intended to make sure Cora Anne received what she wanted. No matter the cost.

The heavy oak door opened slowly, a maid on the other side. "Welcome. You must be Mr. and Mrs. Halloway. Please, follow me."

Neither of them corrected her mistake, though Lou let go his hand as they stepped over the threshold. The woman, her dark hair smoothed into a low bun, her uniform pressed crisp and neat, could not have been older than they.

Except in her eyes.

If he ever had the chance, he'd want to talk to this woman whose eyes would tell him a truer history than any he'd read in textbooks.

She led them through a foyer with polished floor and a parlor of polished antiques. In a sunroom, facing the opposite side of the garden where they'd sat, the others waited.

"How nice of you to join us, Louisa." Charlotte Ravenel Cooper Watson had aged well, her silver hair tucked into place, her mouth pursed in a way David imagined she'd only enhanced over the years. Her brown eyes glittered over them both but settled on Lou. The rustle of her skirt as she rose indicated silk, and David wished he'd heeded both Lou and Grace when asked to wear a tie.

Charlotte lifted one hand. Only the thin skin over a web of veins betrayed her age. "Please introduce me to your husband."

She knew they were no longer married and had intended the insult. He feared for a moment Lou might release her long-held fury, but she took Charlotte's hand and pressed it briefly. "How nice to see you again, Mrs. Watson. This is David Halloway, Cora Anne's father."

She sidestepped the moment with grace. Her mother would have been proud.

Charlotte extended her hand to him, and he took it. Her fingers lacked warmth, much like her eyes. "A pleasure to meet you, ma'am."

"Mmm." The sound was disapproval. "But not so much of one, you dressed for the occasion. Observe my grandson." Her chin tipped toward Tennessee, who crossed his arms over his tie and grimaced. "I have finally won him over to the rules of fine etiquette."

David owed an apology to all these women for doubting their admonitions. He offered atonement to Charlotte. "My apologies, ma'am. I'll do better next time."

"Mmm." That sound again. She rang a small silver bell, its sound like breaking glass.

The maid reappeared in the doorway.

"Chloe, we shall come in for luncheon now."

"Yes, ma'am." She clasped her hands in front of her, eyes down.

The walk across the house to the dining room, with its crystal chandelier and silver candlesticks, seemed a promenade, with Charlotte the queen they all followed. David hated this feeling of servitude.

Beside him, Lou gasped.

He tracked her gaze to the portrait over the fireplace. An oil painting so lifelike it might have been a photograph. Patrick, arm propped on his knee, a spaniel beside him, the two of them offering life back to this mausoleum of a house. He had his mother's eyes, David noted. That is, if Charlotte's had been prone to laughter, like Patrick's. The artist had captured their twinkle, and when Tennessee stopped in front of the mantel for a moment, it was as though the portrait had come to life.

Grace laid a hand on Lou's arm. "I always thought she should have had it done of him with a cast net or a tool belt. Except for the smile, that's not my Patrick."

"No …" Lou's voice sounded strangled. Her eyes darted back to his and he knew. This picture wasn't Grace's Patrick, but the one she had known. His mother had immortalized him as she expected him to be, though the smile beaming down at them all hinted rebellion.

David squared his shoulders. Patrick would have been on their side.

"It is rude to linger in doorways, Grace, and Louisa, I expect better of you. Annie, though she disdained her own upbringing, surely taught you better."

Lou's face paled with the intimate mention of her mother's name.

"Come, Mama, sit by me." Cora Anne smoothed over the moment, reminding them all why they were here, and Lou sat, her back to Patrick's smiling face.

The only seats left were on the opposite side of the table, putting him across from Lou, but between Grace and Charlotte. The older woman's mouth pinched when he pulled out Grace's chair. He ignored her, sought Lou's eyes over the water goblets and centerpiece of sterling roses, and blinked twice in rapid succession. The corners of her mouth tightened in a small smile, just for him. Their old code of communication, when she'd first brought him home. *Tell me if I'm doing something wrong,* his blinking said.

Annie and Thornton Coultrie's farmhouse table, with blue geisha china filled with shrimp and grits, now seemed much farther away than a mere forty-five miles down the road.

He'd worried, but Annie hadn't cared that a boy raised by blue-collar folks never learned which fork to use.

And on it went, during a luncheon David could never have imagined they'd have.

The women didn't argue. David's debate students could have learned a lesson or two about temperate discussions. Charlotte wanted the party to be black-tie and invitation-only. She conceded to Hannah as planner—"only because I have heard she does exquisite work"—and David figured Lou filed that tidbit away to tell her sister. They seemed hung up on the menu, with Cora Anne insisting hors d'oeuvres made the gathering chic—though she probably meant less stuffy. Charlotte sought a three-course dinner.

And all the while, even as she agreed with their daughter and spoke like a diplomat to Charlotte, Lou watched for his signal. He expected it gave her comfort to prompt him, and he allowed her the grace of this small distraction.

"Well, it seems," Charlotte said as the dessert of sorbet and cake arrived, "there is little left for me to contribute."

Silence replaced the chatter. David blinked at Lou. With the tip of her finger, she nudged the dainty spoon and fork, though they were the only utensils left.

Tennessee cleared his throat. "Lunch has been wonderful, Grandmother. What about the cake? This one looks good."

Charlotte cut her gaze around the table. "Chloe, the coffee service."

"Yes, ma'am." The maid skittered away.

"Cake—" and each word came out clipped and measured—"is for a wedding reception. An engagement should have more variety, perhaps. Would you agree, Louisa?"

Lou's gaze darted to his and she blinked twice in succession. He barely lifted a shoulder. No idea about these things. Could they not have pie if cake were meant for a wedding? He glanced toward Grace. Lou's cheeks pinked.

Too late, he realized, he'd broken their game.

"What is it, dear?" Charlotte picked up her spoon now, allowing the rest of them to do the same. "You can no longer state opinions without consulting this man? Seems odd, given your current marital status. But there are many things about you I do not understand, Louisa. Why, for instance, you have moved back to Edisto. Surely your career prospects would thrive elsewhere."

Lou turned only her head, her back stiff as their surroundings. "Currently I am conducting tidal creek research under a grant for the College of Charleston. So you see, Charlotte, my career is quite well." She lifted a spoonful of the sorbet. "But thank you for your concern."

"Well, then, what of your husband?" Charlotte turned her daggers to David. "How are your prospects? Because it seems to me, the only reason you all are here is so I can finance the party you've already chosen. Surely, Cora Anne, your father realizes it's the duty of the bride's father to handle such events?"

David balled his napkin, tossed it on the table, and stood. "The only opinions being offered today are for the party you wish to give my daughter and your grandson. They have told you what they'd like, and yes, there is much you can contribute. But rest assured, Mrs. Watson"— he swung his gaze to Lou—"we are prepared to match you financially."

Lou glanced once at Patrick's portrait. "Though we know it pains you to spend money on an idea that is not your own."

"Mama ..." Cora Anne's hushed whisper echoed off the crystal.

"It is as I suspected." Charlotte folded her hands. "My money is all I am worth to you."

"That's not what she meant." Grace spoke, and she sounded tired, as though she'd already had this discussion too many times.

"I can speak for myself, and yes, that is exactly what I meant." Lou stood and the pink in her cheeks had gone crimson. "No one wants this party, except you, Charlotte. We were all fine with Lowcountry boil and lawn chairs. I don't expect you to appreciate a life you have never respected. Resent me—and my family—all you want. But you should honor these children's wishes because all they have ever done is give you the second chance Patrick never could."

In that moment, Charlotte looked like an old woman, face pale and mouth drooping. But then, her lips curled. "You all took my son from me, and then have the audacity to sit at my table and tell me how to give my gifts."

"Charlotte, please—" Grace's voice quivered.

Her mother-in-law snapped. "Hush, Grace. You've never been very good at speaking up. Don't start now."

"That's enough, Grandmother." Tennessee covered his mother's hand with his.

Lou, one last look flung David's direction, stalked away, the sound of her heels echoing in the empty house.

Chapter 31

Lou flung her van into drive. David jerked open the passenger door. She dropped the gearshift back into park. "What?"

"Seriously? You're leaving me?"

"You left me."

The storm crossed his features and twisted his lips into a grimace she remembered all too well. "Because you asked me to."

"Well, now I'm asking again."

"I thought we were together back there, just now."

She shoved hair behind her ears, ruining the smoothness that had taken an hour to achieve that morning. "I never agreed to finance this event. You and I haven't even talked about it."

He hung his head. "Lou ... I'm not asking you to pay for anything."

She shrugged.

"This really about the money?"

"It's about everything, David. How nothing I do is ever good enough." She had expressed those words before—but he never took her seriously. When she said them today, he whooshed out a sigh.

She knew then. He still didn't hear her. "Let me go, please. I need to clear my head. Ride back with Cor and Tennessee."

"Don't you care? About more than the opinion of Charlotte Ravenel Cooper Watson?" He spit out each of her names and leaned in, his nose almost brushing hers. "Don't you care about us?"

She turned from the intensity of his gaze. "There is no us."

The air around them had been sparking, like an electrical storm about to crack open, but her words shut it down. The heat and the flirting and the hint of possibility there'd been all died, and only the thin coolness of the March air was left.

~~~

After Pat died, Grace regretted her moment of cowardice in Charlotte's parlor. In the happening, it'd seemed prudent to guard her heart from words she could never un-hear, in the hope one day her mother-in-law might rejoice in their choice.

Now she knew, had she stood with him that night, she'd have been prepared for the later and the now, for the battles she had waged alone all these long years without him.

After Lou fled the table, and David followed, Grace retreated from Charlotte's bitterness. Outside, she curled into the largest, lowest branch of that tree like a child—or a coward, once more.

She left her son to pacify his grandmother, as only his blood could.

Grace had believed, so many years ago, Tennessee's birth would be the balm Patrick and his parents needed. But the stubborn pride of her husband's family bound them stronger than anything else. As an adult, Tennessee built the tentative bridge now existing between them and Charlotte.

Tracing her fingers through the grooves of the tree's bark, Grace admitted to herself he had extended what she had not. His grandmother, however, sometimes refused to meet him halfway.

The door of the back piazza opened, and Tennessee strode out, Cora Anne's hand clutched in his. Even from across the garden, she could mark the square set of his jaw, the tension of his shoulders, how his hips didn't sway with his usual easy gait, but clipped each step with finality.

Walking away.

Charlotte had lost again.

He stopped, turned, pulled his girl into his arms. Grace looked away. They deserved this quiet, private moment of reassurance. Patrick had given the same to her, right here under this oak.

Grace pressed cold fingers to her temples. She might have known back then. Patrick's choice that day had been as much for her as for himself, the one time he could be both selfless and selfish. He'd gotten what he wanted, but at what cost?

She'd been left to gather the remnants. Now wrapping her shawl around her shoulders, she trudged back in the house, dutiful and duty-bound.

"There you are, Grace. I assumed you'd left as rudely as the others." Charlotte sat at her writing desk, but no work spread before her.

"I waited in the garden. I thought Tennessee deserved to speak to you alone."

Charlotte's chin dipped, and her strong gaze faltered. "He is much like his father."

"Yes."

"But that girl ..." Her mother-in-law regarded her now. "She is not much like you."

Grace looked away, straight into the twinkling eyes of her husband, watching from across the hall. Immortalized as Charlotte had hoped he would be.

"She told me family and forgiveness were everything to her. That my son's death was not in vain, not if it reconciled that which is broken."

"Has it?" Grace felt the words tighten in her chest. "Reconciled us?"

Charlotte folded her hands in her lap. "Of course not. Because I don't know if I can ever forgive myself."

The words were not what she'd expected. "For turning him away?"

"No, dear." Charlotte's lips tightened. "For failing him. I should have encouraged Louisa. I see that now. Instead, I sentenced them both to a life of sorrow. And Patrick died for it."

Grace hadn't thought Charlotte's words could still cut her. But once more, she found herself bleeding. Stanching her own wound, she spoke words that should have been said long before. "What about Tennessee? You would trade your sorrow for a life that didn't have him?"

Charlotte looked away. "He doesn't want my life."

"No, he wants his own. But he would like to share it with you, and," Grace sucked in a breath heavy with resolve, "so would I."

Her mother-in-law looked her over, as if she were a piece of antique furniture under scrutiny for authenticity. Then, lips pressed tight, Charlotte nodded in a way Grace knew was both a dismissal—and an acquiescence.

Chapter 32

Gainesville, Georgia, March 1978

When his boys took the field, David pressed his fists to his mouth. A silent benediction he hoped the team didn't notice. His nerves weren't this bad the day he tried out for college recruiters.

Could've gone almost anywhere after that tryout, but he chose Emory for two reasons. First it was in the center of Atlanta, not stuck in the middle of nowhere like Georgia College. Second, he'd graduated from high school in Cobb County—actually put in two and a half years there—making metro Atlanta the place he'd lived the longest.

His parents lit out for another new opportunity in Valdosta before the ink on his scholarship was dry. Since then they'd had three different addresses. The latest had brought them just above Gainesville. Close enough for Mom to say they'd come watch him coach his first game, since his C team of eighth graders would be taking on one of the local teams.

But only Lou waved to him from the stands when he took his stance at third base. He swiped the sweat already beading his forehead, pulled his cap low. Early March was still cold, especially on a clouded afternoon. But David felt hot and prickly all over.

As if his whole life might change based on this game's outcome.

The boys played hard. They followed commands and swung when told—except that cocky shortstop. He swung at whatever he wanted. Worked out, too, which is why David had him batting clean-up. But if the kid didn't start listening, he would have to bench him out of principle. His own coaches had taught him—the only thing more important than winning is walking off a field with your character still intact.

Today they walked off with a 7-5 take and more than a little bit of pride.

Lou met him at the gate. He hooked his arm over her shoulders and announced to the boys, "Y'all want to meet my girl?"

She rolled her eyes but played the part. He hoped she'd understood when he talked about the coach's marriages he'd seen. The support they had from their wives at every game. The meals they hosted at their homes. He hadn't technically been fatherless, but if it hadn't been for the example of his high school coach, David wasn't sure he'd know what stability should look like.

Once he'd seen it, security was all he'd wanted.

Lou followed the bus back in her little VW. The boys chanted and cheered, thrilled with their first win. David let them have their moment. Tomorrow, they'd have to address the mistakes that nearly cost them that two-run lead.

Thinking about that meant he couldn't think about his parents and their broken promises.

The bus stopped for a line of traffic snaking around a tangle of an accident. One vehicle overturned in a ditch. Another, a small blue pickup, crushed against the forest of pines.

David's stomach lurched.

"Stop." He stood, swaying with the bus's motion.

The driver eased to the side. "Not a good place to get sick, Coach."

He stumbled down the bus steps, sure he was wrong. A cop held up his hand. "Y'all need to move on, please. We're trying to get this cleared."

He worked his jaw but no sound came out.

"David?" Lou. She slipped behind him, put her hands on his shoulders. Turned him to face her. "What is it?"

He jerked his chin toward the blue pickup a tow truck now attempted to extricate. She sucked in a breath. From here, they could read the bumper stickers, peace signs and "Good Day Sunshine." His mom's favorite phrase—how she'd tell him goodbye.

"Sir?" Lou called the policeman back over. He came, wariness in his eyes, as if realizing what he was about to have to admit. "Two adults in that truck? Man and woman?"

The cop licked his lips. "They're en route to Grady." He looked from Lou back to David. "If you're kin, I'd say get on down there. Might not have much time."

"Thank you." She pulled David's arm. "Come with me. I'll drive you."

"My team …" His voice strangled.

She pushed him toward her car. "You have an assistant."

Lou mounted the bus steps, spoke briefly, and emerged with his bag over her shoulder. He sat, catatonic, for the entire trip into downtown Atlanta. And he still made no sound when the ER doctor, in a pristine white coat, came and beckoned him to the small room off the waiting area. Lou sat beside him, took his hand, and when the words were said, he gripped her fingers as tight as he could.

Never, ever wanting to let go.

Chapter 33

Rain started Friday evening, a pitter-patter on the tin roof Lou found comforting. By dawn, sheets of water cascaded down her windows. She rose in the thin light and sat in her mama's old recliner watching the water pool in the yard.

Just a spring rain, her daddy would've said. Soak that ground good. Make it soft. Pliable. Ready for the turning and the planting.

She'd walked behind him all those years. Tarried along in the wake of his hoe, dropping tomato seeds and whispering words of encouragement to that soft foamy earth.

Then he'd given up the tomatoes in favor of the trees. The little baby saplings bent with a wisp of breath and were sure to be torn from the ground when a hurricane struck. So her mama had said.

But Mama had been wrong. Daddy had walked those tree fields so long and so often, Lou gave up and stayed at the house playing school with Carolina, teasing baby Jimmy. When frost threatened, he'd come in, knees of his overalls mud-stained, his hands chapped red, raw from the salty winds, to tell Mama how many he'd saved.

Never did he talk about the ones he lost.

Lou pushed her bare toes, cold, against the smooth oak floor. Over the mantel, a clipping from *Southern Living* hung framed and matted, paired with a portrait of her daddy in his overalls, looking out over his lines of straight tall pines. He'd made good on a gamble and a risk. Let go of the expected and the certain, reaping a harvest greater than they'd ever seen.

Out of nothing but skinny little long leaf pines that grew a dime a dozen all over this island.

What would he tell her, if he were here?

She rocked herself out of the chair, feeling like an old woman with a bad back as she shuffled across the cool floor to the room where her mama had died. With Cora Anne and David's help, she'd taken out the bedstead and dresser, moving them back upstairs to the little room under the eaves. Boxed the quilts but left the photographs—and the afghan draped over the swaying antique rocker.

The box of letters she'd tucked in the closet, but she pulled it out now, knowing how curious it had made her daughter. But there were some missives in this accounting of her life she didn't want Cora Anne to see.

Didn't want her daughter to doubt, as she did, that she'd never given David the whole heart he deserved.

She tapped one envelope against her palm, the post date reminding her how she'd stood on the sidewalk corner in downtown Atlanta, hovering over the mailbox. Writing these words to her father had relinquished her guard—not something she often did. She'd learned at his knee to keep her emotions close.

August 1976

Dear Daddy,

I'm writing you, though I know you'll likely show this to Mama, too.

That's all right, so long as you know I'm seeking your advice. The practical, not the romantic, because we both know which one Mama is.

Do you like David? Really? Because I know he's not what you expected. A city boy planning to coach.

Truth is, he's not what I expected either.

Maybe I'm still hung up on Pat, I don't know. But I wondered this— you sure weren't what Mama expected and it's all worked out somehow, right? You never worried she might've kept a bit of her heart for that other fiancée, that other life? Because David says that's the only thing that scares him. That a part of me may always love Patrick Watson.

Lou folded the letter and tucked it back in its envelope. The creases of the paper were nearly worn through, proving it had been read—

and prayed over, knowing her parents—numerous times. She stuck the box back in the closet and tucked herself into the rocker, the afghan draped around her shoulders. Years before, she'd tossed out several boxes of memorabilia from graduate school in a fit of cleaning frenzy after David left. No doubt her daddy's reply had been in one. Now she couldn't remember all he'd said, only the one line she'd quoted once to her daughter.

Life's a fight for joy, Louisa. You just gotta decide who you want in that ring with you.

The rain's cascade had eased, and now the drops slid off the roof and puddled softly, soaking into the ground, preparing it for spring.

~ ~ ~

This time she brought chicken pot pie, mashed potatoes and a jar of her sister-in-law's canned green beans. Lou practiced her words as she drove. How easily she told her boys to say sorry.

How much more difficult when one wanted to mean it.

When David had picked them up the past two mornings for school, they'd gone backward in time. Back to the first year after the divorce, when the boys waved goodbye but David and she didn't even exchange looks across the yard.

Despite the consistent drizzle, the boys were in the townhome's tiny yard tossing pop flies to one another.

"Hey, Mom," J.D. opened her door. "What are you doing here?"

Cole was more direct. "We know you and Dad are mad again."

"Y'all shut up and stay out of it." Mac pitched the baseball so high he squinted at the weak sun as it came back down.

She handed J.D. the basket with potatoes and beans, hefting the casserole herself. "I'm here to apologize to your father."

Cole cocked an eyebrow at her—an exact image of David. She ignored him and followed J.D. inside.

"Hey, Dad, Mom's here." J.D.'s chortle sounded through the quiet house. They came to the end of the hall that opened into the living space, where David sat on the couch, grading papers.

He raked his eyes over her, and she looked away.

"We'll be outside if you need us." Their son made a hasty exit. For a moment, seeing how David's lips tightened into a thin line, Lou considered following him right back out the door.

She stepped into the tiny kitchen and set the casserole on the counter, putting the granite between them. "I brought you all some dinner." Feeble words. And not what she'd come to say.

David stood and faced her but didn't come closer. He crossed his arms and glared, and Lou realized the emotion swirling inside her she'd never named.

Shame.

"I ..." The carefully rehearsed words died in her throat. Never, not even when they'd bent over the paperwork in the lawyer's office, had he looked at her with such fury.

She swallowed, tried again. "I'm sorry." It was all she had, and she hung her head and turned to leave.

"Sorry for what, Lou? For leaving me in Charleston? For severing our marriage? For loving Patrick Watson?"

Her frustration flared then, and she spun back to face him. "All of it, David." Shock deflated his stance, but she wasn't finished. Words bubbled up. "But are you sorry for making me feel like no matter how hard I tried, I'd never be enough? Never be what you really wanted— the cheerleader wife on the sidelines?"

She'd advanced with each charge. He rounded the couch to meet her, the tendons in his neck stretched tight. "I never asked you to be something you weren't."

"Not with words."

His eyes widened then and some of the mad sloughed off his shoulders. "I wanted to make things easier."

"For you, maybe." She clasped her arms across her chest, chilled despite her sweater, unnerved by the way his lips softened and a small, sad smile offered her his simple surrender.

"I'm sorry." He spoke the words without intonation, without asking for reassurance. David always meant his apology. She only wished he hadn't needed to utter it so often.

Pressing her knuckles against her mouth, she forced the ache back down, into her heart where she'd learned to live with the battering of choices made. To him, she gave a small nod, a weak smile. "That's my line."

He stepped closer and the ache spread throughout her chest when he slid his hands around her waist. Her mind scrambled and tingles spread into the fingertips she lightly set on his biceps, arms every bit as strong as they had been that day in the creek when she taught him to cast a shrimp net.

Bending his head to hers, his lips grazed her jaw as he whispered, "I like it when you apologize first."

She'd lost the ability to speak, to think, to do anything but stay in this safe circle of his arms—

"David?"

Grace's call reverberated in her humming ears. Lou stepped back, knowing this last chance might erode and wash away, leaving them nothing but the sediment of might-have-been.

Chapter 34

Lou, a blush blooming across her cheeks, slid from his arms and down the hall, sidestepping Grace. David stood still, arms akimbo, feeling he'd just dropped something but was afraid to check and see if it had broken.

"Lou, wait ..." His voice tripped over the words.

"I've got to be going." She paused in the doorway, though, and brushed a hand across her face before striding out.

"I brought you a pound cake." Hastily, Grace set the Tupperware on the counter and looked at him, her own cheeks scarlet. "Go after her, David. My car's got hers blocked in."

The slow-motion replay halted, and time started again. Yes. This time he wouldn't let her leave.

Outside, Lou stood next to her minivan, head hung and hands pressed against the door. Whatever they'd been exploring had definitely broken her.

He said her name and stepped closer, hoping to say more.

She pushed off the vehicle, tightening her sweater across her chest as a wind picked up and blew a chill between them. "I'm going to walk. Clear my head."

"I'll walk with you." Thank goodness the boys had followed Grace's cake inside.

She shrugged and set off toward Jungle Road. Head bent, arms tucked into herself, her grey sweater and dark jeans made her nearly blend in with this stretch of gnarled trees and spiky yuccas.

Like she belonged.

By the time they reached the beach access, he had to ask. Had to stop the wondering. "Would you have been happy if we'd come back here?"

"You didn't want to." Her words landed in that space between them, that chasm of the past as cracked and broken as the worn old road they'd just traversed.

"That's not completely true."

She quickened her stride up the sandy path toward the ocean. "Don't fling about words you might not mean, David."

He upped his own steps to a near sprint, catching her and slipping his hand under her elbow, propelling her to a stop.

She pulled back and wrapped her arms across her chest. The ocean's breeze made her hair dance around her cheekbones. A strand caught in the dampness of her lashes and she hastily brushed it aside.

"I want to try again, Lou, please." The words gushed from him, and he'd been helpless to hold them back—the way the beach gave way to great surges of storm.

Her throat worked. He could see the shimmer of swallows as she tried to gain composure. Both hands dashed at her cheeks as she turned away. "I can't do this. Not now. Maybe not ever."

"Why not?"

She turned back to him. He'd hoped she would.

Fisting her hands on his sweatshirt, she shook her head. "Why would you even want to be with me again? I'm selfish and difficult and—"

"Passionate and thoughtful." He let the corner of his mouth quirk into a half-smile when she dropped her head to his chest, actually laughing.

"I think you mean stubborn and controlling." She lifted her chin, the brief moment of mirth dying with the intensity of her gaze.

Covering her hands with his, he nodded. "I know you can be all those things, Lou. But so can I, and here's the truth—if I'm going to have a family then I want the one I've already made. We both made mistakes, and I think…" He cast his eyes away from hers and toward that ocean churning with the rising tide. "We're finally in a place we can admit them to each other."

She tugged on her bottom lip. "You've barely been here three months. We're not ready."

"I am."

Her eyes, deep blue wells of misting anguish, probed his. "I'm not sure I know how to love like that anymore, David. If we try and it doesn't work—"

"It will work." He snapped out the words, as if saying them with finality made them true.

She loosed her hands, stepped back. "You said that the first time we went to counseling. And every other time when we tried."

Because he never gave up. Quitting had never been in his vocabulary, until he met Lou, who when things became too much to handle, retreated into her shell. Skittering away from reality. He'd pushed her out so many times.

With a sigh, she seemed to fold in on herself. "You're always so sure. You can't understand why I need time to think things over. To maybe try something new."

Or someone new. He heard the unspoken message. "Liam Whiting."

"I don't know." Shoving her hands in her pockets, she turned away. "But I think I owe it to myself—and to you—to find out before I make another commitment that leaves me wondering."

And there they were. Full circle. Right back at Edisto where it all began and all fell apart. Maybe he was being too romantic believing this was the place that would put them back together.

He cut his eyes away from her, over the dunes, focusing on a row of houses Patrick Watson had helped build.

Lou ducked her head against the wind and added, "Besides, I thought maybe you might be getting to know Grace."

She said it so like a child making an excuse, that he couldn't help the laughter bubbling up inside him. He tossed back his head, chuckling long and loud.

"What's so funny?" She scuffed her shoes in the soft sand.

"You are." He laced his fingers behind his head. "You realize we're about to be family with Grace, so given our current history, I can't think of anything that would seem much more incestuous."

"Please. I've seen you watching her." Her eyes narrowed, and a tremor crept into her words.

David rocked back on his heels, shoving his hands into his pockets, willing his smile not to betray what he saw.

Jealousy he could work with.

"We're just friends, Lou. But if you're going to spend all your extra time with Dr. Whiting, I guess I could spend some of mine with our daughter's widowed mother-in-law."

"I didn't say I'd be spending all my time with Liam."

"Good. Because we're supposed to be finding a dog for our kids. And you're supposed to be teaching me to cook."

He reached for her, and when she leaned away, he didn't press. But to his surprise, she took his hand as they turned to walk back.

"When did you become so patient?"

He chuckled again, softer this time, and pecked her cheek gently, lingering only a fraction longer than friends did. "When I married you."

Chapter 35

Edisto Beach, July 1988

"He's awfully sweet with her."

Grace looked from Louisa Halloway, to their children, at the edge of Edisto's island point. Tennessee knelt in the surf with Cora Anne, showing her how to scoop and blow the bubbles. Their family had been out enjoying the sunset when Patrick spotted Lou and David on the deck of Still Waters and waved.

Grace would have walked on by.

"He's kind," she told this other woman, who rarely gave her the time of day when their families were together. Grace suspected—and Annie confirmed—Lou's jealousy. But it wasn't for Patrick, as some might suspect. Lou loved her husband. Grace could see it in the way she leaned into him as they strolled, her shoulders always angled toward his.

Lou resented Grace's place with her mother. Annie had taught her to cook, to set a table with a five-place setting, to sew Tennessee's Halloween costume of a Ninja Turtle. Grace needed Annie's guidance.

Though she wanted a friend.

Like Lou. A woman her own age walking the everyday burden and blessing of motherhood and marriage.

"How old is Tennessee now?" David asked Pat. The two men stood in water up to their ankles, arms crossed. Pat, still in his work clothes, pants cuffed to his knees. David in a polo shirt and khaki shorts. The differences obvious.

The similarities startling.

"He's ten," Patrick answered. "Playing quarterback on his rec

151

football team this year."

Just like that, they were off. Lost in conversation of college team predictions and best plays. Lou walked a few yards further down the beach. Grace followed.

"Do you worry he'll get hurt?"

She swung her head between Lou and her husband. "Patrick?"

"No, Tennessee. He's your only one and Mama told me—" Lou bit her lip. "You can't have any more."

That truth she accepted long ago. Together Tennessee and Patrick filled her so completely, only a bittersweet ache was left. "I could worry about a lot of things, but I choose not to."

Lou clasped her arms across her chest. "David wants us to have another baby."

Grace caught the unspoken current. "But you don't want to."

"Do you think I'm selfish?" Lou's hair blew around her face, a dark cloud of mystery and aloofness. Perhaps behind it lay the real woman, the one who feared and ran.

Her question carried so many layers, Grace struggled to form a response. She prayed, daily, for a friend.

But maybe, she could start by being one.

"We're all selfish. At least a little." She offered a bit of her own truth. "I won't let my own mother come visit. She's not healthy, and I won't let her hurt him like she did me."

"That's not selfish."

"Every time y'all are here, my son asks me why he doesn't have grandparents."

"Your mother is ill. The Watsons are just—"

"Selfish." Grace supplied. "Patrick included. I've begged him to heal the past."

They paused at a wooden bench, and Lou sat, digging her toes into the soft sand. The lazy orange sun dipped lower on the horizon, backlighting her with its glow. "I don't think I can handle any more. My friends with more children … they don't understand."

But Grace did. She tired so often of mothers comparing who had the harder life especially since they all assumed hers had to be the simplest.

"I've gone back to school for my specialist. The curriculum director asked me to chair the science department for the county. But I'm the only one who cooks and cleans, who takes her to the library and piano lessons." Lou hung her head. "David's a good father, but he's so busy already. If he gets the varsity head coach position next year—" her shoulder lifted—"he'll be gone even more. And she's five. Kindergarten, finally."

Grace laughed. "Kindergarten was my savior. I thought he'd break all the furniture we owned before we ever made it." She sobered. "Lou, you're one of the smartest women I know. If you and David decide to have another baby, you'll be able to handle it." She glanced back at their children, who now held hands, jumping the waves. "And if not, at least for the summer, ours have each other."

Chapter 36

Only a week after the disastrous brunch in Charleston, Tennessee and Cora Anne invited everyone to lunch at The Hideaway.

Grace preferred to let Charlotte simmer a few more days, but she knew her son wanted his grandmother's blessing, and she loved him for it. His father may have been stubbornly prideful, but Tennessee shed those attributes the way he sanded drywall. Smoothing out the rough spots.

If Grace wanted to work through her own issues with her mother-in-law, a little smoothing would do her good as well.

However, as she'd told Lou, they needed reinforcements—in the form of Hannah and Carolina.

Lou agreed. "Difficult family weddings are my sister's specialty."

Charlotte brought a demeanor cool as a window unit in a beachfront house in July. Frozen over, but easily thawed when served strawberry pie and vanilla ice cream which Tennessee had specially requested. He knew his grandmother better than she thought.

After dessert, Charlotte dabbed her lips with the corner of her napkin. "Carolina, your business has quite a good reputation. If you're willing to work with my standards, I'm willing to compromise with these young people."

Carolina took a small notebook from her purse. "Hannah and I discussed the event. Evening garden party, string quartet, formal place settings ... seems there was a hang-up on the dinner?" She and her daughter exchanged looks.

Hannah sat straighter. "We propose a buffet because Cora Anne and Tennessee want the evening to be less formal. However, the tables will be assigned numbers and we'll orchestrate the serving so no one is waiting."

Charlotte nodded. "As long as my guests don't feel they've come to one of those places where you stand in line to order, that'll be fine."

Grace stifled a smile. This woman had never stepped foot in a fast food restaurant in her life.

"Now, as for the dessert ..." Carolina consulted her notes again.

"Grace is an excellent baker." Lou smiled at her across the table and Grace wondered what, exactly, Ben had put in the strawberry pie. "Perhaps, though I know it would be a lot of work, she could make some of the desserts and we offer a variety, as you suggested, Charlotte."

"I appreciate that, Lou, but I'm sure Carolina can recommend someone with more expertise." She darted a glance at her mother-in-law, who tapped a manicured nail against her chin.

"The children have repeatedly mentioned wanting all the wedding events to suit their character." Charlotte nodded. "If you would like to contribute, Grace, this is certainly the chance. At the wedding, of course, we will only have the best."

Grace bit her cheek. She couldn't decide if she had been praised—or insulted.

"Make that pound cake, like you brought over on Saturday," David suggested as he eased his arm along the back of Lou's chair, not quite touching her shoulder. "It was good."

Now Grace rolled her eyes. "It was bribery. Pound cake is simple."

"Sometimes—" Charlotte folded her hands, closing the conversation—"simple is best."

After lunch, Tennessee took Charlotte on a tour of his recent projects. Grace, needing to be useful, stayed behind to help roll flatware into linen napkins.

Lou joined her. "What was the bribery for?" She asked the question as if she didn't care about the answer, but Grace saw how the corners of Lou's mouth pinched.

"I need David to watch Hank while Tennessee and I go visit my mother next week."

Lou stopped rolling. "She's still alive?"

Grace shrugged. "Her mind is gone. But Tennessee wants to tell her about Cora Anne." Far as she was concerned, the early-onset Alzheimer's had taken her mother long ago. Her father, too. When he'd left, she'd carried on as best a fifteen-year-old could.

"I guess David is taking him?"

The subject change released the constriction in Grace's chest. "He seemed a little worried because Hank is so big and the townhouse is so small, but I figured, he can't be worse than the triplets, right?"

Lou arched a brow. "I don't know about that." Rolling another set, she added, "But maybe he could stay at the farm instead. It's my weekend with the boys."

Ben must have spiked the pie. Lou accommodating her? "Up to you and David, but I'm sure he'd prefer the yard."

"All settled then." Lou tossed the last napkin into a basket. "I'll tell David. No worries. I can handle it."

Lou needed to prove something, no doubt. Grace lifted the full basket and transferred it to the hostess station.

She knew a thing or two herself about that.

Chapter 37

In her small bedroom, Lou lifted her wedding band from the bottom of her jewelry box. She'd meant to give a lifetime to David. She'd believed they wanted the same thing.

Until the time came they didn't.

She rubbed her thumb across the ring's worn gold. It slipped easily over her knuckle. She twisted it there, feeling its weight, flexing her hand to see if the heaviness of their last tumultuous decade together still bound itself into that simple gold band.

"Mama?" Cora Anne's voice, breathless, floated up that stairs. "You up there?"

Lou twisted the ring. "I am."

Her daughter, cheeks flushed with wind and youth, appeared in the doorway, arms laden with plastic dress bags, hangers clinking. "Do you know the boys want to take Hank out on the boat?"

She turned her back, tugging the ring. It wouldn't move past her joint. But it had gone on so easily. "It's low tide, they won't get far."

"They're already covered in mud."

"What the water hose is for." There. The ring popped off and she bobbled it for a moment before dropping it back in the box.

"What are you doing?"

"Just straightening up." She turned, offered an innocent smile, hoping her daughter wouldn't probe.

Cora Anne merely eyed her, one brow raised, another question curling her lip. "You and Daddy seem to be getting along pretty well lately."

"Mature adults often do." Lou tossed a hand toward the menagerie in Cora Anne's arms. "What's all this?"

"Well …" Her daughter shrugged. "You're not going to like it, but please remember, life is sometimes about compromise."

An endearment Cora Anne had gotten from her father. But compromise often meant one person got what they wanted and the other learned to muddle through. Lou crossed her arms.

Cora Anne heaved the pile onto Lou's neatly made bed. The rickety frame wobbled under the weight of Nordstrom and Neiman Marcus. "Charlotte sent over these dresses for us to try for the party and said if we don't like any of them, she'll take us downtown to her favorite boutique."

Dread curled in Lou's stomach. "Did you pick something?"

"No, I was waiting for you."

Never had Cora Anne waited on her before she made a decision. Lou seized her tight. "I love you."

Her daughter looped her arms around Lou's waist, hanging on. "I love you too."

When she'd been a child, so many times on the sidelines as David coached, her arms would wrap Lou this same way. She'd haul her up, so Cora Anne could get a better view of her father. Sometimes, the only view she'd have all week.

Lou had been freer with *love you* then. She squeezed one more time. She should be again.

Laughing, Cora Anne released her. "But you still have to wear a formal dress to the party."

"No crinoline."

"Really?" Cora Anne plucked a dress from the pile and swirled its skirt. "I think it's kind of fun."

"You sure didn't when I sent you to Cotillion."

Her daughter pulled the dress from its protective covering and swayed with it in front of the full-length mirror. "I appreciate nice things a little more now."

"Well, I can appreciate finery without looking like a cotton ball on a toothpick."

"Oh, Mama …" They laughed together, and even Lou had to admit as she zipped her daughter into a dress the color of her summer ocean eyes, sometimes crinolines were worth the trouble.

"You look like your grandmother." She rested her hands on Cora Anne's bare shoulders. Her mother had preened Lou in this very room, zipping her into a dress of sea foam green with tiny tucks and flounces. Readying for a garden party in Charleston. Another life.

"Really?" Cor twirled a bit, ducking her chin over her shoulder, making faces in the mirror. "It's so girly."

"But perfect."

"Let's see what she sent for you."

They pawed through the bags, and Lou tried on three dresses of appropriate pastels and mother-of-the-bride tea length.

Cora Anne sighed. "I mean, they're all fine, but they're nothing special." Her eyes suddenly lit up. "I know." She practically skipped from the room, returning with a ball gown draped over her arm. "Try this."

"This was Mama's." Lou took the dress that smelled of mothballs and remembered her mother lifting the skirt as she stepped lightly down the stairs. Her father had whistled, and Carolina and she had giggled while Jimmy made gagging noises. "I remember her wearing it but not where they were going."

"Who cares? I know she looked beautiful, and so will you."

Lou stepped into the dress, sure it wouldn't fit, but it slid over her hips and settled on her shoulders, zipping easily. Behind her, Cora Anne tied the satin waistband into a jaunty bow. The bell skirt, a soft luminous grey, swung just above the floor. The studded bodice shimmered and changed colors in the light, hues like a peacock opening its plume.

Decades old, but still made for her.

"Oh, Mama ... definitely this one." Cora Anne breathed the words with reverence. Lou pushed her hair behind her ears with the wondering thought of what David might think.

Or Liam. Better to think about Liam whom she'd already invited. Less baggage on a night destined to already be overrun with memories.

"You need a bracelet. Something simple."

Cora Anne opened Lou's jewelry box. Her fingers stilled. Lou moved her gaze back to the mirror, back to the woman who looked back at her, almost young again.

Almost unburdened.

"Your ring's in here." Cora Anne held it out, nestled in her palm.

Lou adjusted a strap. "I might need to take this in just a bit. Mama was taller than me."

"Right on top, like you just took it off."

She tugged at the strap again. She'd have to buy a new bra. Inconveniences of formal dresses.

"Mama?"

"I just wondered if it still fit." She turned, slid the ring from her daughter's palm and tucked it back into the corner of the box where it belonged. "Unzip me, please?"

Cora Anne eased the zipper down so Lou could slip the dress off her shoulders and pull back on her button-down. She fumbled with the shirt, finally stepping from the gown and back into her jeans, feeling as though she'd shed another persona.

Her daughter perched on the bed, cross-legged, her skirt a confection of tulle. She twisted the ring on her finger. "Do you want to talk about anything?"

"There's nothing to talk about." She reached for Cora Anne's hand, ran her thumb over the simple antique setting. "I'm happy for you and Tennessee."

Downstairs the screen door slammed, and David's voice floated up the stairs. "I brought dinner."

Heat swept her chest, and Cora Anne giggled. "Mom, you're blushing."

"I am not." Lou flipped her hair—maybe it was getting too long if she could do that. Snagging an elastic band from her dresser, she pulled it back. "Dr. Whiting agreed to accompany me to your party."

Cora Anne stood, tugging the side zipper of her dress. "Hope he doesn't get jealous when Dad can't stop staring at you."

Chapter 38

Lou appeared in the kitchen as David loaded plastic containers into the sink. Her cheeks were pink, and she'd buttoned her blouse crooked.

Maybe he could still fluster her after all. "Hey, I picked up she crab soup at King's."

"That's not cooking."

"Sure it is. Last time, I burned a layer into the bottom of my favorite pot."

She rolled her eyes. "You have to keep the heat low."

"I know. Let it simmer." He crossed the kitchen to tug her off-kilter collar, enjoying how he could see her pulse jumping along her throat. "You get dressed in the dark or what?"

His mouth dried with the look in her eyes. One he remembered from years past and embraces stolen in quiet moments, like when they would get caught at the Dawhoo Bridge coming home. He moved his hand to cup her chin.

She stepped back and turned, tugging at her shirt. "Liam's coming over tonight, too."

He tamped down his irritation. "I didn't know that."

"You didn't ask."

Outside, Hank's playful bark changed to a shrilling whine accompanied by shouts from the boys. Lou flew toward the door. David beat her and held open the screen. They stepped out on the porch as Hank streaked up from the riverbank, howling, the triplets in a rush behind. The dog paused to duck his head and claw at something near his ear. Then he rolled, yowling and thrashing his head in the muddy yard.

David looked at Lou. "What the heck is wrong with him?"

She stepped off the porch, and he followed. "I think he's got a crab on his ear. Used to happen to Mama's dog, Beau, all the time. Told them to be careful around the creek."

The triplets formed a circle around the dog. "C'mere, boy." J.D. coaxed. Hank continued to paw at the ground, rubbing his head. As David and Lou neared, he could see, indeed, a fiddler crab attached to one of the dog's floppy ears.

"Shh ... Hank." Lou knelt in the mud and held out her palm. She crooned, "It's okay ..." The dog stopped thrashing and nudged his nose into her hand. With her other she reached and squeezed the claw of the crab, flinging the creature away in one fluid motion.

Hank howled again and barreled into Lou, licking and gasping. She fell into a seated position and rubbed his head while peering at his ear. "I think you'll be okay. Boys, take him up to the house and get him a treat, okay?"

Grabbing the dog's collar, J.D. led the pack to the porch. David crossed his arms and stared down at this woman who never failed to surprise him. She was now as mud-covered as their boys. A streak of muck lashed across her cheek, and the crooked buttons mattered no more. He'd truly never seen her look more appealing.

"Are you going to stand there and stare or help me up?" Lou wiggled her fingers in his direction.

"Oh, no." He knew that impish grin playing at the corners of her mouth. Even if it had been years since he'd seen it. "I think I'll stay over here, high and dry."

She screwed up her face. "C'mon. We're not young and silly anymore. Just help me up."

Sighing, he stretched out his fingers. She grasped them, and with more force than he'd imagined she could muster, jerked him right into the muddy yard beside her.

Mud caked itself to his entire right side and obscured the logo of his new Colleton High School t-shirt. "You—" He lunged for her, but she rolled out of the way and scrambled to her feet, laughing.

"Gotcha." She offered him her hand. "Truce?"

"No way." And he pulled her back down with him, wrapping his arms around her waist as she fell, relishing how even under the sulfur smell of the Lowcountry, the scent of Dove soap lingered on her skin.

"You two are worse than the boys." Cora Anne called from the porch. "I'm locking the door until everyone uses the water hose, Mama."

Lou braced her hands against his shoulders and struggled to her feet, mirth and mischief still dancing in her eyes. "I can't believe I did that."

"I can't either." David hauled himself up and flung his mud-drenched arm around her shoulder. She slipped hers around his waist and leaned into him. His heartbeat stuttered.

"Let's go get some old towels out of the barn." She pulled him with her and they crossed the yard. Inside the old barn, she let him go and lifted the lid off a plastic container full of ratty beach towels.

Through the open door, the late afternoon sunlight lent a hazy yellow glow to the air. Dust swirled around the old farm belongings. Canvases draped tables, protecting the research equipment beneath. One of the sheets had slipped from an easel, and he moved to put it back, but stilled seeing the pictures.

"What are you doing?" Lou's voice took on a hint of trepidation.

He pulled the cloth away.

Beneath was a display board of pictures and graphs, charts and data of research collected from the river. He reached out, one finger gently caressing a photo of the sun rising over the creek, its blend of yellows and oranges lighting the buffer of vegetation like a wildfire. In all of it, he could see her mark. The careful attention to detail, the meticulous calculation of the water's quality as the tides ebbed and flowed.

He felt her beside him, could hear her breathing, ragged and scared. "Lou, this is amazing."

She reached for the sheet and flung it back over the research. "I'm good at documentation is all."

He caught her elbow. "You see what others don't."

But she shrank from him. "No, I'm just a good assistant because I take good notes. Liam is the lead professor."

"You'll get there someday soon."

"Not soon enough." She strode away, but he caught her again before she exited the barn—and their moment.

"What's the matter? You were always good with taking things slow."

"Can we get out of here, please?" She handed him a towel. "Clean off as best you can. I bet you have a change of clothes in the car."

He did because long ago he'd gotten in the habit of keeping one in the trunk for days when practice was especially hot. But he wasn't done with this conversation. "What is it, Lou? I thought you liked the research project."

She snapped her towel open and rubbed it vigorously over her arms. "I do, but it's not medical. It's environmental. That's not what I do."

"So change what you do."

Her movement stopped and she turned, staring at him with such hurt in her eyes he knew he'd treaded somewhere sacred. And when she blinked and swallowed, her throat contracting as she fought back tears, he remembered the last time he'd seen her look at him like that.

It wasn't the night she'd told him to leave. It was the night she showed him an ultrasound image with three tiny heartbeats.

Chapter 39

David, the one who wanted a family bigger than the three of them, couldn't be bothered with changing his practice schedule to accommodate her first doctor's appointment. Last she'd checked, this was why he had an assistant.

Lou chewed her lip and rearranged the crinkly paper gown. Playoffs started next week. Not entirely his fault all this happened at once.

They'd given up hoping, for her part at least. Fertility, one more thing she couldn't quite get right. Instead, she applied for a doctoral program. Biochemistry, perhaps, had fewer variables than her chances of getting pregnant post-thirty-five.

But one round of a drug to stimulate ovulation—"Let's just see if it works. One time." David had coaxed—and the stick came up with two bold lines.

Lou leaned back, trying in vain to get comfortable. Already this pregnancy drained her energy more than the first time. Doctors weren't joking about advanced maternal age being a thing.

But nausea aside, David wasn't the only one who wanted this baby. Though how in the world could she manage everything? At least she was due in January, that dead time of year before baseball took over their life again.

"Good afternoon, Mrs. Halloway." The technician beamed as she came in, scrubs garishly bright. "Looking forward to seeing this little one in action?"

Right now baby was the size of a ripe raspberry. "Doubt there will be much action."

The woman, her tag said Cindy, chuckled. "Well … probably not. But let's find a nice, strong heartbeat, all right?"

Lou held her breath. Cindy spread the cool gel across her belly and moved the wand in slow circles. No reason to worry, and yet, all day she'd had a sense of trepidation.

A furrow started between the tech's brows as she probed. Lou glanced at the screen, grainy and gray.

Cindy lifted the wand. "You're Ruth's patient, correct?"

She nodded. Ruth had been her midwife with Cora Anne, too, ten years and a lifetime ago.

"I'm just going to pop out and ask her to come take a look at something. No reason to worry."

They only said that when something wasn't right.

Ruth came in a moment later and took the tech's stool, pulling it close. "Hey, Lou. How are you feeling?"

"Most of the time, like I've been run over by a Mack truck."

"Morning sickness?" Ruth started the scan again.

"All day. A lot worse this time. David figures that must mean it's a boy."

"Well …" Ruth's tongue poked between her teeth as she studied the screen. "I'd say you've got a one in three chance."

Lou's throat prickled. She must've heard her wrong. "What?"

Ruth tapped the screen. "I'm guessing the fertility drugs kicked your body into high gear. You've got three embryos, Lou. Triplets."

Cold and nausea swept over her like a fog rising up off the tidal creeks. She turned, swung her legs over, and tried to stand. "I'm going to—"

The words strangled as she retched, the last of her resolve coming up with her lunch.

~ ~ ~

David jogged up the front porch steps. Lou sat in the swing, one foot tucked beneath her, the other pushing with slow, methodical pumps. One hand splayed over her abdomen.

Through the window, Cora Anne had her homework sprawled across the dining room table. A science project. He couldn't remember what it was about but knew Lou had it under control.

He went to his wife, dropped to his knees, and laid his arms across her lap to stop the swing's rhythm. "I'm sorry."

"I know."

Her tone made him wince. He always apologized, but he didn't always correct the mistake. She pointed that out on more than one occasion. Still, he tried. She knew the pressure he was under as head coach. "Clint pulled a muscle. Bad enough he might be out for the season. We had to figure out a plan for playoffs."

She nodded. "It's always about the boys. What makes you a good coach."

He rocked back on his heels, studying her. In the dusky evening, her pallor looked gray. "Have you been sick again?"

Her eyes drifted across their yard and neighborhood. Comfortable middle-class suburban Atlanta. Well-maintained yards, painted mailboxes, the laughter of children not yet called in for bed drifting across the streets. Stability was a provision he'd worked hard to achieve.

Easing into the swing beside her, he slid an arm around her shoulders. "Lou? Did something happen?"

She turned over her hand. The other cradled her stomach. A glossy black-and-white image he recognized but couldn't interpret. There were three x's where there should only be one.

Right?

He pulled the picture from her and held it closer. "I don't understand."

"We're having triplets, David." She turned back to him, those blue eyes that had captured him from the first moment awash in tears. "I don't understand either."

"Oh, honey ..." He tucked her head against his chest, letting her tears mingle with the sweat of his afternoon. She never cried. "Everything will be all right. We can do this."

"How?" she whispered. "I'm barely enough for one child, let alone three more."

"You're an amazing mother, thoughtful and dedicated." He pushed hair away from her damp face.

She tugged a piece of paper from where she'd had it hidden beneath her leg. "I can't be dedicated to them and this."

He took it and skimmed the contents. Her acceptance into the doctorate program at Emory University. Even as she lifted her head and sat back, he felt the weight of all he was asking her to give up press against his ribs. "I'm sorry, sweetheart."

She didn't say everything would be okay, but Lou had never been an optimist. She leaned on him for that. Instead, she shook her head. "Some things aren't meant to be, I guess."

He grasped her hand, holding tight to the woman he knew wanted to believe in hope, but struggled with formulas she couldn't see. "I'll help you get your doctorate someday, Lou. I promise."

Finally, a small smile edged her lips. "I'll hold you to that, Coach Halloway. Just you wait and see."

Chapter 40

While she wouldn't exactly say she missed the nine-hour drive between Edisto and Nashville, Grace did find the airplane experience jarred her senses. Once she'd thought the sun might rise and set on Music City. Now she knew better.

They took a cab straight over to the nursing home because Grace wanted to make as much of these forty-eight hours as possible—and because she knew her mother would need multiple visits before she clued in to who Tennessee and she were.

If she did at all.

Under the whiffs of antiseptic and urine, the home smelled of memories. Sense of smell had a powerful effect on a person's mind, so she'd read. There'd been a time she tried to shake her mother out of herself by bringing in a box of Krispy Kremes, hot and fresh, like they used to eat on Saturday mornings.

Mother had flung the donuts at the wall and screamed about how Grace tried to poison her. In the end, the nurses gave her a shot, and she wilted like an old carrot, thin and limp.

Grace had gone back home, driving the whole nine hours with only one stop, coming onto the island in tar-thick black midnight. She'd kicked off her shoes and climbed into bed with Patrick, curling into his side and finally weeping so hard she'd been an old carrot herself when it was over.

Tennessee took her hand, squeezing her fingers gently, and she gave him a thin smile. He'd been nine when the donuts happened. After that, he and Patrick accompanied her on every visit.

Divinity flung her hands to heaven when Grace and Tennessee paused outside the door. This nurse sent Grace monthly updates

171

long as her swinging braids. "Well, I'll be. If it ain't the Firecracker's matchbook. And her young piece of dynamite." Her toothy grin pulled a chuckle from Tennessee.

"How are you, ma'am?" He offered his hand, but she pulled him down for a hug.

"No complaints from me, young man. Now, how's your mama?" Divinity turned and squeezed Grace, tighter than anyone had in far too long.

A lump lodged in her throat, pressed against the ample shoulder. "We're well. How's she?"

"Ah, you know your mother. Every little thing sets her off." Divinity scrunched up her nose. "Just don't get your feelings hurt, all right? She's a mean one, but that's the damage those drugs did for so long when she tried to fix herself. Ticker's going strong, and she likes the new aerobics class." Divinity winked. "The teacher plays that head-banging music, says it's therapeutic. Seems to work for your mama."

In the small room, its walls covered with pictures cut from magazines and newspapers, taped haphazardly in a way that made sense only to her, Mother sat in bed, head lolling against her shoulder, her vacant gaze fixed on a point out the small, cloudy window. Her chin snapped up when the door caught. She jerked the sheet up and screeched, "Who are you? Get out of my room."

"It's me, Mother. Grace. And my son, Tennessee."

The grip didn't relax but her eyes darted back and forth, as though in time with the synapses surely firing in her brain, trying to make sense of names she thought she ought to know.

"I don't remember you." A blunt statement, but not laced with malice.

Grace took the worn chair and pulled it beside the bed. For a state-run facility, the home was more than adequate. "That's all right, Mother. We remember you."

"What do you want?"

Tennessee settled his hands on Grace's shoulders. "We just wanted to see you is all. I've got some news I thought you'd enjoy." He went to his bag and retrieved the engagement announcement that had appeared in Charleston's *Post and Courier*. His grandmother took it, fingers trembling, and smoothed out the crease.

She squinted at the print then lifted her eyes to his. "This you, boy?"

"Yes, ma'am."

"Going to marry a pretty little girl."

"Yes, ma'am."

"I had a pretty little girl once ..." She swung her legs over the side of the bed. "Gracie was her name. I think she got married, too."

Grace stood, thinking to help her, but Mother shuffled right over to a box, riffled through and produced a roll of Scotch tape. She spoke to her back. "I did get married to Patrick. Remember? Tennessee is our son."

Her mother's hands and head shook together. "Gracie's only a girl. I sent her away to live with someone better. Maybe someday I'll see her again." She stuck tape to the wall, her tongue between her teeth, her only focus hanging the picture of the family she no longer knew.

~~~

"Tell me about it." Tennessee's words came quietly, over the platter of fried green tomatoes at the bustling restaurant downtown. Grace hadn't wanted to eat. She'd wanted to do nothing but wash the visit with her mother down the drain of the hotel shower and collapse into bed, before the memories reared up and took her under those waves of grief she'd long ago learned to ride.

But her son wouldn't let her wallow, wouldn't let her drown. So much like his father.

"She's been sick a long time." The easiest explanation, the one she gave those kind ladies on the prayer team at church whenever someone got a whiff Grace had family of her own.

He shook his head. "I know, and the Bells brought you to Edisto. When did you decide to find her?"

"I didn't. She found me—in one of her more lucid times. By then

I was a mother myself." She offered him a half-smile. "And I couldn't imagine someday not having a relationship with you. But ..." She twisted the napkin in her lap. "She would never get the treatment she really needed, and mental illness was harder to handle then. Patsy and Robert helped me get her into the home." How she missed those kind souls. They'd have been her son's surrogate grandparents, as well, but they'd both passed when he was young.

"You're a wonder, Mom. How'd you survive?"

"I had your father." Patrick Watson with his easy smile and strong arms, taking her wobbling tray of sweet tea glasses before they could spill. She could see him in Tennessee—every day.

"I'm sorry you've lost so much." He hunched forward, his eyes soft with tears she didn't often see him shed. "It's not fair."

"I told you a long time ago, life isn't fair, but God is good." Though sometimes, like when she came here, that was hard to remember.

Chapter 41

"What do you think, Dad? Major League here, huh?" Cole flexed and mimed pitching a ball at the back of his brother's head as they rumbled home from practice.

"Sure thing, if you work hard." David tried not to be one of those dads pinning all his dreams—and Cole's—on the Major League, but the tantalizing what-if was worth a try sometimes.

"We could be the Halloway Triplets. The crowd would love it."

In the front seat, J.D. raised his head from his algebra homework. "I'll go to college and play as long as it's a good one, but that's it."

Mac leaned forward and rapped him on the head. "Listen, Einstein, not all of us have your brains."

"You could if you'd crack those books occasionally." David swung the car into the farmhouse drive, where the canopy of trees had begun to bud for spring. He pulled behind Liam's Land Rover and swallowed the growl that rose in his throat.

"Dr. Whiting's here again?" Cole rolled his eyes.

"Again?" David kept his voice even, though he fisted his hand around the seatbelt release. Not a day went by he didn't regret this deal Lou and he had made. Maybe it was time to figure out just how serious Liam Whiting may be.

"Yeah, he took Mom to dinner the other night," Mac reported, swinging from the jeep. "She let us stay home and watch *Star Wars*."

Lou was nowhere in sight, but David spotted Liam down near the dock. He lifted an arm in hello before unloading the bat bags. By the time he'd stacked everything on the porch, the boys were pillaging the kitchen, and Liam headed his way.

"David," he called, "Lou asked me to tell you she took Hank over to Grace. I expect she'll return soon."

David nodded, sizing up this man who had given Lou back her sense of purpose. He couldn't resent someone who brought a light back into her eyes, much as he wished the professor would confine himself to Charleston. Liam stood relaxed in his waders and fisherman's jacket, thick gloves slick with pluff mud.

Behind him, at the creek, David could see a half-dozen college students with nets skimming the water. "What are y'all working on today?"

"Observing the shrimp spawning."

"Sounds interesting." He followed Liam down to the water's edge.

The professor showed him the tiny creature. "They always return to the same place." He spoke with reverence. "Amazing what nature can do that we cannot."

David's jaw twitched. "But sometimes we can." He changed the subject. "What did Lou document today?"

"So she's shown you?"

He bristled at the implication Lou's research was a secret he might not have known, one kept between her and this man who shared her sense of order and pattern with the natural world. "Of course. She's very talented."

"I've encouraged her to present it at the symposium in May. Will help set her apart for a doctoral program."

"Doctorate?"

Liam paused in the packing of his supplies. "You didn't know?"

David rolled his shoulders. "She's mentioned it before."

Years before. When he'd wanted to have more children and she'd wanted to get out of the high school lab. They'd agreed. Baby and then Lou would be back to school. He'd manage the household while she pursued her dream. But that baby had turned into months of trying, then a round of fertility drugs, and then they were having triplets. Lou didn't mention her doctorate again and neither did he, even as she sank under waves of grief from which he couldn't pull her out.

David turned his gaze to the spartina grass that waved in the evening breeze, protecting the delicate ecosystem from which came miniscule creatures who knew nothing but their way home.

He forced out the words. "Thank you for encouraging her."

Liam swung the bag on his shoulder. "I can't take all the credit. She told me the timing really couldn't be better, since you were here."

"Glad to be of service."

The professor walked with him back toward the house, students trailing behind. The boys were swinging on the tire again, making the tree branch groan in protest. David cupped his hands around his mouth and called, "One at a time."

J.D. and Mac jumped off and began pushing Cole wildly.

Liam laughed. "Brothers."

"You have any family around?"

"Nah … just me. And the ex." Liam lowered his voice like a conspirator. "She sure doesn't offer to help me cook dinner."

David stepped back, trying to read this man, but Liam had turned to his students. "Got everything packed? Let's head on back." He returned and extended his hand to David. "I'll see you Saturday night?"

The engagement party. David gripped Liam's hand in return. "Saturday night."

"Your boys Braves fans?"

The question was so off-kilter, David nearly stumbled. "Of course."

"Yankee doubleheader on Saturday. Guess I'll slip in my ear buds." Liam shook his head. "But from how Lou's described Mrs. Watson, I fear the wrath."

"You most definitely should." He clarified. "Fear the wrath."

"If I risk it, you going down with me?"

The offer was tempting. He'd groaned checking the schedule and seeing the conflict. But—"I'd be as afraid of Lou as I am Charlotte Watson. You're on your own."

"Ah, well. Only live once, I figure."

"Heads up!" The boys had abandoned the tire swing to throw the football left on the bottom porch step. Cole's enthusiasm meant J.D. needed to go long and he might have made it—if Liam hadn't snagged the ball neat as a running back on Friday night.

He fist-pumped the boys who made suitable exclamations.

"Whoa, Dad, did you see that?" Mac caught the return spiral, shaking his head. "And he's older than you."

If his boys hadn't been so wide-eyed, and so oblivious to the awkwardness swirling around the air that spun that football, David might have been offended. But he couldn't help but laugh.

Liam joined in. "Are they saying that was pretty good for an old guy?"

"It was, professor," one of the male students confirmed.

"Well, in that case, as you all say, I'm out." Liam stuck out his hand. David shook it again, feeling he'd just agreed to dinner with his enemy and yet, strangely, cheered by the prospect.

The group emptied the drive and only a few moments later, while he proved to his sons that he, too, could still catch a decent pass, Lou pulled in.

"Hey." Her generic greeting was surely meant for them all, but when the boys just waved, her gaze went straight to his.

He threw the ball back to Cole and turned from the game. "How was Grace's trip?"

"I don't really know. She was pretty quiet. Seemed glad to have that beast back though."

J.D. jogged over, ready for Cole's pass. "Can't believe you didn't let us say goodbye, Mom. No fair."

"Y'all said goodbye this morning and then changed and left me a muddy mess in the laundry room. Once was enough." Looping her purse over her shoulder, Lou rubbed her temples.

David wanted to slip his hand under her short ponytail and knead her neck into a different kind of tension entirely. Instead, he stuffed his hands in his pockets. "By the way, I got a lead on a golden over in Ravenel. Want to drive over and check it out next week?"

Her eyes skittered across the yard. "Hank's been a handful."

"Not all dogs are like Hank."

"Thank goodness for that."

"Are you saying you changed your mind?" David kept his voice neutral. He counted on this. Something else they'd have together.

"I might need more time to think about it is all."

"Let me know what you decide."

Lou winced. Almost as if she'd prefer to have him tell her she'd had enough time to make up her mind. She huffed out a sigh. "We can go look."

He let the grin spread wide, knowing if he offered it to her just right, his smile would edge one from her. Lou pursed her lips, and then pressed them flat, the corners just tipping up.

Satisfied, David followed her up the porch steps. "Need any help?"

"With laundry?"

He shrugged. "With anything."

Her laugh sounded brittle. "Don't get me started." She pulled at the screen and stood, holding it open. "Come on. I'm about to make a mean frozen pizza."

He took the door from her and they stood, framed in it, like a photograph from the past, frozen in time. Reaching out a hand, he stroked her cheek with his thumb, heard her catch of breath. He let his hand linger against her jaw, felt her swallow as her eyes searched his. "I mean it, Lou. Anything you need."

She nodded against his palm, and he withdrew his hand and himself, giving her back the only thing he really could. The space between them and the freedom to choose.

Chapter 42

Lou considered herself detail-oriented, but dealing with Charlotte reminded her of working needlepoint with her mother, and it gave her nearly the same headache. Every detail of the party had been scrutinized—though with very little compromise. The boys would have to wear tuxes. No two ways about it.

"The tailor will deliver directly to me on Saturday morning." Charlotte told Lou. "Less risk of ... contamination, shall we say, before they arrive?"

Contamination, her foot. Lou swept furiously at the mud dried on the porch. She'd give Charlotte something to be contaminated about.

"Whoa, Mom, you trying to take the paint off with the dirt?" Cora Anne stepped back from the steps as Lou flung the last of the clods toward the yard.

"Sorry. Didn't see you there."

"You must be in a real tizzy if you didn't even hear me drive up."

Lou shrugged. "Got a lot on my mind, sweetheart. What are you doing here?" She leaned on the broom handle, admiring her daughter. She never tired of these impromptu visits. Their relationship had been dry as the porch's mud tracks for far too long.

"You know I've got this photography project I'm working on for the museum, and thought I'd run a couple of the unknowns by you."

"Sure."

They settled on the ratty sofa in the den. Cora Anne pretended it was hard to get comfortable—the family's new tactic for suggesting she replace the furniture. Lou might come around to it faster if they'd all stop acting like it was such a big deal.

Cora Anne spread five photographs in the sepia tone of the seventies across the table. "These are definitely from the building of Ocean Ridge after David Lybrand had to sell Oristo. We've identified him." She tapped a man in the photo's center. "But we need help with the rest."

Lou pulled a photo close to her nose and squinted. "How'd you miss picking out Patrick?"

"What?"

She pointed to a tall man in profile with the other five, leaning on shovels and wearing hard hats. "The Ocean Ridge Resort was his first job out here. What he did when his parents cut him off."

"Tennessee never mentioned it."

"Maybe he just forgot, but I can tell you." Lou swept the rest of the pictures into a stack. "I can't help you, but Grace could. They met while he was on that project."

"Guess I'll head over there then."

"Why don't we go down to the beach and get dinner? The boys won't be back until later. Dad took them for their tux fittings."

Cora Anne cringed. "Sorry about that."

"Not your fault." Lou stood, raised her arms over her head, and stretched down into the small of her back where she held all her stress in a knot. If she could figure out just the right way to bend, maybe it would loosen and she'd be flooded with all those endorphins athletes spoke of—a sudden rush of ecstasy and relief.

"Mom, I do have one more thing I wanted to ask." Cora Anne bit her lip and ran her fingers over the loose threads in the plaid weave. "Can I move in here until the wedding?"

"Really?" She dropped her arms with the rush of delight. Maybe she'd untethered that knot after all.

"I was only in the cottage through winter, remember? Tennessee wants to rent it this summer and put the extra income toward our new house." Cora Anne's eyes sparkled. "We'll keep a week in July open for the reunion, of course."

"Of course ..." But Lou's mind leapt ahead to logistics. "I could move downstairs." She'd already been using the room where Mama drew her last breath, so surely that would be all right. The wedding was in June, so this would only last a few weeks, really, since it was practically April—

"I thought you might move into Nan and Granddaddy's room upstairs, and I'll take yours. Seems the most practical."

Practical. How impractical to keep her parents' bedroom preserved. Once she'd been able to make decisions based on practicality—and then learn to live with them. Joy evaporated as a cloud of grief descended, but Lou shook it off. She could do this. One small change at a time. "Mama ..."

"You'll have to help me." Her voice broke.

Cora Anne stood and pulled her close. "You know I will."

Upstairs, Cora Anne passed a hand lovingly over her grandmother's vanity. "Can't you just see her sitting here, primping those curls for church?"

Lou had a different vision. She saw herself, seven years old, face pulled into a pout as her mother brushed and tugged and smoothed her long dark hair into braids for school. When she'd finally had enough of the scalp torture every morning, she'd taken Mama's sewing scissors and cut those braids off with one decisive snip.

She winced at the vanity. "You can have this if you want."

"I'd love it." Cora Anne sat on the stool and gently pulled open drawers that rattled with perfume bottles and ancient pots of rouge. Lou turned and braced her hand against the doorframe, overcome by the floral smell that evoked her mother's presence.

"Mama?"

When David's parents died, she'd thought him strong and stable until the day came that the closet in the bedroom was the only thing he had left to empty. And she found him, curled in the corner, weeping into his mother's bathrobe, which smelled of cigarette smoke and peppermint. She'd gathered him in her arms and promised him she wouldn't leave too.

Cora Anne touched her shoulder. "Mama?"

"I can't do this right now." The sob catching in her throat spilled over and she pulled away, seeking shelter in her own room, where the scent of roses didn't linger.

The shadows had stretched long across her chenille bedspread when the gentle tapping on her door stirred her awake.

"Lou, can I come in?"

She pushed up on her elbow, disoriented, wondering why David was here—

And all the past few months came back in a rush that took her breath. Collapsing back against her pillows, she must have made a sound that alarmed him because he entered without her consent.

"Hey ..." He came over to the bed and sat beside her, stroking back the hair now stuck to her puffy cheeks. "What happened?"

"Mama's vanity smells like her perfume."

He needed no other explanation. Gathering her into his arms, he held her while she wept again, all the racking sobs of an orphaned child masquerading as an adult.

Chapter 43

Today, Grace made pies. She cut cold butter into flour and turned the dough with her fingers, disdaining the use of her food processor like the Food Network star recommended. She flattened and rolled and filled the dishes with dried apples like Annie had taught her. Cinnamon came next and she sprinkled liberally, having read that the spice prevented inflammation and could ward off depression.

The sweetness sent her back. Her father laughing on school mornings as he sprinkled cinnamon sugar thickly over Texas toast. Tennessee sitting at the tiny counter in the caretaker's house at Cooper Creek, wearing footed pajamas because as a first-time mother, she believed he must dress according to the calendar rather than the weather. A ratty blanket dangled from his lap, as he watched her make breakfast, asking nearly every day for cinnamon toast.

Now her only baby was marrying and leaving her too. She was entitled to the wave of tears that almost splashed her pie.

A knock sounded, and Hank leapt from his bed at the foot of the fireplace, looking like an advertisement for Lands' End. He shattered that illusion by sliding across the floor. He never could seem to grasp that running across her hardwoods offered him no purchase.

"Hush, boy." She snagged his collar. "Did you behave like this while I was gone?"

She swung open the door to find Cora Anne, her arms full with a box and a stack of magazines.

"I can assure you he behaved exactly like that." Her daughter-in-law-to-be kissed her cheek and swept into the room. "What are you baking? It smells amazing."

"Apple pie."

Cora Anne had been around long enough to know Grace baked from scratch only when anxious or feeding someone else. Her blue eyes searched Grace's face, a gentle probe. "I'd love to hear about your visit."

Except Grace didn't want to talk about it. "Put this down first." She hefted the box and set it on the coffee table. "What's in there?"

"Photographs. Mama said you could probably help me identify some of the people. We're working on organizing all the old photos at the museum. This batch is from Oristo. And these"—she fanned the magazines—"are ideas for the party and wedding." Cora Anne's cheeks glowed. "I'd love you to do my hair, if you don't mind."

"Why in the world would I mind?" Grace took the stack, grateful she'd worked her worries into that pie dough and could focus on happier times. "You know your Aunt Carolina's wedding is how I got my job at the salon, all those years ago. The owner was shorthanded and asked me to help out."

"Really?" Cora Anne tucked into a corner of the couch and Hank joined her. Laughing, she rubbed his ears. "Don't worry, boy, soon you'll have a new playmate."

"Did they find a puppy?"

"Headed there tomorrow, I believe."

"That'll be good ..." Grace wanted to be happy for David and Lou, for the seaming together of their cracks that might give them a new future. But her own loneliness clouded the desire. She flipped open one of the style magazines. "What are you thinking?"

"Up for the party because Grandmother Charlotte hinted that's appropriate, but down for the wedding because Tennessee likes it."

Grace studied this girl her son loved, a girl who'd been so damaged, so broken, Grace worried he would break his own heart helping her heal.

Charlotte must have felt the same about her.

With the realization, she startled, and the magazine slid to her feet.

"You all right?" Cora Anne scooped it up and pointed to the open pages before Grace could formulate a passable answer. "Here's one I thought would be good."

A simple chignon, swept up with tiny white flowers. "Yes. That would be perfect."

They flipped glossy pages, laughing at impracticalities and sighing over whimsical shots, soft with light and chiffon.

"Tell me about yours and Patrick's wedding." An innocent statement, since Cora Anne might not have asked if she'd known.

The oven timer beeped, and Grace welcomed the distraction. She lifted pies and set them gently on the counter, so as not to let the crust fissure and the filling spill out. How did she tell her there'd been no fairy tale wedding? Only a pledge at the Charleston County courthouse and a walk on the pier. A stranger had taken their picture, and she'd worn a borrowed dress.

"I know all about Mama and Daddy's. Presbyterian Church, reception at the farm. Of course, you would know, Aunt Caro and Uncle John got married at St. Michael's because his family are members. I bet even Charlotte would approve of a St. Michael's wedding."

"No doubt she would. Be right back, sweetheart." Grace ducked into her bedroom and retrieved the silver framed picture. She passed it over. "We kept things simple."

Cora Anne caressed the glass, tracing Patrick's smile with her fingertips. "You both look so happy. Even in their wedding pictures my parents ..." She set the picture down. "They looked nervous."

Relieved at the turn in the conversation, Grace leaned on the counter, letting the pie's steamy cinnamon scent settle her. She'd had a courthouse and a happy marriage. David and Lou had a church and years of discontent. Patrick had always told her it didn't matter what a wedding day looked like. What mattered were all the days that came after.

"Your mother and father need to find each other again, that's all." She folded a dishcloth, fingers fumbling. "They seem to be working on it."

Cora Anne shrugged. "Mama's bringing Liam to the party."

"Your mama likes things neat and tidy." She set the cloth aside and twisted her hands. "I'd wager divorce is messy, and repairing a relationship after? That's like suturing up a wound. Looks awful until the scars heal." Her scars still pulled tight like scabs.

Cora Anne set the picture aside. "Sounds like something Nan would say."

"Well, you don't style a lady's hair for thirty years and not learn a thing or two."

Outside a door slammed and Hank jumped again, this time knocking the box of pictures to the floor in his pursuit.

"Hey, babe." Tennessee pushed Hank out of his way and kissed Cora Anne, lingering a bit longer than was necessary, given they were in his mother's kitchen.

Grace cleared her throat.

He grinned that hundred-watt smile that got him and his father out of trouble almost every time. "Sorry, Mom. Your pie smells good." She arched a brow, and he amended with a kiss to her cheek. "I came over to hear about those Ocean Ridge photographs. How come I didn't know Dad worked that project?"

"I don't think he cared much for building a golf course, but it paid the bills."

They gathered the spilled photographs and spread them across Grace's dining room table amidst the centerpieces of driftwood and shells, fresh flowers and hurricane candles she always kept it set with. A bit ridiculous since, when alone, she ate at the counter or on a TV tray.

"I love how nice you keep things," Cora Anne said cradling a piece of wood. "Makes a house a home."

"Learned that from your grandmother as well." Grace smiled, sifting through the photos. Snapshots taken a lifetime ago.

"She taught you to make her crab cakes, right?" Cora Anne's question carried wistfulness.

Grace set down the pictures and pressed the girl's hand. "You know she did."

"Mama doesn't like to make them. That's the only recipe she says she can't do justice and plus, it takes like ten pounds of crab to feed the boys."

"I better start teaching them to set their own traps then." Tennessee brought wedges of pie to the table. Grace smiled at the size of the piece he'd served himself. Probably ought to teach Cora Anne that recipe as well.

"Maybe we could come over when you make them? I'm not very good at picking the meat." She wrinkled her nose and Tennessee tweaked it.

"You'd be better if you'd relax more. They can't pinch when they're cooked." He scooped a bite of pie in his mouth, swallowed, and grinned. "Or maybe we could just come over for dinner every week since someone doesn't have the patience for pie crust either."

Cora Anne threw her napkin at him, laughing. "You said you weren't marrying me for my culinary skills."

"You did learn to fry chicken, so I figure we'll survive."

Grace shook her head with their playful banter, relishing the simple sounds of laughter in her kitchen. "You all come over whenever you want. We can make it a standing date. There's always more than enough."

Perhaps she wasn't going to be quite so alone after all.

Chapter 44

The triplets, born right before Christmas, stayed in the NICU together for thirty-one days.

J.D. came home first with the strongest lungs, even though he weighed less than Mac. Mac Truck, the nurses called him because he was the biggest of the three, broad-chested and thick, even as a 34-week preemie. Lou could lay her hand on his chest without her fingers wrapping around like they did on the others.

Mac remained another five days, and when they brought him home, he immediately abandoned the NICU schedule. J.D. had been easy from the get-go. Eat, sleep, change, repeat. The perfect baby for Lou's charts.

Mac refused to sleep anywhere except right beside his brother, so David finally broke down one of the cribs. By the time they were allowed to bring Cole home, the baby with the weakest lungs and the toughest spirit, Lou hadn't slept more than a three-hour stretch in two weeks.

Cole, at least, kept his schedule during the day, making the long hours between when David and Cora Anne left for school and returned manageable. The church ladies came by, of course, and Mama stayed the first two weeks they were all three home. Mac settled down so long as they co-slept, but Cole couldn't abide the dark.

One night, bleary-eyed and strung out, Lou nestled Cole into his crib and switched on a gift that had been dropped off that afternoon. A nightlight beamed stars all over the ceiling. Lou crept out, knowing she only had about an hour before he wailed.

They all slept solidly for the next four.

She jerked awake and rushed from the king-size bed.

The stars danced across the nursery ceiling. The babies stirred, mewing like newborn kittens rather than shrieking like little banshees. The clock's blue numbers glowed three a.m.

The first time in a month she hadn't seen every hour all night long.

When the trying for another baby turned into five years of waiting and wondering, Lou told herself it didn't matter. She'd been content with their life, just as it was. But the hopefulness in David's eyes—the joy she'd seen when the doctor told them they'd have sons—had been worth the difficult pregnancy and the fearful hospital days. She'd finally given him something he'd always wanted, a family that would grow to be big and boisterous, like the one she'd brought him into.

Surely now he would want to be a part of it all. Would realize she and the children needed more from him than provision.

Cole squealed first, so she scooped him up, his tiny head against her hammering heart. He stopped the moment she tucked him under her chin, and for the shortest time in the middle of another long night, Lou found herself content.

And terrified the feeling wouldn't last.

Chapter 45

"You're not saying it right." Lou's laughter filled the jeep, and David grinned at her. He had no intention of correcting himself if that's all it took to hear her laugh like that, belly deep, the way she had the first time he'd hauled in a shrimp net.

"Listen," she pursed her lips then drawled out, "Ra-*vah*-nel." Her breath sighed on the middle syllable as though the word needed to rest under the weight of all the connotation that name carried around here.

He knew how to pronounce the small community where he'd found the golden retriever breeder. He'd heard it said more than once when referencing Charlotte and her blue blood ties. But his North Georgia tongue sometimes tripped over the soft syllables and the word came out wrong. An innocent mistake that had set Lou to teasing.

And he liked her this way.

"Ruh-*vahhh*-nel," he intoned, straight-faced. In the jeep's backseat, crowded knee-to-knee, the boys groaned.

"Dad, you're going to make us sound like a bunch of hicks." J.D. leaned forward between the front seats. "I think he's pretending, Mom."

"You think?" She wagged her brows at David, almost suggestive, and he risked taking his eyes from the road to wink at her.

She swatted his arm. "You're a mess."

"Like father, like sons."

"As usual, I am outnumbered. Should've made Cora Anne come along."

"The night before her fancy party, I'm sure she has better things to do than pick out a dog with us."

"Hannah whisked her off, and I think champagne and pedicures were involved."

"I rest my case." He navigated into a narrow, pot-holed drive that bore a sign hanging from its mailbox: Certified Golden Retrievers Available.

"Anyone else hear banjos?" Cole asked.

"And you thought we sounded like hicks." Mac elbowed J.D. The boys scuffled, a daily occurrence.

"Boys." Lou twisted around. "Behave or we won't pick out a puppy."

They spilled from the car as soon as he stopped, and David turned toward her with a grin. "Don't say things you don't mean, remember?"

She arched a brow. "I never say things I don't mean."

He thought they were still teasing one another, but just to be on the safe side, he grabbed her hand and squeezed it. "I know."

The boys were already at the pen in the scruffy yard, kneeling down and calling to the puppies, still in that fur-bundle stage where they tumble over themselves walking. Beside them, a man in overalls tipped his straw hat. "Howdy, folks. I'm Earl. Y'all the family wanting a puppy?"

David extended his hand. "We are."

"Well, I got some good 'uns right here. Their mama's born three litters and every one of 'em's survived and thrived. Not a runt among 'em."

The puppies were a range of color—whipped-butter yellow to reddish gold. There were six in all. After their initial sniffing of the boys' fingers through the wire, they scurried away and burrowed under their mother to nurse. She lay on her side, her coat the color of rich honey, her eyes tracking every movement.

"She's got more red in her than the daddy did. Why they've got such variety to pick from." Earl produced a photo from his front pocket of a dog poised on a well-manicured lawn. He had a strong, wide face and the classic coat of a golden retriever.

"He's beautiful." Lou took the photo from David and examined it closely. "We had a dog like that growing up."

"Well, miss, if you're looking for his spitting image, you'll like that 'un right there." Earl pointed to the puppy on the end, whose tail wagged in time with his suckling. "He's the biggest and has those sturdy legs and bigger head, like his daddy."

"Can we hold them?" Cole looked ready to climb the fence.

"Oh, yeah. But only four of 'em are for picking from. Got two promised already. Glad y'all could come on out. Three more folks coming by tomorrow. Likely they'll all be spoken for by the next week."

Which meant they needed to decide today. David glanced at Lou as Earl loosed the gate. Soon as they stepped inside, the puppies abandoned their mother and swarmed. The boys scooped them up one by one for comparison, getting licked, and in Mac's case, marked.

"Oh, gross!" He released the red-tinted puppy he held and winced at the stream on his jeans.

"Just means she likes you." Earl pushed a wad of tobacco under his lip.

The puppy he'd pointed out to them had come straight to Lou, who lifted him to her chest and rubbed under his chin. David winced. A man ought not be jealous of a dog.

"I like this one. What do you think, boys?" She handed him over to J.D. They passed the pup around, and he wriggled and squirmed until David returned him to Lou.

"Guess we know who he likes best."

"Are you just a mama's boy?" She cooed, letting the pup swipe his tongue across her chin.

David swallowed, his throat thick, seeing her soften and smile without the taint of grief or anger. He'd take home each and every one of those puppies if it meant Lou would become herself again.

"You want to speak for that 'un?" Earl hooked his thumbs in the front of his overalls and grinned wide—despite the chaw in his cheek.

The puppy nosed under Lou's chin again, settled his head on her shoulder, and went limp as she held him like a baby. "He's definitely a sweet one." She turned to David. "What do you think?"

"You going to tell him he has to love us all equally?"

She stroked the pup's soft coat and shifted her stance until they were nearly hip-to-hip. "I make no promises."

"Hey, Mom, this one's cute." Cole held up the reddest pup of the litter.

"She's already spoke for, son. That girl's gonna be a breeder like her mama."

At Earl's statement Lou's brows contracted and anger whisked across her face—disappearing before David could process why. She set her lips in a thin line and turned back to the scruffy man. "Are all your girls spoken for?"

"Yes, ma'am. Only had two. Folks picked 'em first because breeding purebreds ain't nothing to sneeze at when you wanna make some extra bucks." He puffed out his chest. "These here pups are $250 a piece, but I can get $300 for the girls."

Lou squeezed the pup she held and kissed his head before setting him gently on the ground. "Go on over there and see your mama, little one." The dog obeyed, trotting over to flop beside the mother's head. Wearily, she licked the pup's ears as though to remind him who would always be his mother. Lou straightened, arms crossed, and looked to David.

He could see the frustration simmering just below her surface. For the first time, he wondered if that's how she'd felt, pregnant with triplets when she hadn't even wanted another baby. Weary and resigned and overcome.

"We'll take that one. Right, boys?" They shrugged and grinned, still playing with the others.

"He'll get tired of Mom because she won't play fetch, so don't worry, Dad. Soon he'll love us too."

David grinned at J.D. and his practicality. Then he turned to Earl and closed the deal. "If anyone changes their mind about one of those girls, you let us know. We'll take her too." He heard Lou's tiny gasp as he and Earl shook.

"Come on back in a couple weeks. They'll be weaned and ready to go."

As they walked back to the car, the boys distracted by an argument over who would sit in the middle this time, she slipped her hand into his. Returned his gentle squeeze from earlier. "Thank you."

There would be plenty more to say, maybe in the days to come. But for today, with the sun setting low through the copse of pines, he kept her hand and opened the car door like he had on their first date. "You're welcome."

Chapter 46

The rain came in again Friday night. This time with a king tide— the full moon pulled at the ocean and the creeks, making the water rise higher and higher. Lou, in her kitchen at the dimmest hour of early Saturday morning, thought she ought to load up the boys and head on into Charleston before the roads flooded. But that creek edging her daddy's pastures had never breached its banks. The water seeped up through the vegetation buffer, receded quickly once the tides turned, washing clean salt-tinged water back out to the sea. The sediment settled on the creek bottom where it would become part of this teeming ecosystem Liam so adored.

Liam. She turned her thoughts to that good, solid man. He'd promised to arrive early and stay in the background, fetching her drinks he said, to combat the social anxiety greeting all Charleston gentry.

But she knew, when her pulse raced and her breath quickened, when she couldn't take one more introduction or piece of small talk, David would press his hand to the small of her back and help her make an exit.

She hadn't asked him for that. But always, he could tell when she needed a breath. He'd taken her out during her father's receiving line at the funeral home while hordes of people came to shake her hand and hug her neck until she thought she would suffocate. "Breathe, Lou," he'd whispered, sitting her in a chair away from the crowd. "Just catch your breath, and you can do this."

The wind set the rockers on the porch again to swaying and a memory surfaced. David sitting with her after Mama's funeral. Bringing her food and telling her if she could come back to Edisto, well then, so could he.

Yet, she continued to see what might happen with Liam. A stab of guilt pricked her conscience. She'd never led a man on before.

Although Patrick Watson may have begged to differ.

The rain shifted, and a gust blew harder through the oak's leaves, the tire swing whirling and twisting in the air. The old ropes might snap at any moment. But then the wind died, as if that had been its last hurrah, and the rain slacked as the sun's fringe glowed through the pines.

~~~

"Louisa, how nice of you to join us." Charlotte swept down her curved staircase, dressed in a pantsuit, neck and wrists heavy with pearls. "We've so much to do and so little time."

For a party that didn't start until six, coming into town by noon should be sufficient. Lou pressed her lips into what she hoped passed for a smile. Six hours. They had six whole hours.

"I've prepared the pool house for their entertainment." Charlotte flicked her wrist toward the triplets. "Surely they can manage without supervision."

"Lady, we haven't had a babysitter in years." Cole's mouth needed a dose of soap.

Lou pinched his elbow and forced a smile at Charlotte. "They'll be just fine. Through here?" She marched down the hall and out the back of the antebellum mansion, through the garden heavy with roses that sparkled in the sunlight. The rain had left a heady, earthy smell in direct contrast with the expensive perfume of the house. She settled the boys in the pool house where their tuxes hung in crisp bags, shoes shiny and lined up neatly. There were snacks, a pool table, and a television already set to Major League baseball on ESPN.

"I'll send your Dad over when he arrives, all right? Don't break anything, and Coultrie," she only used their full names when serious and they knew it, "don't let your lip get the better of you, got it? Your family lineage is just as impressive as Charlotte Watson's. Understood?"

Three sets of eyes rolled, but they nodded. "Hey, Mom," J.D. called as she turned to leave.

"Yes?"

"You know the difference is, we don't care about that lineage stuff, right?"

She put her hands on his shoulders. "Baby, you may not care, but these people all do, an awful lot. So don't shame the memory of your grandmother by not being proud of the blue blood that runs in your veins."

"Ugh, now you sound like Cor." Mac groaned and flopped on the couch.

"Who sounds like me?" Cora Anne appeared in the doorway, her hair in rollers, a platter of sandwiches in her hands. "I intercepted these from Chloe. She says if you guys need more, just come see her in the kitchen."

Lou followed Cora Anne back through the garden and toward the house. "They should be fine for a couple hours at least. Your dad's coming soon as he's finished his duty at that track meet. Of all the days to have a conflict—"

"Mom." Cora Anne slipped her arm through Lou's. "It's fine. Everything's going to be fine."

How much Lou wanted to believe that.

The cocktail hour began at six, but Charlotte had Chloe pop a bottle of fine champagne and pass around glasses before they dressed. After hours under the woman's scrutiny, Lou's nerves were raw—and Grace's seemed downright frayed. After finishing Cora Anne's hair, she mentioned a headache, and Lou passed her an aspirin before she went to change.

Charlotte, now dressed in deep blue chiffon and a diamond necklace that probably could've paid for the triplets' college education, entered while Cora Anne fought with Lou's zipper. Her brisk knock had evidently only been a warning.

"Cora, darling, let Chloe do that."

In the mirror, Cora Anne met her mother's eyes, irritation tugging at the corner of her lips. She'd already told Charlotte she preferred her double name. "I've almost got it. These vintage dresses just stick sometimes. This was my grandmother's."

Charlotte's fingers fluttered to her throat, patting the diamonds as though she needed reassurance they were still there. Perhaps the mention of her once best friend was a reminder she didn't want. Lou focused on her own image in the mirror, how the dress hung exactly right, hugging curves she hadn't realized she had. Her arms were lean and toned—must be from all the months of hauling equipment and furniture and endless boxes in and out of that house. She smoothed her hair behind her ears, pleased with the product Grace used to tame it so it fell just right, grazing her bare shoulders.

Charlotte cleared her throat with a strangled gurgle that had Lou turning, concerned. "Are you all right?"

For a moment, Charlotte's face betrayed her true age. Her mouth pulled into a bow and her cheeks seemed sunken, her skin washed with a milky pallor. But then she transformed, drawing a deep breath, relaxing her jaw into a smile that almost seemed a grimace.

"How much you resemble your mother, Louisa. Particularly in her old dress." Her inflection landed perfectly on the last words.

Lou took the earrings Cora Anne held, fitting them despite her trembling fingers. "If I can be half the woman my mother was, Charlotte, I'll count myself blessed. I told you we appreciated your offer for tonight's ensembles, but I preferred this one." She slipped the back of the second earring into place, despite quivering fingers, and forced the lady's smile her mother had taught her to use, even in uncomfortable situations. "After all, it's nice for Cora Anne's grandparents to be remembered this evening, as well."

Charlotte clasped her hands, tight-lipped. "If you're ready, we'll form the receiving line. Louisa, your beau has arrived, I believe."

Poor Liam. No doubt he'd been accosted. Hugging Cora Anne, whom Charlotte wanted to hold for a grander entrance, Lou hurried down the stairs. As she rounded the curve at the stairs' bottom, the toe of her shoe caught at the hem of the long dress and pitched her forward.

"Whoa, there." Liam's strong arms caught hers. One corner of his mouth tipped up and he winked at her, roguish as Rhett Butler. "I seem to have a habit of rescuing you." He kept his hands under her elbows and pulled her closer to his chest, whispering in her ear, "I kind of like it."

Her cheeks tingled. He leaned back and tracked his gaze from hers down to her toes and back up again. "You're beautiful, Louisa."

"Indeed she is." David's voice sounded sharp. He stood behind Liam, arms crossed, jaw tight and eyes narrow. A defensive look she recognized from years of watching him coach.

Liam released her, and she lifted the edge of her dress to step down. "The boys ready?" She chose not to look at David, because she felt smoldering anger rolling off him in waves.

He made a conscious effort to control it, though. She could always tell that too. "They're ready. Waiting on Charlotte's command."

"Well, aren't we all?" She wished, for once, Charlotte would appear with orders that whisked her away from standing between these two men.

David reached for her hand, brought it to his lips, and kissed her knuckles gently. "You are beautiful, Lou." Without moving his softened eyes from hers, he added, "Liam, you'll keep an eye on her tonight? Don't let her worry too much."

David released her hand, as Liam took her other one. "That is why I'm here. To enjoy the company, and the refreshment." He tucked her arm into his elbow. "Let's get you a glass of wine, Lou, before the party starts."

She let herself be led away as David held up two fingers. Not the peace sign, their sign. *See you later, I've got this.* And though it was Liam, the date she'd chosen, whose steady hands had saved her from embarrassment, David's touch lingered on her skin.

Chapter 47

David stared after them as Liam led Lou away. He'd move on when the twitch in his jaw stopped. Heels clicked on the hardwoods behind him.

"You know, there's nothing more disheartening to a woman than to spend hours primping to enter a room, and when she does, all the men are looking at someone else."

"Grace." David kissed her cheek in brotherly fashion. "You look lovely." She'd chosen a dress of turquoise blue with a billowy skirt and the barest hint of cleavage, he couldn't help but notice.

"Charlotte didn't like my choice any better than she liked Lou wearing that gown of Annie's, but what's a party without a little drama?" She wiggled her brows at him.

"You're in a good mood."

"I took the pre-Charlotte cocktail of Xanax and champagne."

"Should you mix those?"

"I'm a widow at my son's engagement party in my mother-in-law's house, David. Hold your judgment."

He winced. Too busy thinking of himself and Lou and their predicament, he hadn't considered how hard this evening would be for Grace.

She laughed, brittle a bit, but still real. "I'm kidding. I had aspirin and a power nap. Hid from Charlotte, so she couldn't tell me again she ordered a few cheesecakes for dessert back-up."

"In her defense, she'll need them once the triplets are loosed on your pies."

Tears glistened in her eyes, but Grace blinked and tossed her blond curls. "Let's find some champagne. Celebration, of course."

He tucked her arm into his, as Liam had with Lou. "Of course."

The garden had been transformed with little lights, candles, and white linen everywhere. Hannah, a headset tucked discreetly in her ear, passed him right on by muttering something about ice. Her mother, Carolina, was across the small yard lighting the last of the votive candles. With those two at the helm the party ought to run smooth as a well-kept trolling motor.

Which reminded him he'd told Lou he'd look at the motor on the little johnboat the boys liked to use. Meant to do that last weekend, but an extra baseball practice had beckoned.

Cora Anne appeared on the back steps, hand tucked in Tennessee's elbow, breathtaking in a dress that made David wonder how they'd gone so quickly from the father-daughter Valentine's Dance to this. He took his place beside Lou in the receiving line. She slipped her hand into his as Tennessee thanked everyone for coming, giving a special nod to Charlotte for hosting. She demurred, of course, as though it had all been nothing.

Watching how gracefully his daughter and future son carried this burden—three generations of thwarted relationships before they would become family—David thought he maybe understood a bit why Charlotte insisted on this party. At the toast, he lifted his bottle toward her and nodded.

To his surprise, she returned the gesture.

Dinner was seated and plated. David sat with Lou and the boys— and Liam, of course. They talked of fishing and the spring rains, while the boys ticked off the schooldays left.

"Still six weeks to go," Mac moaned into a huge bite of his Chicken Provençal. "Mom, you should make this sauce stuff sometime. It's pretty good."

"You should swallow before speaking, son," David reminded.

But Lou chuckled, rather than admonish. "This dinner cost more per person than I spend on three meals for the three of you, so enjoy it now. Tomorrow we're back to pot pie."

"Good thing I like pot pie too." Mac grinned.

After dinner came dancing. Hannah grabbed David by the elbow and pulled him to the floor for the father-daughter dance he hadn't known was scheduled.

"Didn't you read the itinerary?" His niece rebuked. "Uncle David, I sent it to your email over a week ago."

He shrugged and let himself be handed off to his daughter, who wore a mischievous smile he hadn't seen in years. "Guess what song I chose, Dad?"

Somehow, they'd repaired what had been broken, and his family felt almost whole again. Only hairline cracks left.

The music started, and he tucked her against his chest like she was six years old again. "You remembered."

"I never forgot."

He twirled her around the dance floor, the big band strains of Etta James swelling with the fullness of his heart. David hadn't had many perfect moments in life—but nearly every single one he could recall involved the five people in that garden who bore his last name.

When they finished, he saw Liam hand Lou his handkerchief. Jealousy stabbed like a stitch in his side.

The evening carried on with simple toasts from Hannah and Ben as maid of honor and best man, and an address from Charlotte. She allowed herself to be led onto the small stage but disdained the microphone. Instead her voice, with no warble of age, carried across the garden. Difficult as the woman may be, she wore the mantle of matriarch well. She thanked the guests for coming, making special mention of those who would expect a calling out of their social standing.

"As you know, my son Patrick, had he been here tonight, would've been overjoyed at the union of these two families. Louisa and he were dear friends." Her eyes tracked the crowd, passed over Grace, and settled on Lou as she spoke. "Of course, I once counted her mother among my dearest friends, as well. Let us take a moment now, in quiet remembrance of our departed, who surely are showering this union..." Her gaze moved to Tennessee and Cora Anne. "With the blessings of heaven."

The crowd bowed as one, in reverent silence, for the second time that evening. After her soft thanks, the band lifted instruments and the quiet tempo of an old Elvis song filled the air.

The tightening in his throat—and the pang in his gut—told David it was now or never. He turned in the crowd, stepping over to the corner of the dance floor where Lou stood beside Liam.

"Dance with me?" He'd have begged, if necessary, but she turned from Liam, her eyes still damp, that ghost of her old smile—the one he'd seen with the puppies—playing on her lips.

"I'd love to."

He took her onto the floor and pulled her hips to his, where she'd always fit just right. She curled her arm around his shoulder, her other hand tucked into his, and they swayed cheek to cheek as their wedding song played. "Can't Help Falling in Love" had been chosen, he'd joked then, because Lou would never have rushed in.

But she'd taken his hand so easily all those years ago, when he helped her back to her feet after knocking her down. That had been their relationship from there on out—knocking each other down only to help each other back up. This time David wanted them to stay on their feet.

She sighed, a wisp of breath against his cheek.

He caressed her bare back. Whispered, "Please, Lou, let's try again."

"I'm scared."

"Me too."

She leaned back, enough to see his eyes. How she'd always gauged what he really meant. He knew why she hadn't looked him in the eye that night on Edisto when she'd asked him to leave.

"Have you really forgiven me?"

He pulled her tighter. How else could he make himself clear? "Did you forgive me?"

Her lips pressed together, and her eyes darkened a fraction. "You always pushed me."

"I know."

"I don't like to make snap decisions."

"I know."

Her lips softened back into a small smile, chin tilted up, and he wondered what Charleston and their children would think if he kissed her right then and there on that dance floor. "I came home on a whim, though, and that seems to be working out."

"This can too."

She chewed her lower lip, her tell that she was nervous but hopeful. He bent his head and let his lips graze her cheek, right where the hint of a rosy flush crept up from her neck.

"People are watching."

"I don't care."

"I do." Leaning her head away from his as the song crested toward its end, she added, "Can we get through the wedding? I don't want to start something and have it hovering over us. The pressure feels like too much."

She made him ache in all the ways a husband should—and in plenty of ways he shouldn't. But he nodded, agreeing. This party was only a precursor to the next several weeks. He'd seen Lou's calendar, tacked on the wall in her makeshift office, and he knew despite Cora Anne's newfound ability to relax, his daughter still lived by a planner.

He placed his cheek against hers again. "After the wedding, I want to take you on a real date. Just us and the sunset."

Her skin heated against his, and she nodded. The song ended, and he let her step away from the circle of his arms. But she kept his hand. "Charlotte's toast was gracious, don't you think?"

He glanced over her shoulder. Grace stood on the outskirts of the dance floor, swirling the contents of her drink. "I think she left someone out."

Lou followed his eyes. "I can't fix their issues."

"Didn't ask you to."

She dropped their linked hands. "Since when are you so concerned with Grace's well-being?"

He hadn't forgotten her jealousy, but he thought it had gone dormant. "Aren't we all friends, concerned for one another?"

Lou folded her arms. "Still, it was kind of Charlotte to remember my mother."

"And it would have been kind for her to remember Tennessee's mother."

She whirled back toward the bar. He stepped close behind, snagged her elbow. "Why are you mad?"

Pulling free, Lou rolled her shoulders. "I'm not mad." He waited. She sighed. "Grace is always the one everyone wants. She's kind and generous and doesn't give in to despair ..." Her eyes finished the sentence for him. *Like me.* "Sometimes it feels like she took my place in this world." She waved her hand around the garden, but he didn't think she meant here.

Or with Patrick, either.

"Grace and your mother needed each other, Lou."

A muscle jumped in her jaw, as if she were fighting to hold back words that might ought to have been said years ago. When Annie could have heard them. "I needed help too."

He understood the implication. Over and over, he had failed her. Why couldn't he get this right? What did she really want?

"But right now, I need a water. With ice, that's all." She found his gaze, held it. "I think I'm a little overheated."

He nodded. "I'll get it."

When he brushed past her, she pressed her hand to his shoulder, leaned against him for a moment. A brush of bodies and regret. "David ... there are many things we need to say."

"That bench we sat on?" He turned his head, searching the darker edges of the garden, her lips a breath from his. "I'll meet you there."

Chapter 48

"Louisa." Charlotte's tone halted Lou's stride into the shadows. She turned. "Yes?"

"I believe the evening has been lovely. Would you agree?"

Lou didn't think for a moment Charlotte needed her praise, but she nodded anyway. "Of course. Delightful."

"What of Grace? Does she think so as well?" Charlotte adjusted a diamond bracelet on her narrow wrist. Already disinterested, Lou supposed.

Maybe she could fix something—or at least give it a wrench—after all. "I think Grace would have appreciated not being overlooked. Tennessee is her son."

Charlotte's hands dropped to her sides. "Grace allowed Patrick to disdain his upbringing. I am certain she does not mind being excluded from it now."

"But she might mind exclusion from her only family." Lou wished she'd kept walking. This conversation was headed nowhere—except to remind her she had no reason to be jealous herself. David was right. Grace had needed her mother. And Lou couldn't fault her for that.

"Do not cast stones, Louisa. I saw you dancing with your ex-husband." Now her features pinched, smug as a cat with cream. "I wondered, why is it you are no longer together? The breach doesn't appear to come from him."

A deep breath of the garden's scent—azaleas, gardenias, camellias in full ruffled bloom—reminded Lou of her mother. She drew herself up to her full height, though even in heels she was no match for Charlotte's regal stance. "My marriage is my business, and I'll thank you to keep your opinions to yourself."

"Your mother was a great woman, Louisa. But stubbornness was her downfall."

Lou twisted away.

Charlotte's words carried after her. "Don't let it be yours."

She wouldn't give Charlotte the satisfaction of seeing her cry but the woman followed anyway, greeting those along the path Lou wove through the crowd.

Where was David? How long could it take to get water? She headed toward the house. He must have gone inside for some reason. She snipped up the back steps, heels sharp on the bricks, and dragged open the heavy back door.

Stubbornness, her downfall. Charlotte was one to talk—

Inside stood David, his arms around Grace.

~~~

Pushing Grace aside—gently—David streaked down the steps after Lou. She moved quickly for a woman who had been complaining about hurting feet earlier. When she ducked into the pool house, he followed.

The bathroom door closed. "Lou?" He rapped on it.

"It's fine, David. Go back to the party. To Grace."

He exhaled through clenched teeth. He hadn't been with Grace. The bar was out of ice so he'd gone to the kitchen.

Chloe had been there, wiping counters. "Mr. David, you're going to be in trouble. Get out of here."

"Ice water first, please?" He held up the glasses and she obliged.

"I saw you dancing with Ms. Louisa."

"Spying on the party out the window."

"Best way to see everything everyone else misses." She topped the waters with sprigs of fresh mint. He wondered what else Chloe saw out the windows of this big house. As he headed out, the back door opened, nearly knocking the water from his hands.

"David. I'm sorry." Grace stood there. This time her frantic blinking hadn't kept the tears from streaking her face.

"You all right?" Ridiculous question, he knew.

She shook her head, that fragile laugh again. "Clearly not. I mean, it's hard enough remembering Charlotte certainly didn't celebrate her son's engagement like this. But then she can't even mention my existence in front of her friends—oh, no. It's Lou and Pat who were such good friends ..." She flapped her hands as if she could fan away her tears. "Meanwhile he may be gone, but I'm still his wife." She spat the words and David knew what was coming next. He'd seen enough women lose it in his day.

Her shoulders heaved. "You probably all knew the truth—that we got pregnant and had to get married. Everyone thinks he chose me out of love, but the longer he's gone and the more I have to be here, I think maybe he chose me out of desperation to escape." Her voice pitched. "How better to rid himself of this life than to marry his pathetic, pregnant girlfriend who'd already been abandoned by her own family?"

Her dam broke and David set the glasses on the side table—with a fleeting thought that Charlotte would have a coronary over the water rings—so he could wrap his arms around Grace's quaking shoulders. He had no words to give right now. Telling her he'd had no idea of the circumstances behind her and Patrick seemed fruitless. Instead he rubbed her back and shushed, the way he often had when Lou fell apart and actually allowed herself comfort.

Lou. He'd looked up to find her, thinking he could signal for help.

Of course she'd gotten the wrong impression. Though how could she, after their dance? This time he banged on the bathroom door.

She yanked it open. "What is your problem?"

"You, most of the time." She started to close the door again, but he stuck his foot inside and braced the door with his shoulder. "We need to talk."

"I thought that was the plan, but you changed your mind."

"Lou, she was upset."

Her shoulders slumped. "I know. I saw."

"Then why are you mad?"

"I'm not mad ..." She sniffled, and rubbed her eyes, leaving behind a black smear. Lou took a while to work up tears, which meant she'd been crying before she saw him with Grace.

The realization hit David like a line drive. He'd always put everyone else's needs first—except hers.

Chapter 49

Grace accepted abandonment. But still, when David let her go so he could streak across the garden after Lou, she climbed the stairs on trembling legs. Very much aware she was nearly as alone now as she had been on that rainy day in March her father left.

She had been fifteen years old. He'd packed a bag before dawn and left without saying goodbye. The clicking shut of the front door had woken her from an already fitful sleep, and she'd crept downstairs just as his taillights pulled away from the drive. She'd wondered where he was going so early.

The note had been left on the kitchen table.

I'm sorry but I cannot do this anymore. Grace, you take care of your mama, now.

She didn't realize what he really meant until days later when he still hadn't come home, and she had to call Patsy to help her because Mama hadn't gotten out of bed in three days.

At the moment, Grace wanted to climb into bed for a few days herself. Charlotte had offered her a guest room for the night. Before she'd confirmed her place in this world, Grace had thought it an act of kindness. No matter. She would stay, because even this house of frost would be better than driving home alone to the black night that waited on Edisto.

In the opulent bath, she peeled away her dress that smelled of gardenias and heartbreak. The shower water ran hot enough to tint her skin pink before she turned it cooler and lathered her hair, rubbing small circles into her scalp.

But she couldn't massage out the ache that had only ever dulled, and sometimes, like tonight, sharpened. Making her into a woman filled with doubt and fear. Her breath caught against her ribs, and she braced her arms against the tile walls. During these moments, she missed Patrick the way she missed breathing easy, the way she missed the life they had made their own.

When she emerged, wrapped in the softness of a guest robe, as though Charlotte's were a fancy hotel, a soft tapping broke the silence. Chloe stood on the other side of the door, hands clasped like Lula May used to hold hers when she waited on the dining room.

"Miss Grace, she'd like you to come to her sitting room, please."

Grace put a hand on her hip. "I've told you—like I told your mama—do not call me *Miss*."

The corner of Chloe's mouth tipped. "Grace, bring yourself down to the sitting room, so I can go on to bed. Please."

"That's more like it."

In the small—almost cozy—sitting room off her own bedroom, Charlotte sat in one of the chairs flanking the fireplace.

"You looked like you could use this." Charlotte held out a small glass. Grace took it and sniffed. Bourbon. The expensive kind. "It will help you sleep."

"Will it help me forget?" She leveled her gaze on her mother-in-law, noticing Charlotte's eyes were rimmed red.

"Only what you want to forget."

They sipped in silence, the drink burning Grace's throat. But it seared away her tears.

"You looked very nice tonight." Charlotte's words came out formal, clipped.

"But still not good enough for your friends?"

The older woman sighed and lowered her glass to her lap where she spun the bottom of it against her palm. "They do not know you, Grace. They never have. Patrick—and then you—made sure of that."

"You made sure of that." She drained the last of her drink, feeling reckless and sad. A reminder of why she didn't drink.

"I never thought you wanted this life he'd rejected." Charlotte's voice betrayed her. The tiniest crack.

Grace pulled up her knees and sat like a child. "I only ever wanted your acceptance."

"I heard what you said to David tonight. Saw him leave."

"He had to catch Lou before she got the wrong impression."

"That seems to happen to them often."

Grace rolled her neck. "Some people aren't easy to love."

"But you love them anyway." Charlotte stood and collected the glasses. "Patrick, he could be selfish, strong-willed. With Louisa, he'd have remained that way. With you ... he became better than the man I raised." The corner of her mouth turned up. "I've never admitted that to anyone before."

Grace rested her cheek on her knee, regarding her mother-in-law with wary wonder. "Thank you for saying that."

"You know we offered him many options when he brought you home and announced your marriage."

"That's one of those things I'd like to forget."

"He should not have sent you out that night. You deserved to hear him. If you had, there would be no doubt." Charlotte's voice thickened. "My son cleaved himself to you out of love."

Grace believed her, because this admission probably hurt Charlotte more than the other. Then to her surprise, her mother-in-law extended her hand, cool and smooth. Grace took it, felt how paper-thin Charlotte's skin had become.

"And if you'll have me, I will try to do the same."

Chapter 50

The phone rang over and over Sunday morning.

Each time Lou answered, David started with, "I'm sorry." Why didn't he get her frustration wasn't about Grace? It was his promises, broken. How he always cast her desires aside to do what was best for everyone else.

"David, I'm tired and busy. We'll talk later." Then she'd hung up. Every half-hour later, he called back.

David had the ability no one else ever had. He could make her fall in love with him, and he could splay her heart wide open. She'd already put it back together once. She couldn't do it again.

On the fourth ring, she snatched the phone and snapped, "I told you I'm fine."

"Well. Good morning to you too."

She gasped. "Liam. I apologize."

"I take it I'm not the man you expected."

"No." Her mind scrambled. "I mean, yes." Liam was exactly who she'd expected him to be. It was her ex-husband she could no longer understand.

He chuckled, but there was regret in the sound. "It's all right, Lou. I watched you and David all night long. You belong together."

"Too bad we're divorced."

"Too bad neither of you seemed to remember that when you were dancing."

She tucked the phone between her ear and shoulder so she could finish assembling a cardboard box. Today was as good a day as any to start cleaning out the closets. Kept her mind off what Liam had just hinted. "I'm a terrible date."

Now his laugh sounded real. "But you're a wonderful research assistant."

"Know your strengths."

"Do you?"

Pausing, her hand on the closet door, she wondered. Did she?

"Because I'd like to bring you on full-time. My next grant will provide a decent salary and look great on an application for a doctorate of environmental studies."

"What makes you think I want to be an environmentalist?"

"The way you get so excited when I tell you how the recent sediment samples show an ecosystem revitalization."

Lou tugged open the closet door and dropped the box from under her arm. Nearly dropped the phone as well, but not because Liam's words made her anxious. They made her happy. "Samples from the vegetation buffer zone?"

"Those are the ones."

One side of the closet was all plaid shirts and overalls. Her mama had never emptied her daddy's farmer's attire from the rack.

"Lou?"

She reached for a sleeve, blue and green, the color of healthy water after all the debris had settled to the bottom. Water ready to wash back to the sea. "I'll do it."

"In that case I'm coming over with the contract before you change your mind."

"I won't." This time she was sure.

She hung up as rain splattered the windows again. Surely the parting in these spring storms had been an omen of good tidings for Cora Anne and Tennessee. Cheered by the thought, she pulled clothes from her mother's closet, packing donation boxes, making room for more in this house.

The way her mama would have wanted.

"Mama," J.D. called up the stairs. "Ms. Grace is here."

A silk blouse crumpled in her hands. Lou bent her head and breathed in her mother's strength, surely the vestige of it still clung despite the dust and mothballs. Downstairs, she found Grace in the kitchen with her boys. They'd filled the kettle and set out the tea, as if her mother's presence really did linger in that kitchen.

"I should've called." Grace lifted her hands in apology. "But I needed to tell you—"

"Boys, can you go haul down those boxes of clothes I've already packed? Just put them straight out in the back of the van so I can take them in the morning." This wasn't a conversation for their hopeful hearts.

"Aw, Mom, it's raining." Cole blew across the hot chocolate he'd made for himself.

"Slacked off, actually." Grace chimed in. "Better haul while you've got a break."

Once their footsteps clambered up the stairs, Grace turned to Lou. "I was crying, and David acted like a friend. Don't make this into something it's not—and has never been."

Lou fiddled with a packet of chamomile tea as she chose her words. "David is like you. Kind to a fault."

"I didn't know kindness could be negative."

"He takes care of everyone else."

Grace caught her breath. "Except you."

She lifted one shoulder. "I gave up my plans, followed his because I thought one day they'd intersect."

"He followed you here, Lou. What about that?"

"And I thought …" She twisted the teabag's string around her finger. What had she thought? "I thought I could do this without him, but he's made me need him—want him—all over again."

"So give him a real chance."

"Maybe we're already past that." Lou gave Grace a small smile. "Maybe, instead, he deserves the chance for someone new."

Grace shook her head. "You're crazy, Lou." She said it with a hint of laughter to take away the sting. "Sometimes I think you're just looking for excuses. Like you're punishing yourself because Patrick died and you grieved."

Her fingers stilled on the wrapper. All the years of prayers and therapy, yet no one had ever said those words. And the moment they landed in the space between her and Patrick's wife, Lou knew they were true. "He went after her because she's my daughter."

"I know that."

"And he died."

"No greater love than a man lay down his life for his friend." Grace wrapped her fingers around Lou's wrist. "I don't come by my love for Cora Anne easily, Lou. But I've lived in a world where everyone takes the easy route out—the running away believing something's better on the other side. I've chosen to remain right here, to make my life *here* better. But sometimes," she let Lou go and reached for a napkin to wipe her eyes. "Sometimes I forget how loved I truly was, and that's what happened last night. Charlotte hurt my feelings—"

"Oh, she's good at that."

Grace snorted. "Yes. But she also apologized."

Lou wouldn't have thought Charlotte even knew how. "Impressive."

"You ever think how we're all just living in the wake of someone else's choices? You chose graduate school, and Patrick chose me. Charlotte chose anger for a long time. Cora Anne chose guilt."

Lou flicked her gaze out the kitchen window. The boys must've finished with the boxes because they were giving the tire swing a whirl. Liam's Range Rover pulled in.

"There's another good man. Not sure what you did to deserve two of them." Grace's eyes crinkled at the edges, and Lou found herself smiling back. Teasing between girlfriends. Not a concept she knew well.

But maybe she could learn. "Grace, I—"

The crack sounded like a gunshot. For the briefest moment Lou thought some hunter had strayed into their pasture.

J.D. screamed Cole's name and Mac shouted hers.

Wrenching open the screen door, she ran outside. That wide, sturdy limb of the oak—where the tire swing hung for decades—had split and lay in a heap on the soggy ground. Sticking out the tangle of splinters and Spanish moss were Cole's feet. He wore his new sneakers and her wildest, fleetest thought was she'd told him not to.

Lou grasped one of the branches, trying to see her son's face. At her side, Grace reached for another.

Liam ran across the yard from the barn. "Don't move it yet." He skidded to his knees in the mud, felt underneath the debris, sweeping aside leaves until Lou could see Cole's face. Liam's hands probed his neck and splayed the branches to expose his chest. "There's no puncture wounds, so let's move it off him gently."

The thickest section of limb lay across Cole's midsection. Liam wrapped his arms around it and heaved as Lou and Grace pulled. The boys ran over to drag the rest off their brother. Cole splayed atop the tire. Bile burned her throat with a glance at his right arm bent at an unnatural angle. The splintered bone poking through a gash. His head lolled back, eyes closed and still.

Lou bent over his face. She touched his cheeks—only now losing their little boy roundness. His skin was clammy. His lips tinged blue already. The rain started again, splattering him with drops, and she could barely feel his shallow breaths against her jaw. "Get me an umbrella or something to keep him dry."

"Lou, honey …" Grace knelt beside her and swiped at her cheeks with her fingers. "It's not raining."

Liam paced at Cole's head, a phone pressed to his ear. J.D. and Mac squatted on their brother's other side. The triplets were not identical, but in that moment their ashen faces mirrored one another.

"Mama, he's going to be okay, right?"

She couldn't answer.

~ ~ ~

Now she was the one who called four times. Twice from her house to his while the paramedics loaded Cole onto a backboard in the rain.

Again from the ambulance, leaving yet another message, this one on his cell. The fourth from the hospital waiting room, just before Grace came in with the other boys. "Please, David," she whispered the words to the sterile walls. "I need you."

Liam brought her coffee, while Grace told her Tennessee and Cora Anne would track down David and be on their way. She nodded and tried to sort out what the paramedics had told her. Concussion definitely. Bad break to that right arm, looked like the elbow. Spine hopefully all right. Would need an MRI to know for sure. A nurse brought her paperwork to sign. She stared, the letters and sentences swarming together like a hive of bees around her mother's rose bushes.

Liam took it from her hands. "Where's your insurance card?"

She dug it from her purse and handed it over, aware she was the one who'd become catatonic. The words Liam told the nurse barely registered. "Her husband will do the rest."

Husband. These were the times she needed him to be that, but they'd erased it all with signatures on another line, another paper of squiggles that had swam before her eyes.

Chapter 51

The parking deck at MUSC was a maze, and by the time he wound his way to the waiting room on the third floor, he'd muttered more curse words than he'd used in the last year. Surely God forgave overwrought fathers.

Surely wives forgave idiot husbands. Even ex ones.

Lou sat limp and pale in the corner. He crossed the room in three strides and swept her up. She crumpled against his chest. Next to her, the frightened faces of Mac and J.D. told him plenty.

"Shhh, it's going to be okay." He pressed his lips to her hair, breathing in the scent of rain and lavender.

She pushed her hands between them. "Where were you, David? I called and called."

"I went for a run. I'm sorry."

Lou started to say something, but shook her head. "Thank you for being here."

As though he'd want to be anywhere else. But they couldn't deal with that right now. "What happened?"

J.D. and Mac slipped between them, both talking at once.

"We're sorry—"

"We didn't know the tree—"

"Mama, Daddy." Cora Anne rushed off the elevator. "How is he?" Her arms stretched around them all, knitting their family together—if not whole.

~~~

"Concussion, but not too bad. Lucky he didn't snap his neck, and spine checks out all right." Dr. Woods was all business. David wasn't impressed. "But it's this," the doctor snapped an x-ray onto the wall and flicked a light switch. "That has me worried. Compound fracture to the elbow. Broken through right here." He tapped the image where the skin below Cole's elbow would be.

David whistled softly between his teeth. One didn't need a medical degree to decipher that picture. The bone had snapped in two places and stuck out at odd angles. "How long until it heals?"

"Not going to without major surgery." The doctor flipped off the switch. "Swelling needs to go down first. Have him on the schedule first thing tomorrow." He continued giving details in a brisk, precise tone. "There's also a risk of infection, especially given where he landed, but we debrided the wound as well as we could. We'll keep a close eye on him for symptoms—fever, chills, the usual."

Nothing about this was usual.

His son slept, thanks to the pain meds, head turned to the side on his hospital pillow. They'd have to get his down-filled one from the house. That kid had been particular about pillows since he was three and Lou finally got over her fear of SIDS. Jaw slack, his whole body relaxed by the medicine pumping in through the IV, but all David could see was Cole on the mound. Chin tucked into his shoulder, eyes squinted at his target, lips curled in concentration—and an attempt to intimidate. Letting loose a curve ball so sweet he had the best pitching record in their region.

"Thank you, doctor." Lou nudged him. David managed a nod of acknowledgement as Dr. Woods left.

She crossed her arms. "Thanks for checking out."

"I heard every word he said."

"Really?"

He ground his teeth. "I heard him say they're going to fill our son's arm with pins and bolts, that he'll need weeks of physical therapy, and it could be at least a year before he has full-range of motion again. If he gains that back at all."

Bending over Cole, Lou brushed the honey-colored hair back from his forehead. "He's tough, remember? He was the smallest but had the most fight."

"He could've had a chance to go all the way. Best arm I've ever seen in a kid his age."

Her fingers lingered on Cole, as if healing him with her mother's touch. When she spoke, her voice hollowed. "That's all that matters? He could've broken his neck, and you're upset he may never throw a baseball the same way again?"

If she didn't understand, he couldn't make her. This wasn't about him or his expectations. When their son woke up and realized what had been lost, his devastated dreams would be harder to set back together than that bone.

Like trying to fit together the pieces of their marriage. Sometimes, the fragments just couldn't be found.

Chapter 52

Edisto Beach, July 1993

Lou never lost her temper like she had that afternoon when Cora Anne threw a fit—and all the babies' new toys out into the ocean.

She'd slapped her, and when her own mama grabbed her wrist, Lou expected another smack across her own face. Which she deserved.

David was certainly no help. He sat in the kitchen most of their last afternoon, on the phone finalizing next season's schedule. Lou wanted to scream like their daughter had—"You never pay attention to me."

But she was a grown up, not a child.

"Go out to dinner with Carolina and John," her mother suggested after Cora Anne was sent to the room she shared with Hannah. "You need a little break."

"I need a little help." The beach bag straps scraped her sunburned shoulders, and she trudged to the house, where an eruption of baby wails echoed across the dunes.

They went to the Dockside for dinner. Only because Mama took over as soon as she came in the house. As they left, Lou saw her father press a folded bill into David's hand. Her husband pushed it back, but Daddy refused.

"Did you tell them we need money or something?" David whispered, jerking open the back door of John's car.

"They have eyes, you know. Ears too." The thin walls of Still Waters hadn't disguised their nightly arguments, though usually she fell into an exhausted sleep before fully voicing her frustrations.

Dinner improved Lou's mood. No one spit food in her face or knocked over a drink. David softened after a beer and a plate of fried shrimp. He ordered key lime pie with two forks and offered her the first bite, which he knew she liked best.

Carolina, eyes shining with excitement, explained her new wedding planner business. "I've already booked the rest of the year. Can you believe it?"

John hooked his arm around her sister's neck and smacked her cheek. "I'm so proud of her."

A quick glance at David showed Lou a hint of regret in the slump of his shoulders. When they stood to leave, he slipped his arm around her waist. "Can we walk?"

Would keep them away at least another half-hour, but surely her mother could handle it. So long as Cora Anne didn't add to the tears again.

David snagged her fingers as they strolled away from the restaurant and veered onto the bike path. "I think we need to talk about some things."

Finally. She breathed out, the humid air comforting and quiet. "Yes, we do."

"I know I'm busy and it's hard for you to balance work and the kids."

Lou smiled. He had noticed.

"So maybe we should consider a change."

She wanted to leap in the air and shout, the way he did once he'd won a game. But she held herself in check, just to be sure. "You'd consider it, then? It's a big move."

"If you're sure it's what you want—"

"Yes. Yes." She flung her arms around his neck. "I know it's going to be hard for you, but you'll get another job and everything will be so much easier—"

He untangled her arms. "What are you talking about?"

She stepped back. "Moving here. So my parents can help us, and then, later, I can go back to school."

"That's not what I meant." He scrubbed his hand over his head. "Lou, I ... I thought you might want to stay home and not work for a little while."

Swimming in the ocean, waves broke over her head. Drowning out all sounds and sense of stability. Every time, she lost her footing. That reason, more than any other, was why she didn't go in the water and swim with her daughter. Now, standing on the narrow path as the sky overhead darkened, the same sensation swept over her.

All grounding gave way.

"Working is the only thing I'm good at." She put more distance between them. "The only time I ever finish anything. How could you ask me to give that up?"

"Daycare eats every penny you make, Lou. You know that. This would just be temporary—"

"No. I already gave you what you wanted. Another baby, remember?"

"Don't cast that up to me. Neither of us had any idea we'd get triplets."

"And only one of us understands how hard it is. I need my mother's help."

He reached for her. "I'm supposed to help you."

"When, David? Because you are never home. Someone or something else is always more important."

"I coach kids from underprivileged families. They need a father figure."

"Well, you know what? Your own kids need one, too." She turned, shoulders back. Done. Shortcutting through backyards, Lou left David to follow. Wondering, if she had the courage to pack them up and come without him, he'd follow her then too.

She heard the screaming as soon as she turned onto the block Still Waters anchored.

"Patrick!" Her father's voice.

"Dad!" Tennessee Watson's.

She broke into a run, and David streaked past her. By the time she made it down the access path over the dunes, he and Daddy were dragging a limp body from the ocean's edge. David flipped Patrick Watson over.

Blood seeped from his head, coloring the clean sand dark. David knew CPR. Years before, when life glowed rosy at its edges, he'd come home from coaches' training and joke he needed to practice mouth-to-mouth.

He pumped Pat's chest.

Pat, who had once cradled her face and called her beautiful. Promised her this world if she wanted to stay.

David counted. "One-two-three—" He lowered his head, gave back life.

But Patrick's chest didn't rise.

Lou crumpled to her knees. Grit and shell pieces bit her skin. Her vision and hearing tunneled. All she could see was her husband desperately trying to save another man who'd once made her promises she knew he couldn't keep.

And she felt the life she knew shatter like fragments in the sand.

Chapter 53

Grace knew there were plenty of things she didn't do well. Punctuality, for instance. Balancing her checkbook. Organizing events.

Come to think of it, having Cora Anne for a daughter-in-law might be like having a personal assistant.

While they waited out Cole's surgery, they made a list of meals to stock in Lou and David's freezers. While Cole should be able to come home the next day, there would be a lot of back and forth for follow-ups and eventual physical therapy. Grace figured Lou wouldn't turn down homemade meals.

She also rolled out four dozen sugar cookies and made a chocolate cake. Which depleted her flour stock and required her to call up The Hideaway and order a dozen cheddar biscuits to go along with the shrimp chowder she was taking over to David's tonight.

Foresight. Another lacking trait.

In The Hideaway's kitchen, Jeanna piped mashed potatoes into something special and clucked like a mother hen as Grace selected the fattest biscuits from the warmer. "You know that man's still in love with his wife."

"I don't know why everyone keeps supposing I'd go after my daughter-in-law's father."

"He fits your—what's that the kids call it?" Jeanna snapped her glove-covered fingers. "M-O."

"My what?"

"Vulnerable. Needy. You fill a void. Right now with food—maybe later, emotionally. You can't save every stray, Grace."

Her friend's words stung. "I'm not trying to save anyone. We're all

233

friends helping each other out." She folded the lid of the box. "Family, really."

Jeanna stripped off a glove. "Honey, I know this is hard with Tennessee getting married. You must miss Pat something awful."

The box's lid refused to cooperate. Too many corners for her stiff fingers.

"But you've waited all these years, saying you didn't need another man. That he was enough love for a lifetime." Jeanna's voice thickened. "I'm worried you're going to get hurt when David and Lou finally work this out."

She quit fumbling with the ridiculous box lid and let Jeanna squeeze her hands with all their years of friendship in her touch. "I'm not attracted to David. I'm just—" Heavens, could she even say it? "I'm lonely."

Jeanna rubbed her knuckles as if applying a soothing salve. "I know, honey. I've been there."

"But you have Lenny now and your kids are still here."

"So is yours."

She grabbed a paper towel to dab her cheeks. Gracious, she'd cried enough the last few weeks to fill that big soup pot on the commercial stove several times over. "He doesn't need me."

"Oh, Gracie …" That nickname never bothered her coming from Jeanna, who always spoke in affection. "Everyone needs you, but I think it's high time you let yourself be on the receiving end." Jeanna patted her back and deftly shut the box lid on the biscuits. "Now go run these over to David's and come on back. I need a taste-tester for tonight's special." Jeanna winked. "You just never know who's coming through those doors."

~ ~ ~

The spring season was still early and the restaurant all but emptied by eight o'clock. But come summer, the place buzzed until eleven. Jeanna told Ben, as Grace and she wiped counters, time to start hiring the seasonal staff. Grace smiled at the words.

Seasonal staff. Sometimes those were the ones who learned the ways of all the seasons this place held, so they stayed.

Like her.

Jeanna handed her a simple glass of water, fresh and cold with lemon and mint. "Go on out to the porch and sit awhile. The break'll do you good."

The spring rains had moved on, and the stars found their brightness again. Not crisp like all winter, but soft and twinkly like the lights in Charlotte's garden for the party.

Grace lifted her arms and stretched, elongating her back's tension. Between the dinner rush and the delight of the salmon special, she'd barely given a thought to the Halloway family. Guilt crept in with a whiff of the pluff mud coming off the creek. Low tide now.

All the sediment settling.

"Well, hey there." Liam Whiting pulled a chair beside hers. "Mind if I join you?"

Shoulders relaxed, she eased back in her chair. "Plenty of room."

Liam tipped his head back as well. "Look at that sky."

"I know. Warm weather's coming."

"I'll have to work harder at fishing. They'll all go to the bottom, looking for the cooler temps."

"What a hard life you lead," she teased.

He smiled back and she noticed, for the first time, how his eyes crinkled with age—and wisdom. Dr. Whiting might wear the youthful air of a hip college professor—all worn jeans and tweed blazers—but his eyes betrayed him. Loneliness plagued him too.

"You talked to Louisa today?" The question lost its innocence when he said Lou's name, a breath of a sigh on the soft syllables.

"No, but Cora Anne called. Said the surgeon came by and was pleased with how he looked. Might let him come home early as tomorrow."

"That's good then." He swung his beer by the bottle's neck, arm hanging down, still pretending.

Grace offered what she could, even though she knew the words would chaff. "I've known Louisa a long time. She can be slow to make up her mind, but when she does, there's usually no going back."

He waited. She figured he wanted to hear the words—permission to let this hope dissipate. "She loves David. Always has. Even my husband saw it when she couldn't."

"Tell me about him."

"David?"

"No." Liam drained the bottle. "Patrick. He's a legend. Tell me why."

She laughed. "He's no legend. Just a man who loved his place in this world, once he found it."

"Not Charleston."

"Not his mother's Charleston."

"Ah." Pushing fingers through hair grown long over his collar and sprinkled liberally with salty gray, Liam sighed. "How'd you meet him?"

"Waiting tables at the Dockside. Summer after he and Lou broke up. When he was still nursing those wounds, I was his rebound. And then," she splayed her hands across her knees and let the moonlight glint off the ring she'd never removed. "I was his wife."

"Must've been more than a rebound then."

"Sometimes we go looking for what we think we want." She lifted her face to the stars, thinking of Pat's impish grin. "When what we need is sitting right beside us all along."

Chapter 54

"Figured you'd need this." The morning after Cole's surgery, David appeared right as the clock registered seven. He handed her a large cup of coffee.

"Thanks." There was a cheese Danish in a paper bag, too. Lou lifted the corner of her mouth in a half-smile. He hadn't forgotten.

"May I?" He gestured to her makeshift bed and she scooted over to make room. "How'd he do last night?"

"All right. They kept the pain meds in him, right on schedule."

His shoulder pressed against hers. There were shadows beneath his eyes and he'd skipped the razor that morning. The stubble coming in on his cheek and chin made him roguish, despite its silvery color. He tipped back his head and closed his eyes, as if to catch a few more moments of rest. "Cora Anne has the boys. Taking them to school. Then she said something about the florist."

Lou gasped. "Is that today?"

"I don't know." David kept his eyes closed, and his voice slurred.

He was really falling asleep? She scooted off the couch and retrieved the calendar from her purse. Yes, meeting with the florist at ten that morning. She'd never make it. The tears came sudden—too quickly for her to stop them. Shoulders rounding she dropped back to the couch, trying to quiet the sobs she didn't understand.

David slid his arm around her waist and pulled her to him. She doubled over in his lap, felt him slip the coffee from her trembling fingers, as the frustration and fear and fatigue wracked her body. He kneaded his fingers beneath her hair, saying nothing, letting her muffle her cries so she wouldn't wake Cole. When the wave finally subsided, she lay limp, stretched across David, more intimate than they'd been in years, even in the ones leading up to the divorce.

She finally spoke the words plaguing her all the time. "I can't be everything for everyone."

"You're not supposed to be."

"I promised her I'd go to all the meetings, be involved."

"She understands you need to be here."

Lou sat up, pushing damp strands of hair from her face. "She didn't before."

"She was a kid, then. Now she's an adult." David took her hand, squeezed it in his. "Lou … I can help. With everything."

She wanted to believe him. "I'm a mess." She slid her hand free, straightened her shirt.

David smoothed a hand over her hair. "Not to me."

His words curled around her like a warm blanket and she wanted to sink into them—into him—and believe they could simply step back in time and undo a long tangled history of regrets.

But maybe, instead, she could try going forward without dragging along the past. "What if I go to the florist and you stay here?"

His hand moved to cup her chin. "You're going to trust me?"

She moistened her lips. "I'm going to try." This time she embraced the way her grounding shifted, and she moved with it.

A gentle whisper of her lips against his. A banked ember flickering back to life. He tasted of coffee and spearmint, of the past and the future. And he leaned into her, hands cradling her face. The moment, slow and quiet.

A knock sounded. They broke apart. Trembles cascaded down Lou's body.

Dr. Woods stuck his head in the door. "Good morning. Let's see how he's doing."

Lou stood, pushing her hair behind her ears. "Just a minute, please." She ducked into the tiny bathroom and splashed water on her face. They hadn't kissed like that—

She couldn't remember the last time kissing him had felt like coming home. Like everything in the world was right and true and good and easy. Lou gripped the edge of the sink. Nothing was that way anymore. She needed to remember reality, not be caught in a net of emotions.

When she returned, David bent over Cole's bed, easing him awake. Dr. Woods prodded Cole's fingertips. "Circulation looks good. How are you feeling?"

"Horrible." Cole moaned. "The food here is terrible and this bed is the worst."

Dr. Woods chuckled. "All right then, I'd say we're ready to go home." He nodded at Lou and David. "I'll send the nurse in with discharge instructions and orders. You'll want to go ahead and get those prescriptions filled, and we'll set up an appointment for next week. Main thing is rest, let the body heal itself." He patted Cole's other shoulder. "Always does, you know, given enough time."

"How long until I can play?"

Dr. Woods looked between Lou and David, who pressed a fist to his mouth and turned away. The doctor sighed. "Cole, it will be awhile. That's the best I can tell you."

"You're saying I may not be able to play ball again?" Cole's words lisped like when he'd been four and needed speech therapy. It was the L's that got him, turning ball into bawl. Lou wanted to bawl herself as her son's eyes swam with tears. David might have been right.

"We're just going to take it slow." She sat beside him, away from the configuration holding his arm in place, willing David to pull himself together.

He turned back, nudged her aside. She relinquished her place, knowing he was who Cole needed. "We'll see, son. Let that bone heal on up, rest, do the physical therapy. Never know what's going to happen." He laid his hand on Cole's chest, and it rose and fell with their son's heaving breaths.

"But Daddy," rarely did their boys slip back into that endearment, "I'm a pitcher." His voice pitched too, on that word. Dr. Woods slipped out. David bent over Cole, holding him as he wept. Lou wrapped arms around them both.

She no longer wanted to tell Cole it was just a game. That there would be other opportunities. David's bad knee—the one he had stretched out as they sat together—told another story. One accident and he'd become a coach instead of a player, changing the whole trajectory of his life.

Sending him careening straight into her.

Pulling back from the embrace, she rested her hands on his shoulders as he comforted their boy. Hoping he could feel in her touch the same understanding she'd felt only a few moments ago when he grazed her lips.

And despite the way his mouth still molded to hers, the way her body seemed made to fit his, she knew. The might-have-been lingered in his every day.

Just not with the same bitterness she'd let steep in her.

Chapter 55

"Hey, someone order a pizza?" Tennessee waltzed through the door, box in hand, Cora Anne behind him holding a spring mix of flowers David couldn't even pretend to name.

"I hope those flowers are for Mom and the pizza's for me." Cole tried straightening up in the bed but fell back wincing. David reached behind and tugged him up.

"Do you think I'd waste tulips on you?" Cora Anne dropped a kiss on his forehead that he promptly wiped off.

"Please tell me there's olives and sausage."

"Pepperoni and banana peppers too." Tennessee set the pizza on the side table and swung it under Cole's nose. "Happy now?"

He inhaled like it was his last meal. "If I didn't already have two brothers you'd be my favorite."

Tennessee laughed and leaned against the wall between the machines. "Guess I better up my game. Brought the pizza for us men so your sister can get your mom out of here for a while."

Lou had her nose in the bouquet, breathing deep, and David knew she was ready to eradicate the hospital smell—and all its memories—from her mind. He hugged his daughter to his side. "A rescue, huh? She's probably got a good hour before they'll let him go home."

"Probably more the way this place works." Lou set the flowers on the windowsill. "How was the planning?" She hadn't made it after all, but David had been right. Cora Anne understood.

"Easy peasy. I kept my mouth shut and let Hannah and Aunt Caro do all the talking."

Lou's worry crease came back. "Are you getting what you want?"

"Absolutely. We had some parameters." Cora Anne giggled and

Tennessee's baritone chuckle joined in, their voices a medley of joy David never imagined he'd hear. No wonder he was crazy enough to think he and Lou could try again, after seeing what time had given his daughter.

"Come on, Mama." She took her mother's hand. "Get your purse. We'll go around the corner to that little place Hannah likes and I'll tell you all about it." Cora Anne blew a flirty kiss to her fiancée and David glanced away when Tennessee's cheeks reddened. His daughter was the only person who ruffled that man's feathers.

"Gross," said Cole. "Can I have my pizza now?"

Tennessee passed out slices on paper towels. "I'll get us some drinks from the machine. What do y'all want?"

"Mountain Dew?" Cole raised hopeful eyebrows at David.

"Don't tell your mother." He stood. "I'll come with you. See what my options are."

"How's he really doing?" Tennessee asked soon as they were out the door.

David sighed. "We'll have to wait and see how the arm heals."

"I'm so sorry." This man who would be his other son clapped him on the shoulder like a brother. "I should've checked that tree. Mrs. Annie had been worried about it before. Said it was like a magnet for lightning strikes."

"Pretty sure Lou's daddy hung that swing for Jimmy. Between him, storms, and the triplets, that old tree was bound to give out sometime." David crossed his arms and studied the machine's offerings. All Pepsi. Sometimes he really missed Atlanta.

"How's she holding up?"

He punched the button for Cole's Mountain Dew, wishing he had something besides a vending machine to hit. "She's Louisa. Tough as nails."

"Sharp as nails, too, I imagine." Tennessee reached around him to feed the machine more quarters. "Like mother like daughter." He frowned, and for a moment, David saw Patrick—and the steel set of his jaw that day in another hospital waiting room when he'd offered his blessing. "Can I ask you something?"

He nodded, wary. No one should ask him for relationship advice.

"You think you and Lou will get back together? I'm only asking because your daughter's putting all her hopes on it, and if she's going to get crushed again, I'd like to know."

David crossed his arms. "Doesn't make it your business."

Tennessee cocked a brow. This *was* his business—and Cora Anne's—and David knew that. He blew out a breath and punched the machine again. This time root beer bore the brunt.

"I'm doing all I can. Can't control Lou's reactions." He gripped the cold bottle. He could shake it and watch it spew, the way he wanted to release months' worth of pent up frustration. Maybe then he could breathe past the tightness in his chest every time he thought he'd missed his chance to make things right.

Tennessee took the bottle from him. "I figure, can't control anyone but yourself. But if you want to hit something again, I got a few more quarters."

How this kid managed to make him grin, even with his fury still flickering, was a mystery. Actually, a gift. David took the offered change. "Thanks."

Another bottle of Mountain Dew later and he felt a little calmer. They fell into step headed back to the room. "I'm trying hard as I can, you know."

"Nah," Tennessee chuckled. "My mother always says you can never try too hard to make a woman happy."

David stopped mid-stride. Maybe it really was that simple. His phone buzzed in his pocket. He pulled it out, squinting at the unknown number. "Hello?"

The gravelly voice on the other end spoke slowly.

David held up a finger for Tennessee to wait. "All right then, we'll take her. Yes, will pick them both up tomorrow. Check all right?"

Tennessee crossed his arms and leaned against the wall, watching him. David grinned as he pocketed the cell. "What did you say about making a woman happy? Because I think I just hit the jackpot."

"With what?"

"A little something for her to love. I'll tell you and Cole together, but you have to keep a secret." David clapped him on the back as they went into the room. "I seem to remember you're good at that."

But in Cole's hospital room, he found his son listless, picking at his pizza rather than inhaling it in three bites. David removed the tray and leaned over him. "You all right?"

Cole shrugged and looked at Tennessee. Thirteen years old and he didn't want his future brother-in-law to see him cry. David got that.

So did Tennessee. "Hey, I'm going to go check out the cafeteria. I like to wash my pizza down with ice cream, personally."

That drew a slight grin from Cole and a request for Rocky Road. When Tennessee left, he let his head fall back on the pillow, tears leaking from his eyes. "I'm scared, Dad. What if I can't play again?"

David flexed his knee. "We'll figure it out. You're young and medical breakthroughs happen all the time."

The afternoon sun dipped and came flickering through the blinds, pooling on the bed. Cole agitated, flinching when the movement shifted his arm.

"Hang on." David twisted the blinds closed and shadows filled the room. A chill trickled down the back of his neck. He went to Cole and stroked back his hair, the skin hot to his touch.

Punching the nurse's button, he kept his voice calm. "Cole, listen to me. Do you feel okay?"

"Just cold ..." He mumbled, chin nodding toward his chest.

This wasn't happening. They were having pizza and going home and fixing everything. He could make their life good again. He could. David pressed his thumb into the nurse's call button and held it.

A moment later Judy, Lou's favorite, poked her head in the door. "What's wrong?"

"I don't know. He's burning up."

A wisp of worry crossed her features as she pulled the cart with its high-tech thermometer bedside. She took his temperature. "Lay back for me, baby." Judy lowered the bed and tucked Cole in with a mother's touch. "Likely an infection. We'll get some antibiotics going and run some labs."

Her words rang clear and sure—but David knew better than to trust clarity in the darkness.

Chapter 56

As Grace drove out to the Coultrie farm, the moon ghosted in the late afternoon sky. A common sight as the seasons shifted into one another with the earth's tilt. Her little world seemed to have tilted too.

Away from Patrick as the sun.

His voice no longer echoed in her every thought, every decision. Instead, the truth Jeanna had spoken filtered through, reminding her to everything, there was a season. She parked and waved to Liam's group, swishing nets in the water and making notes. In Lou's freezer, she nested the lasagna between a chicken casserole and pot roast. Down in the creek, Liam's baritone carried out over the buffer of vegetation, lecturing about living shorelines and environmental sustainability.

"If you don't believe me"—he tossed a grin her way when she walked onto the dock—"just ask Mrs. Grace Watson. She's lived on Edisto how long now?"

He might be baiting her to guess her real age, but she gave him the true answer anyway. "Thirty years."

One of the girls sighed. "I couldn't imagine living all the way out here for that long."

"Sure you could. I had everything I needed. Family, friends, church." She nodded to the water puddling in the pluff mud. Tide coming. "Half my groceries once came from these creeks."

"How'd you know what to do with it all?"

Grace's brows puzzled together. She shot Liam a look. These poor kids memorized facts, but they didn't know anything that mattered. "When I needed help, I read a cookbook. Or asked a friend."

"We roasted oysters, remember?" A boy with impish features elbowed the girl. "It wasn't that hard."

"Did you really dig the oysters out of these creek banks?" Her persistence made Grace laugh.

"Oh, honey. You aren't from around here, are you?" Patiently she told them how Tennessee caught crab and flounder. How they netted shrimp and dug oysters, and that once, a friend had shown her how to make terrapin soup.

"Terrapin?"

Another student leaned over and whispered to the girl.

Her mouth gaped. "You made turtle soup?"

The group laughed, and the sound was like balm to Grace's soul. Liam winked at her as he gave instructions for gathering the equipment. She wondered what it would have been like to have a professor like him, one passionate about his study.

The students still asked her questions as they loaded up, so she reached in her purse and dug around until she found a business card for The Hideaway. "Here, this is the best restaurant on the island. Go there, ask for Ben, and mention Grace sent you. He'll tell you where everything on your table came from and exactly how they prepared it."

"Sounds like a semester end celebration to me." Liam leaned against his car door.

Amidst the echoes of affirmation, Grace felt her purse buzz in her hands. She dug around for her cell phone. Tennessee. "Hey." She listened, face tightening with the words.

Liam must have noticed because as soon as she clicked off, he said, "What's wrong?"

"It's Cole." She explained what he'd told her. "Tennessee says they're moving him to ICU."

"Well, get in. You can ride with me. I know how to avoid the rush hour traffic."

"You'll have to bring me all the way back out here."

He shrugged. "I can think of worse ways to spend an evening."

So could she. It had been a long time since she'd spent an evening with a man.

Guilt nagged a bit as they drove. She shouldn't be planning how to make this worth his while. But her mind shifted through possibilities. Shrimp chowder maybe. Homemade biscuits. A bottle of wine.

Liam talked about living shorelines and marsh migration as though she understood the terms. She had only memories of Patrick mentioning similar ideas, and she knew it had to do with keeping the creeks and waterways healthy and fertile.

"How'd you become interested in all this anyway? It's very …"

"Niched? I know. The powers that be remind me all the time."

"But important."

"Maybe not as much for those who aren't going to live and thrive here."

She shrugged. "Maybe more so. People want places like this to last, at their disposal for vacation. Patrick said we were like the land's mother, and the tourists were like the aunt we have to invite but can't wait to send home."

Liam laughed. "He'd have been a great guest for my class."

"He'd have been great for a good many things."

"Can I ask you a question?"

She raised her brows. Figured she knew what was coming. Always did, sooner or later.

"How'd you let the grief go? Enough that Cora Anne will be your daughter-in-law."

"There's no such thing as letting go. There's just forgiveness, plain and simple. Sometimes every day, over and over." She moistened her lips, chapped with the spring winds, and glanced out the window. The landscape faded from the sanctuary of Edisto into the outskirts of Charleston. But still rural and rough. Gentry didn't live here. Real people did, and these people carried ancestries of forgiveness for afflictions far worse than hers. She turned back to Liam.

"It wasn't her fault. She was a child. Lou and David—" She bit her lip before she said something that had been hammering around inside for a while.

"They should've been there." His hand slipped off the wheel, found hers in the middle of the seat. "I've noticed. This thing with them—

they've let it cloud for a long time."

She said nothing in return, unwilling to betray the friendship she'd worked hard to carve from the hardened history.

Liam squeezed her fingers. "Maybe this time they've finally let the truth filter though."

He couldn't have known her earlier thoughts, but when he spoke, she heard the echo, loud and clear. As if Pat were right there, whispering in her ear, telling her it was time to embrace the new season.

Chapter 57

Lou's whole life reminded her of riding with her daddy up and down those tidal creeks. Easy trolling at high tide when the water rushed in to fill all the shallows. But if they stayed out too long, the motor might sputter against the muck, and what had been a peaceful afternoon turned sour as the smell of pluff mud.

She laid the back of her hand against Cole's forehead. Even though the nurse said the fever was down, his skin still warmed hers. By the time she and Cora Anne had returned from lunch he'd been lethargic, barely opening his eyes when she bent over him. She hadn't been this frightened since he lay in that incubator wearing more tubes than he had limbs.

David stood behind her, his touch feather-light on her shoulders. "Why don't we let him rest? There's folks out in the waiting room who'd like an update."

When the results came back with sepsis, Cole had been moved down a floor into the ICU. The room's walls, all laden with machinery and wires, closed her in already. But she wouldn't leave him. Not alone. Not like when she'd had to leave him in that NICU.

Her chest heaved with a shaky breath. David rubbed her arms, his hands sending a gentle message. "I'll stay, Lou. He's not going to be all by himself. You go get a breath of fresh air."

Fresh air. She wasn't sure the last time she'd breathed air that wasn't tainted with memories or medicine or death.

"Just for a minute."

She pulled away from David's arms. She wanted to let him be her rock, but what if she slipped again? Another fall would kill her spirit. She had these boys to raise. Boys who deserved a strong mother like she'd had.

Who deserve to believe love conquers all. She shook the thought away. Love sometimes brought about the fall.

J.D. and Mac were hiding around the corner from the waiting room, sitting on the hospital floor, backs against the wall, as if waiting on an all-clear from a tornado drill at school. They were bent over a game, but she wasn't fooled. Her boys were only still and quiet when worried.

"Mama?" J.D. scrambled to his feet. "Can we go back there?"

They were thirteen. Old enough by the hospital policy, even if not by hers. But she'd learned long ago, when they squirmed in her arms, being together contented her boys.

"It's two at a time and Dad's back there. Y'all have to take turns." She tucked J.D. into her side. "Who are you hiding from over here?"

Mac jerked his head toward the waiting room as he stood. "Cousin Gloria just showed up. But Ms. Grace intercepted her."

Gloria. Mercy, she didn't have the patience for that right now. Lou bit her lip hard. She hadn't wished for her mama in seven months. As if even thinking the thought would be a betrayal to her mother's dying hope that she'd find her own contentment. But in this moment, she'd have given anything for Annie Coultrie to be at the helm.

"Can I go first?" J.D. moved a step down the hall.

"As long as I don't have to go in there with all those people." Mac turned pleading eyes to her—and his back to the waiting room.

She nodded. "I'll let everyone know how he's doing. Really he needs to rest and let the antibiotics kick in." How confident she sounded.

J.D. scurried away, and Mac followed. Lou squared her shoulders. Her mother would have thanked everyone for coming and sent them on home. She could do that. And if they didn't go … well, David wanted to be helpful, so she'd send him out. He'd be less genteel, but these were desperate times.

The crowd quieted as she turned the corner. Of course they'd stop talking about her when she came in the room. Lou scraped her bottom lip, searching for words, when she realized they hadn't quieted for her.

The heads in that tiny room were all bowed and folks were backed up against the walls, hands joined in an infinity circle that twisted all the way around to the center of the room, where Tennessee had knelt with Cora Anne at his side.

"Father God," he prayed. "We ask first and foremost, always, for Your will to be done. For You to make our hearts open and soft toward whatever that may be. But we ask, for this family right here, that You lay healing hands upon Cole …"

Tears swelled, blurring the scene before her. In the corner of the room she saw her brother Jimmy and his wife, Susan. They'd brought the boys over from school. She saw Cousin Gloria, her hand linked with Jeanna Townsend's, her lips moving with prayerful words of her own. She saw Ben and Hannah, shoulder to hip, and her sister Carolina and brother-in-law John. Which meant Caro had shut down early—or left someone she only half trusted in charge.

Across the room, she recognized Liam's head bent toward—Grace's? Lou's breath caught at the sight, and she nearly laughed aloud, interrupting the reverence of a moment meant to cloak her family with love. But how perfect, and why had she not thought it before?

She rubbed her temples as Tennessee interceded on her behalf—as he asked God for strength and—oh, heavens—patience. She'd asked for that once, too. The triplets were no doubt an answer.

"We thank You, Lord, for first loving us. Loving us in our failings and shortcomings and mistakes. Loving us in our stubbornness …"

Her own eyes cast heavenward. Way to call her out without saying her name.

"We thank You for Cole, for the gift he and his brothers are to all our lives. Amen."

The room echoed and rustled as one, and Lou found herself enveloped in arms that passed her one to another. For once, she didn't long to run away, to find someplace new. Finally, her roots had reached out and taken hold and anchored her right here, to these people and this purpose.

Even Cousin Gloria's presence was welcome, as she pressed Lou's nose to her silk blouse, near the base of her throat, where the scent of White Roses lingered. Mama had worn the same perfume, a touch to her throat and wrists, every Saturday night date or Sunday morning. She'd been wrong. She'd never been alone.

Her mama's presence was all around, in these people, in this place. Right where she belonged.

Chapter 58

J.D. hesitated in the doorway, so David motioned for him to come on in. Hard as it might be, the boys needed to see their brother. Might be time to bend the rules a bit, though, since Mac peeped over J.D.'s shoulder.

Two visitors surely only applied to adults. After all the boys had shared a womb, so David figured that made them a three-for-one deal. Not to mention, a moment ago there'd been some flashing lights and scurrying of nurses somewhere else, so now was a good time.

He waved again. "Shut the door."

J.D. and Mac slipped in, clicking the door so softly behind them, it edged back open an inch. David chuckled. "Y'all might want to learn to do that with your mama's screen door."

Mac shrugged. "We'll work on it."

J.D. moved to the other side of the bed, staring at Cole's arm wrapped completely from fingers to shoulder. "Tell us the truth, Dad."

If only it were that easy. David shook his head. "He's pretty sick, guys. Infection likely came from the mud, and his body's been too weak to fight it off. But give him a few days and a few bags of that medicine, he'll be good as new." His voice trembled. Maybe the boys wouldn't notice.

"No, he won't." J.D. quaked over the words and crumpled beside his brother. "Should've been me."

What was he talking about? "Listen, son. This was an accident."

"No, Dad. I saw the rope fraying and that the limb was cracked. I was going to tell Mom, but we thought—"

"Cole and I thought, not you." Mac interrupted, squeezing J.D.'s shoulder. "You're the safe one."

"I shouldn't have let him get on that tire. I had a bad feeling …" J.D. bent his head again. "And now he's hurt so bad he might not get to play. It should've been me. I don't even care if I can't play baseball. I just do it because—"

When J.D.'s voice hitched on the words, Mac finished for him again. "He just plays because we like it and so do you, Dad."

"Oh, son …" David moved between the bed and the machines, doubting he'd held his boys this close since they'd been infants. "You never have to do anything to please me."

"I pushed him extra hard." His son's sobs broke his own heart. "To prove my point we shouldn't be on it. I thought it would crack more and he'd get off—I didn't think—"

"I pushed him, too." Mac wouldn't let his brother take all the blame, and David was grateful. They had each other, someone to lean on. Unlike him growing up, which was why he'd always found solace in a team.

"Boys, no one is to blame. Maybe it wasn't a great choice, but what happened wasn't intentional. And Cole," David glanced at his son's narrow form, so still under the white sheets. "He's going to be just fine."

"Don't lie, Dad."

"I'm not lying." He stood, arms crossed. "I'll tell you a story, okay, but don't tell your mom?" They nodded.

He'd tell her himself, eventually. "That night your sister almost drowned—and Tennessee's dad did—I blamed myself. I should've been there to go in after her. But I made us late getting home because I wanted to walk. Your mom wanted to ride with Carolina and John, but I needed to talk to her.

"By the time we got to the beach house, Cora Anne had already gone in that water and the accident had already happened. But if we'd been sooner—" His breath caught over confession.

"But it was an accident, Dad. You've all always said so." J.D. snagged a paper towel to swipe at his nose.

David clapped him on the shoulder. "Exactly. I spent a long time hating myself for letting it happen, but truth is, Pat saved me too. What if I'd gone in after her? What if I'd been the one to hit my head on those rocks and drown? I'd have left your mother with four kids—three of them you rascals"—he cuffed Mac playfully under his chin—"and how would that have been? Certainly not better, I'll tell you that."

J.D. leaned against him, as if he was five years old again and they were reading before bed. "Think it's okay if we pray for a miracle?"

"I don't know a lot, son, but I know asking for a miracle is always okay." He hugged his boys close again. "But you have to understand, if it doesn't happen our way, if Cole can't ever play again, that doesn't mean things aren't working together for good. Just takes a while, sometimes, to see it."

~~~

Outside the room, Lou stood, her temple pressed against the coolness of the metal doorframe. The door hadn't caught and through the inch-wide crack, she'd heard David's deep, strong voice over her boys muffled ones. Enough she could piece it all together. Her sweet, tenderhearted J.D. ... she wouldn't let this drag him down like she'd let herself—and Cora Anne—drown under grief all those years ago.

Then she heard David's admission, and she pressed knuckles to her mouth, holding in the words she should've already said. Had she ever had the thought? That he should've saved their daughter?

No, her only thoughts all that time had been selfish. That she'd never really told Patrick how much he'd meant to her. She'd let him die believing she never really cared. But the truth—that murky truth that was never clear and never seemed right? She'd loved him because he let her go, rather than make her stay.

And in that moment, leaning against the doorframe of her son's ICU room, she realized why she'd been so insistent David leave.

She needed to see if he'd come back.

Chapter 59

Edisto Beach, July 2001

"I think we should get a divorce." Lou spoke the words haunting her. Not defensive. Arms limp across her lap. Not angry. Eyes straight ahead, though.

Not looking at his.

"Because you don't love me anymore or because you're done trying?" David's voice broke on try, and he hung his head.

No, she didn't want to try anymore.

And love? She loved their kids with passion that frightened her. For them, she'd let go of who she once wanted to be, so she could become the mother they needed. But her husband of twenty years?

For him, she felt only frustration.

"We could try counseling again." David spoke through the dark. Ahead the ocean rippled in and out. A refrain of tug and pull with the moon, whose light shimmered on the waves.

Lou understood the ocean. She too surged forward and back, her instinct always constant.

She could not do this anymore. In fact, since she'd decided, she'd been like one of those pelicans cresting up and down with the tide, never moving. Constant.

That's what she needed.

"We've talked ourselves out of this, David."

He turned his head toward her, but she remained stoic. The pelican on the waves. She could wait him out.

"You have never believed in divorce."

She turned to him. Just enough so he could see the tears she felt pricking her eyes. So he would know she wasn't giving up without hesitation. "I'm not sure what I believe anymore. But I know it's not this marriage."

He stood then, tall and straight, his profile momentarily blocking the moonlight pooling on this worn back deck of Still Waters.

"I'll go home in the morning and be out by the time you return."

He clipped down the rickety steps and crossed the narrow boardwalk with long strides. By the time he hit the beach, he was running.

Away from her.

With clenched teeth, she worked the ring free from her left hand, twisting it over her swollen knuckle. Would she feel free now? To come back here? To pick up the pieces of a forgotten life?

The drops fell, a puddle inside the ring lying in her palm.

Chapter 60

D avid's knee hurt.
Lou knew because he kept stretching out his leg and flexing his foot. His long legs weren't made for the boxy hospital chairs. The waiting room had emptied hours ago, but they stayed, sipping coffee and making small talk.

Every hour they would take turns going back to the ICU, but the hospital had rules about them staying all night in there. Instead, they were in a quiet room off the main waiting area. It boasted one narrow couch and the two chairs. A nurse had brought a couple flat pillows and thin blankets.

At first Lou had sat awkwardly on the couch. It was the same as the one she'd slept on in Cole's room. Where David had kissed her only that morning.

They hadn't talked about that.

She'd moved into the chair beside him and resorted to picking at her cuticles. A habit she'd broken in seventh grade.

David would stretch and sit up. Fidget and shake one leg. Stretch again. They'd exhausted all their safe topics, and she was afraid to ask him about the kiss. Likely just a momentary lapse in judgment, despite what he'd said while they danced.

His knee popped this time when his leg elongated. David winced. Lou quit her cuticles and dropped her hands, positioning one just above his kneecap and the other just below. She kneaded.

David's head lolled back and he groaned. "You haven't done this in a while."

"They're calling for more rain. No wonder you hurt." She pushed her thumb deeper into the tight muscle. "Did you take something?"

"No."

She released him and grabbed her purse. Dumped two ibuprofen into his palm. He swallowed them down with the now cold coffee. Lou resumed her massage.

When they were married, she did this after almost every game. At least the ones when she was still awake when he got home. The long hours standing, chasing his runner down baselines, and jumping in victory meant he came home limping. Somehow, her touch always seemed to work.

At least that's what David said.

She slid one hand below his knee, left the other on top working small circles. A moment later, his hand covered hers. "Thank you."

"You're welcome."

"I did, you know." He still had closed eyes, head tilted back against the pale wall.

"Did what?"

"Forgive you."

Her hand would have slipped if he hadn't gripped it. Lou passed her tongue over her bottom lip before biting hard. Not because she didn't want to say the words.

But because she should have said them first.

"I was wrong."

"No ... you were right. I didn't see you like I should have. I wanted ..." His eyes opened. Found hers. "To be a person others could depend on. But I failed to be someone you could depend on."

"You did try, David." He had. After Pat's accident, but the trauma of that one year had consumed their family. "I shut you out." She laid her head on his shoulder. "But I'd like to let you back in."

His lips grazed over her forehead and she turned into them, hoping—

A soft knock sounded on the door.

They broke apart, and David said, throat a bit raspy, "Yes?"

"Mr. and Mrs. Halloway?" A young nurse had opened the door. "We thought you'd like to know, his temperature has been normal for almost an hour. The antibiotics are working. Likely we'll transfer him back upstairs later today."

David pulled her to him, hugging her tight, the taste of desire not gone, she imagined, from either of them. Merely shifted aside by this even sweeter moment.

Chapter 61

The garden at MUSC reminded Grace of Annie. Azaleas neatly pruned and budded, paths sculpted and lined with pavers. The glory of roses climbing the trellises overhead. Come summer those blooms would intoxicate the whole place, shielding those who might sit here, heavy with worry.

She thought about the miracle of modern medicine and how those machines pumped purification right into Cole's blood. How they all lived with that need to be cleansed.

"Hey there."

Grace looked up at the sound of Lou's voice and scooted over on the wrought iron bench. "Hey yourself. How is he this morning?"

"He's awake, but not himself. Still, it's good to see his eyes open." Lou crossed her ankles and folded her hands in her lap, every bit still a girl raised to be a debutante, whether she'd wanted that life or not.

Next to her Grace sat one knee over the other, lazily swinging her foot, grateful the warm weather meant she could wear sandals most of the year. The morning sun warmed their faces. Grace turned hers toward the light.

Lou shielded her eyes. "It's nice out here."

"You'll never guess whose donation made this possible."

"No ..." Lou's dark hair brushed her cheeks as she swung her head.

"She protects herself with ice, but Charlotte has a few secret projects that betray her."

They sat silently again, and Grace marveled that they could. The evening they'd met on the pier, she'd told Patrick she and Lou would never be friends. Then, when Annie and T.C. took him under their wings, inviting them over for Sunday dinners and family reunions, she'd been sure the awkwardness would never pass. They'd sidestep around one another, and Grace knew now she bore a responsibility for retreating. How long had she waited for Louisa to come to her—to accept her? When she could have done for this fellow mother what she'd done for Cora Anne. Lived up to her name.

"Thank you for all you've done." The words didn't seem forced, but Lou pressed her hands against her knees as she spoke them.

"We're family," she covered Lou's hands with her own, "and we have to look out for one another."

Lou nodded, and then glanced at the sidewalk leading to the hospital entrance. Grace followed her gaze. Tennessee and Cora Anne strolled, hand in hand, but before they got to the entrance, he said something to make her laugh. She tipped her chin to the sky, peals of joy obscuring the fear—if for only a moment. Tennessee slipped his arm around her waist and pulled her close, kissing her without a care for the busy sidewalk in downtown Charleston.

"All things for the good ..." Lou murmured.

Grace turned to her. "What?"

"Something David said to the boys. All things work together for the good. Like them." She nudged Grace's shoulder. "Like us."

~~~

"The boy will need a good bit of therapy, then?" Charlotte dabbed her lips and rang the bell to signal Chloe they were ready for dessert.

"No doubt." Grace folded her linen napkin. "His brothers are praying for a miracle, hoping he'll be able to play ball again."

"Might be simpler to ask for basic function." Charlotte shook her head. "A break like that can set a body back. I always wondered ..." She sighed. "No matter."

But these weekly dinners they'd been having, this dance to finally understand one another, gave Grace the courage to probe. "Who was hurt?"

Charlotte looked to the mantle. They'd had an informal—at least for her mother-in-law—dinner beside the fireplace. A picture of her brother in his Navy uniform had occupied that corner for all the years Grace had known her.

"My brother, Andrew, caught a bad break during the war. Healed nicely, but he didn't have the dexterity he once did. He'd talked about designing his own buildings, but he could no longer draw. Instead, he took charge of the business's finances. I've thought before it was the … deformity… that made Annie leave him."

In the silence Chloe set down dishes of ice cream with fresh berries. Grace offered thanks as was her habit, and Charlotte dismissed Chloe with a wave, as was hers.

Grace picked up her spoon, trailing it through the glaze drizzled on top. "I don't think Annie was that shallow."

Charlotte savored a raspberry, then lay down her spoon. "I don't either…. and I wish I'd told her so."

Too little, too late. How often had that been the price for burdens carried? Grace ate her dessert, but in her mind, she recalled her last moments with Patrick. He'd gotten up early and brought her coffee in bed before he headed out for the day.

"I'll be gone till dark, likely. Got to get all the new windows installed in that place next to Still Waters. Good thing Tennessee can help. Going to take the whole crew to get it done before the storm blows in tonight."

"Be careful. I'll keep supper hot." That was what she'd always said, the same words nearly every day. A code of sorts for all she didn't take the time to voice. *I love you. I'll miss you. You're my whole life.*

She swallowed, the cold searing her throat. "Charlotte?"

"Yes?"

"You should tell Lou. And Carolina and Jimmy. About Annie— what she was like growing up."

Charlotte's eyes widened. "Do you think they would want to know? She was different, then."

"No, she wasn't." Grace smiled. "The spark that made her give up everything for Thornton? I bet it was always there."

A small smile started, just barely, at the corners of Charlotte's mouth. "You mean, like it was for Patrick as well?"

Grace lifted the silver coffee set and poured. First for Charlotte, then herself. "You really knew I was more than a whim?"

"Oh, my dear. I knew the moment I met you, this was no fling or retribution. He could've married Louisa, and they'd have been happy, but they'd never have been," Charlotte delicately wet her lips as she lowered her voice to say, "passionate."

Grace chuckled into her coffee, watching as mirth—an emotion she'd never seen from her mother-in-law—danced in Charlotte's eyes.

The older woman laid her hand, blue-veined and adorned with jewels, atop Grace's. "Tell me, how is your mother?"

Grace pressed her lips together, the answer always heavy, but her mother-in-law's touch light and hopeful. Perhaps, like the ground outside now covered over in evening dew, Charlotte was warming with the spring.

Chapter 62

Edisto Island, August 2006

Lou slid a clean pillow behind her mother's head, the casing trimmed in embroidered handiwork. Pulled from the back of the linen closet where Mama stored items more precious than generic ones plucked from the K-Mart shelves.

"Thank you." Her mama's voice shook, weak as transparent tea.

Lou's chest pinged and the pain of grief radiated through her limbs. "You're welcome, Mama. Anything you need, we'll get it."

The hand lying across her mother's stomach lifted. Beckoned. Lou leaned closer to hear. "I need you to come home, now."

"I am home. We brought you to the farm, remember?"

Mama's hand turned and her eyes tracked the sunbeams through the window. Dust danced in the slight breeze from the ceiling fan. "I know where I am. Where are you?"

Lou choked down the fear rising like bile in her throat. "I'm right here, Mama. Carolina and Jimmy, too. Should I get them?"

"No …" She blinked and tears leaked from the corners of her blue eyes. "Louisa. You need to come home. It's time."

"Time for what, Mama?" Constriction bound her torso. Shallow breaths barely filled her own lungs, much less her mother's. Surely Mama couldn't predict her own death to the moment.

"Time to find where you belong. Your daddy's waiting."

The doctor said her mind would wander. Lou nodded. "All right. I'll go see Daddy in a minute."

"No, baby. You can't see him. You just have to feel him. Down by the creek. He wants you to help."

"Bring in some shrimp for supper? I will."

"No …" Mama's voice strengthened. "Listen to me. He wants you to come home and take care of his creek. Like you promised."

Lou winced. She'd never told Mama about that conversation. "Daddy's gone, and I took a different path."

"And now it's time to take the one that comes back home." Mama's chin dipped and her exhale deflated her narrow form.

Lou waited until her mother's chest rose again with breaths of uneven rhythm, but regular all the same, before she slipped out of the room and down to the dock. There the creek shimmered under the August harvest moon, hanging low and golden round in the sky.

Water brushed the pilings, murmuring waves of long-forgotten times. Whispers of the might have been—and maybe the meant to be.

Chapter 63

The puppies yipped in the backseat even though Mac and J.D. held them gentle as babies.

The male, his head really almost as big as J.D.'s, lunged across the seat and licked David's ear as he turned onto the dirt road. "Hey, I'm trying to drive here."

J.D. reined him back in. "We gotta name 'em, Dad. Can't we at least tell Mom we got the boy?"

In Mac's arms, the girl with the honey coat wiggled. David hoped his gut was right this time.

"It's a surprise. You can't tell." Mac admonished as he stroked her between the ears.

"Just for today, guys. Once Cole's home and settled tomorrow, we'll all be together and we'll name 'em then."

J.D. whispered something into the dog's ear probably only intended for him, Mac, and their new acquisitions. David pretended not to hear, but his heart quickened anyway with his son's quiet plea that they all be together, all the time.

They got the pups settled in the barn—he wasn't crazy enough to bring them in the house without Lou's permission—and he left the boys under Cora Anne's watchful eye. She and Hannah were on the porch with glasses of tea and a folder full of wedding plans that needed finalizing.

In less than six weeks he'd give away his only daughter. He dropped a kiss on her forehead when she looked up to tell him bye.

"You're only going to be gone a few hours, Dad." But the smile tugged up the side of her mouth. With the wall she'd built as a teenager, he stopped offering fatherly affection. Now he had to make up for lost time before Tennessee Watson stole the last of her attention.

His gut tightened. He liked that boy, really did, but his daughter deserved to know her father loved her first. "Hannah, will you fix me some of that tea in a thermos to take Lou? The hospital's is all syrupy and she complains."

"As she should. Tea's not hard to make, so I don't understand these people who have trouble." Hannah strode into the kitchen, catching the screen door before it banged shut behind her.

"Listen, Cor," he moved the folder from under her hands so she'd focus on him. "I need to tell you something."

"You're kind of scaring me. Is Cole not getting better?"

"No, it's not Cole …" He searched her eyes for any trace of resentment. But her wide irises, blue as her grandmother's hydrangeas, stared back. Unafraid and unencumbered. "I'm sorry I wasn't the one who saved you that night."

She blinked rapidly. Tears came easily for his stoic daughter these days. For her mother, as well, come to think of it. "Daddy … you weren't there."

"I know. But I could've been. And after, I definitely should have been."

Her breath came out slow, as though the words she wanted to say required all her strength. "I forgave you—and Mom. Finally. None of us need to carry that anymore. We washed it out with the tide, remember?"

Those old Edisto superstitions.

"Can I ask you something?" She pressed her lips together and eyed him suspiciously—like when she was a little girl pleading for a stop at the Krispy Kreme hot sign. "What's up with you and Mom?"

David shrugged, but heat crept up his neck.

Cora Anne giggled. "Oh, Daddy. You've got it bad."

He wagged his brows at her, the moment suddenly light as one of Grace's angel food cakes. "Think she feels the same?"

"I'm praying."

"Me, too, baby girl." He wrapped her in his arms while he still could claim her solely as his. "Me too."

Chapter 64

Lou eyed David as he helped Cole navigate his t-shirt. If she didn't know better, she'd call him giddy. But that would be ridiculous.

"Mom, can you go out while we do my pants?" Cole asked, his voice still raspy weak. The shock of hair tumbling across his forehead made him impish—even if he didn't want her to see his underwear. No matter she was the reason it was clean.

She stepped outside the door and Judy waved her over to the station. "Y'all about ready to go?"

"His father's helping him get dressed. Guess that will fall to his brothers at home since I'm good enough to fold his boxers, but not to actually see them worn."

Judy snickered. "He is thirteen, after all. Dad can't help him at home too?"

"Oh, well …" She fumbled, uncertain. Did the staff not realize the situation? Why would they? The paperwork was a blur but surely she'd marked somewhere on there this was shared custody. "We don't exactly live together anymore."

"Don't exactly or just plain don't?" Judy tilted her head, sizing up Lou the way she sized up Cole's vitals. "Because you two don't strike me as divorced. Strained a bit, but who isn't when under a stressor like this?"

"We've been divorced nearly five years." Even as she said it, she heard how ludicrous she sounded. Had it really been that long?

Judy huffed. "If that's true, you're the poster children for amicable."

"Lou?" David leaned out the door. He wore jeans and a polo, a grown-up, polished version of her boys—and the young man who'd knocked her down on the college green.

But his voice alone made the flush start on her cheeks. Powerless to stop it, she ducked her head and called back, "Be right there."

Like a conspirator, Judy leaned over the counter. "My professional medical opinion is, if he can make you blush, you just might want to rethink that whole status."

"We're ... talking."

Judy arched a brow. "Your thirteen-year-old boy is probably 'talking' to a girl. You're a grown up." She swatted Lou playfully with a chart. "Act like it."

"Thank you, for all you've done."

"Oh, honey, he's been a joy. Now take him home and feed him some real food."

She nodded and stepped away.

"Mrs. Halloway?" Lou turned back. Judy's expression had sobered. "Be happy."

Like a blessing she'd have received in church, Lou felt the buoyancy of the words stirring inside. Finally, she might have permission to be just that.

~~~

David tapped his fingers on the steering wheel, out of time with the radio, until Lou reached over and stilled his hand while he waited to make the left-hand turn onto highway 174.

"Please stop. You're making me jumpy."

He slid one hand from the wheel and held onto her fingers. She didn't pull away. In the backseat, Cole had his head against the window, eyes closed. Every now and then a wince of pain would flit across his brow and the crease between his eyes deepened. David should have both eyes on the road. Instead he had one on his son, and the other darting glances over at Lou every few moments.

She let him keep her hand, but she gazed out the window. Her hair brushed behind her shoulders, the longest it had been since the triplets had been born. The neck of her pale blue shirt scooped wide enough he could see her collar bone. A tiny gold cross that had belonged to her mother nestled in her clavicle. He used to kiss her there, soft feathery kisses along her throat, hoping she'd tilt her head back so he could pursue more.

David swallowed and refocused on the road.

When they turned under the canopy of pecan trees that sheltered the farm's drive, Lou gasped. "Look." Along the fences supporting the rarely locked gate, tiny yellow roses had burst into bloom. She sighed. "Those are Mama's sweetheart roses."

"Sweetheart?" In the back, Cole stirred.

"They only bloom in the spring." Lou twisted around to grin at their son. "You know, when love is in the air."

Cole pretended to gag, and Lou laughed. On the porch steps, J.D. and Mac waited, all dirty jeans and big smiles. David had figured they wouldn't even make it into the house. His boys kept secrets about as well as fishermen told the truth about their catch.

Lou hugged them. "What in the world have you boys been up to?"

Cora Anne held up her hands. "Look, I did the best I could under the circumstances." She bounded down the steps and side-hugged Cole on the way to her car. "I'm sorry to go, but I've got to run up to the museum and then meet Hannah at The Hideaway."

"Thank you." Lou caught their daughter in an embrace that squeezed David's heart.

As Cora Anne pulled out of the drive, Mac beamed. "We've got a surprise."

"I hope it's that you look like this because all your other clothes are clean and neatly folded and put away."

"Yes, ma'am. Dishes too." J.D. glanced at David, excitement written all over his face.

"I'll have to go check this out." Lou started up the porch steps.

"But Mom—" Mac was cut off by David's hand on his shoulder.

"Let us get Cole settled first."

"Yeah, very sick person here." Cole pretended the steps could be too much to climb, so Mac ducked under his good arm and helped him stagger as though he really were helpless.

J.D. hung back, helping David unload the jeep, his brown eyes blinking trepidation. "You think he's mad at me?"

"Did he seem mad?"

"No."

"Then don't be putting on emotions that aren't there." How he wished he'd said that eons ago to their mother.

Cole made it all the way to the couch where the boys had prepared the Xbox. "At least my thumb still works." He grasped a controller and propped his feet on the coffee table alongside his brothers. Lou opened her mouth, no doubt to admonish the feet on the table, but closed it quickly.

"I'm going to see what we can pull together for supper." She backed away to the kitchen, the boys already immersed in a world they could control. "You know I hate that thing," she reminded David as she opened the freezer, "but at least it will keep his mind occupied for a bit."

"For a bit," he agreed.

She had her head in the freezer but pulled back to stare at him. "Did you do this?" The tiny freezer was stuffed with neatly labeled, foil wrapped casseroles and containers.

"I asked Grace if she'd put together a few things." Bless that woman and every other cook at the Presbyterian Church.

"The end times could come and we'd still be eating lasagna." Her sarcasm didn't fool him. The slight tremor in her voice gave away her emotion. Lou had grown used to doing everything on her own. He had no one but himself to blame for that.

He hefted one of the lasagnas from the stack. "Why don't I get this going? Frozen casserole is one of my specialties."

"Oh, really? And what are your others?" They ought to close the freezer door before her nearness created enough heat in David's chest to thaw all those casseroles. But he didn't move.

Instead, he leaned into her and whispered, "I'm getting real good at turning something sour into something sweet."

"What are you two doing in the freezer?" J.D.'s voice jolted them apart. Lou turned her back, searching, he was sure, for a dish to wash or a counter to wipe.

He faced their son, the frozen foil dish now burning his fingertips. "Fixing dinner."

"Right ..." J.D. stepped to the porch. "I gotta go check on ... something." He winked since his mother's back was still turned.

David showed off his salad-making skills while their dinner bubbled away in the oven, and Lou pretended to be impressed.

"I mean, it takes a lot of skill to tear lettuce," she joked, sipping her wine and seeming more at ease. He threw a carrot at her and she ducked, laughing. Then her brow wrinkled. "What's the noise?"

He cocked his head toward the living room. Yup. The boys had smuggled in those puppies. He'd know that girl's yip anywhere.

Lou's eyes narrowed. "David, why do you look guilty?"

Laying down the knife, he held up his hands. "Let's just keep in mind I said barn only."

"What ..." She scrambled from the table to the living room. He followed, hoping he was quick enough to see her face—and uttering a split-second prayer his gut had been right.

Lou stood, hands on hips, studying their boys who had thrown their grandmother's hand-crocheted afghans over themselves—and the mysterious wiggling lumps on the sofa. "What are y'all doing?"

"Just playing Xbox, Mom." J.D. was all wide-eyed innocence.

In the middle, Cole cradled his damaged arm atop a heap of multicolored blanket. "Yeah, nothing happening here." But then the puppy reared and they both yelped. Cole from pain—the pup from fear of suffocation, probably.

David lunged and grabbed the boy puppy from Cole's lap. J.D. scampered up, the girl tucked in his arms. Cole's cheeks drained of color as Lou stepped around the coffee table and gaming wires to ease him back against the cushions.

"It's okay ..." she soothed. "Deep breaths." She breathed with their son like he'd seen her do in the NICU, sitting by the incubator, stroking tiny fingers and practicing breaths that matched the ventilator. Cole's cheeks pinked again.

"I'm going to get you an ibuprofen. Dr. Woods said you can have it in between the pain pills. Just be still." Lou turned her eyes from Cole. On him, the blue had been gentle as summer sea, but David knew she was aiming a storm his way. "Then maybe someone can tell me why these dogs are in my house?"

"Don't be mad—" Cole panted a plea. "They wanted to surprise us, and look, Dad got you the girl puppy so you don't have to be alone."

That hadn't exactly been why, but before David could intervene, Lou stood. "Well, then, if she's going to keep me company when all you boys are at his house, maybe she needs to start learning the rules of this one. Such as, no animals on the furniture"—she swung a heated gaze between the other boys—"or around your brother's very painful, still healing, broken-in-three-places arm."

"I'm fine, Mom, you just scared her."

Mac interjected. "Yeah, Mom. Sometimes you have that trouble voice and it's scary."

She crossed her arms and threw a glare David's way. "I don't have a trouble voice." He resisted the urge to laugh—or agree.

"It's really deep like this," Mac somehow managed to assume a falsetto that also carried thunderous tones. "You boys better get that homework done or I'll throw the Xbox in the creek."

The boys and David exploded in laughter. The pups, unsure of what was happening, began to yip and struggle.

The corners of Lou's mouth twitched. "I don't sound like that. David, do I?"

He grinned and passed the wriggling dog to Mac, so he could throw an arm around her shoulders, casually of course. "Only when they deserve it."

Her light punch against his chest only made him want to embrace her more, letting this new life unfold around them. One where she laughed more easily and cried more readily and let him be a part of her carefully constructed world all over again.

"Fine. I won't use my trouble voice to scare these babies." She reached for the girl J.D. held. "But how in the world did we wind up with two? I thought Earl said all his girls were spoken for."

"Breeder changed his mind when he saw her. Said she'd never be a good litter-bearer because she's so small. And I figured," he caught her eyes, back to their summer blue, with his, "you didn't care about that."

"Not a bit. She's perfect just the way she is."

"Can we name them now, please?" J.D. sat back down on the sofa beside Cole. "We decided you could name the boy and Mom could name the girl, but the rest of us get one veto each."

"How diplomatic." Lou grinned at David over the pup's head. *Thank you*, she mouthed. He nodded and winked—and hoped she'd sense more than *you're welcome*.

"Let's name her Ravenel. That way she'll always know where she came from." She snuggled the pup close. "Except your dad will have to learn to say it right."

"Good luck with that." He wrinkled his nose as if the name left a bad taste in his mouth when in truth, it made him eager to see how long he could run that family joke.

Mac sat on the coffee table, letting the boy pup sniff at Cole's knees. Cole reached out a hand and stroked the dog's muzzle. "Can we name him Russell? Like the creek? Then they'll both know where home is."

"What do you think?" Mac lifted up the dog and looked him in the eye. "Are you a Russell?"

"Maybe Russ," J.D. said. "And Rav, you know, until Dad learns to say it."

"Names they can grow into." Lou slipped from David's side. He felt the emptiness as soon as she pulled away. She passed Ravenel back to J.D. "Like you boys."

As she crossed back to the kitchen, she looked at him, eyes lingering in a way he hadn't seen for a long time. A look that kindled all the hope he'd been nursing.

One that told him she'd found her way home.

Chapter 65

When Lou came downstairs after tucking in the boys—as if they were toddlers again, and she'd never confess it but she missed those days sometimes—the kitchen smelled of coffee. At the kitchen table, David jotted a schedule for Cole's prescriptions. He'd lined up all the medicines in their orange bottles like sentinels across a placemat.

Seeing her, he propped his chin in his hand. The worry of these last few days had darkened his hazel eyes to the color of the coffee percolating in that old pot of her mama's. "He's asleep?"

She dropped into a chair. "Soon, I think." Weariness settled into her bones. They were home.

Together.

Even Cora Anne had breezed in after dinner, saying she needed a hot bath and a break from wedding magazines. She'd plucked *Jane Eyre* from her grandmother's shelf of classics and retreated upstairs asking if they could all catch up in the morning.

David poured Lou a cup of coffee. She knew it would somehow taste of this house—sweet cutting the bitter. Why she'd keep the old pot until it gave out. Some things didn't need to change.

But other things did.

"The other two are in sleeping bags on the floor, insistent they're taking turns keeping watch." Safely accounted for with no IV drips and all twelve limbs spread akimbo across the tiny room.

David tipped a tired smile her way. "They're good boys." Some of the worry faded from his eyes. "We didn't ruin them."

She blew across her coffee. "No, we didn't."

"I need to go back to work tomorrow."

Of course he did. She didn't expect him to be here, all the time. She flicked her gaze toward the door of her office, creaked open as always. Her work would simply have to wait.

David hunched over his coffee. "There's a game—Mac and J.D. want to play but they don't want to upset their brother."

Lou pushed her cup away. She and Cole would figure out this different way forward together.

"There's a position for next year they've asked me to consider. Ninth grade and JV coach." He sounded hopeful, and she wanted to let him be.

"Sounds perfect." Lou bit her lip, willed back the tightening in her chest. "You'll be busy next year." She avoided his eyes, focused instead on the center of her table. Painkillers and the pill cutter replaced the salt and pepper. She grasped the bottle. "Better get another one ready. Nurse said stay ahead of it."

But when she positioned the white pill—still so little to be too large a dose—beneath the blade, her hands trembled and slipped, slicing off only a miniscule corner. Frustration and fatigue rose in her throat.

David covered her hand with his. "Let me do it."

"No." She jerked away. What if she'd been letting her emotions get the better of her? Reading into his gaze promises that no longer mattered? "You aren't going to be here all the time. I can handle this."

He pulled her arm away and held it. His thumb dug into her palm and his eyes pooled again into dark irises. Intense and focused. "Who says I'm not going to be here?"

She turned her head.

But he put his other hand on her chin and made her face him. "This time you're going to look me in the eye and tell me I have to go. You do that and I'll walk away and end this. I'll be a father and an ex-husband and we'll live those separate lives you thought you wanted."

She couldn't look at him. Her lashes matted with tears. "Why would you want to stay?"

His exasperated sigh ended with a chuckle, and he drew her face close to his. "Because I love you. I have always loved you, even when you made it nearly impossible. Even right now, in this moment, when

I don't claim to know what you want."

"I want to stay here." The admission came freely. "Liam's going to bring me on full-time to conduct environmental research."

"Is that all?" David's voice hitched. "Everything you want?"

"No." She gave him everything, heart wide open. "I want you. I want our family. I want our home. I want more than the marriage we had."

For once, he waited. Didn't rush her.

"But I need to know, David. Are we going to be a priority? It's taken me over twenty years to believe I can be content with motherhood and Edisto. I'm here, now, and I'd rather do this with you than without you."

"Why?"

She blinked, clearing her vision, and saw the smirk started at the edge of his lips. And she knew what he wanted. "Because I love you."

With those words, his hands kneaded her neck, gently, the way she soothed his knee. "I'd rather teach our boys to catch in the backyard than lose this all over again."

"I'm not saying don't take the job—"

"You're saying, let it be a job. And those are far easier to come by than this."

Tears slipped down her cheeks.

David brought her lips to his and kissed her without hesitation or regret or fear. Not the gentle caress of a hopeful lover but the exaction of her husband taking what he needed—what he wanted. Urging her closer, deeper, he offered more than an invitation to more than a kiss. This was a commitment, not a second attempt.

His arms grasped her waist and tugged. She moved into his lap, making out at the kitchen table like they were college students again. Her only thought how he made her feel alive and warm. Her tears rinsed both their faces like the creeks washed away unwanted sediment clouding fresh water.

He broke from her mouth only to trail kisses down her jaw to her collarbone, and there he paused, his nose against her skin, breathing heavy as she trailed her fingers through his hair.

"You've lost weight." He whispered the words against her shoulder.

She leaned her head back to give him access to the hollow of her throat where he'd always plant a kiss after—

And he paused. "I need you to decide real quick, Lou. Church or courthouse this time?"

She set her palms against his cheeks, pulled his gaze to hers. "I think I can only handle one church wedding at a time."

"Good thing, because we're going to have our hands full housebreaking Russell and Ravenel."

In the corner of her kitchen, the pups tumbled over one another, trying to make the bed cushion soft as their mama's belly, no doubt. A lump rose in her throat. Shoulders quaking, she let her head fall against his shoulder.

His hands stroked up and down her back. "Shhh ... I promise, this time, it's really going to be okay. I can make that roast in the Crockpot. Easy."

Lou sat up, still laughing.

"What's so funny?"

"You said Ravenel." She leaned forward, pressing her lips to his. "The right way."

Epilogue: The Wedding

In her mother's old room at the farmhouse, in front of the full-length mirror, Lou set Cora Anne's veil in place. She pushed in the last pin and folds of lace-edged tulle cascaded down her daughter's back. Her girl stared at herself. Likely marveling how one white dress could change a life.

With an embroidered handkerchief that had belonged to her mother, Lou dabbed the corner of her eyes.

"Crying already, Mama?" Cora Anne looked like a dream in a strapless gown, overlaid with more lace that grazed the floor. Into her crown of hair, Grace had woven small white flowers, all twisted and curled and tumbling across her shoulders in dark waves.

Lou stroked one of those curls, tucking the flower more securely. "I believe I'm entitled to a few tears."

There was a knock on the door. "Mama?"

"Y'all can come in."

The triplets staggered inside. Mac's shirttail untucked, Cole's tie hung loose, and J.D.'s coat thrown over his shoulder like a debonair gentleman out of a movie. Lou raised brows at her daughter, and Cora Anne lifted her bouquet in front of her face so they couldn't see her laughing.

Definitely not a dream.

Hannah and Carolina gasped and flurried about fixing the boys. Lou let them. Today she only looked after her daughter.

"How did you know?" Cora Anne wet her lips, shimmery pink with Hannah's administrations of makeup, and made a face at the taste.

Lou smiled and passed her a bottle of water. "How did I know what?"

"That Daddy was the one."

As if she had spoken him into being, David appeared in the doorway. He wore a blue suit and a paisley tie Cora Anne had bought from a men's shop on King Street. Last week he'd gotten what he called his wedding haircut and now a few days later, the shock of the crop had worn off and softened along his ears. The silver edging his temples stood out more these days, but when he beamed at her, all she saw was the man she'd married all those years ago. Young, eager, content to spend a lifetime making her happy.

He'd looked at her the same way, in the judge's chambers of the Charleston County courthouse last month.

"Y'all doing this traditional, I assume?" The judge fixed his glasses on his nose.

Lou rolled her lips so she wouldn't laugh, but David, completely straight faced, said, "Yes, sir. We're pretty traditional."

When they'd repeated the vows following the judge's drawl, Lou felt certain she had never understood them before.

"Do you, David James Halloway, take this woman to be your lawfully wedded wife?"

"I do."

He linked his fingers through Lou's. From the corner of her eye, she saw the triplets all shift their gazes elsewhere. They were excited, but in the words of Mac, "Don't let us see you kissing, okay?"

"Do you, Louisa Coultrie Halloway—" The judge's gray brows wrinkled together. Lou couldn't help it this time. She giggled. "Did I miss something?" The poor man readjusted his glasses.

"Second time's the charm, right, sir?" David urged her closer, and she complied, their bodies a mere breath apart.

"Let us hope so." The judge meandered on. "Do you, Louisa Coultrie Halloway, take this man to be your lawfully wedded husband?"

"I do."

They repeated the other sacred words—to have and to hold, to love and to cherish, for better or for worse—and then, on "till death do us part" their eyes had never wavered from the other. This time, Lou had understood what that meant.

Now, she embraced her daughter. "How'd I know?" Lou drew back and looked straight into Cora Anne's blue eyes, mirrors of her own. "I knew because I could live without him." Her smile came so easily. "But why would I want to?"

As she stepped back so David could get a good look at their daughter, Cora Anne twirled and beamed. "What do you think, Daddy?"

David stared. Then he crossed the room in two strides. "I think," and he pulled her close, "Tennessee Watson is the second luckiest man alive."

"Really? Who's first?"

"Me." He let her go and reached for Lou. She stepped into the circle of his arms, and he pressed a kiss on her cheek, close to her hairline, lingering a bit to inhale the White Shoulders she'd dabbed at her throat. "Hey, there, Mrs. Halloway."

His hand slipped into hers, fingering the gold band he'd put there again.

~ ~ ~

The reception at The Hideaway promised to last long into the night, though David suspected Tennessee was ready to whisk his bride away. Not a thought he wanted to have.

He fixed a cup of coffee and rejoined the boys at their reserved table. The pillar candle's flame sputtered and shook as Cole tried to use his good fingers to snuff it out. Still a daredevil, though David would do his best to break that tendency. He thumped his son's hand as if he were two again.

"Don't you like at least having the ability to zip your own pants?" Cole's second surgery had been successful. David had never seen someone so proud to wiggle his fingers.

Cole grinned, sheepish, as his brothers chortled. "Sorry, Dad."

"Go get me some more cake, would you?" He passed over the delicate china plate. This party was every bit as refined as Charlotte's. Except for the country music. Cora Anne was on the dance floor now with her wedding party and Garth Brooks.

Across The Hideaway's porch, Lou tilted her glass toward him. He lifted his cup in acknowledgement. They'd done it. Passed over their girl and become family, finally, with Charlotte Ravenel Cooper Watson. Judging from the way Charlotte had Lou's ear bent to hers right now, she would no doubt be assuming a matriarchal role with them all.

A wind from the creek made the candle's flame flutter again. The candles in the church had done that too, the whole ceremony. He and Lou had lit ones for their parents, while Tennessee and Grace lit one for Patrick. But those flames hadn't glowed strong and full; they'd all waved as if wisps of wind floated about.

Of course down here, folks would tell him that was the spirits walking. If that was the case, he figured they were all pretty happy to see the Coopers and the Jenkins family finally making the match that was meant to be. When he'd walked Cor down that aisle, Tennessee's grin had spread wide and crinkled his eyes.

David felt the same look on his face every time he looked at his wife. A marveling at how things work themselves out.

J.D. slid his cake across the table as Cora Anne called, "C'mon, boys. Nobody around here gets this song." Alan Jackson's "Chattahoochee." David chuckled and ate his cake. His kids may have the blue blood of the Lowcountry, but they had a little rural Georgia too.

"May I?" Grace dropped into a vacant chair. She was stunning in sea glass green, vintage hair combs sweeping back her blond curls.

"I hope someone told you how beautiful you are tonight."

"Now David." She leaned into his shoulder, teasing. "You're a married man."

"Miraculous, isn't it?" He searched the room again for Lou, and found her, still talking to Charlotte and standing in the soft glow of the outdoor lights. She turned her head as if sensing his gaze, and he caught his breath at the way her hair grazed her shoulders and her lips pursed in anticipation of a promise meant only for him.

Beside him Grace laughed, softly. "I hope you told her how lovely she is tonight."

"Only about a thousand times."

"We never get tired of hearing it."

He sat back and surveyed the room. "Where's Dr. Whiting? Didn't I see you dancing earlier?"

Grace ducked her head, and David chuckled. He hadn't realized, but now it made perfect sense why Liam hadn't put up more of a fight.

"There's never really been anyone since Pat ..." She fingered the ring he'd never seen her take off. "But maybe it's time for a new beginning."

The music shifted. Definitely time. He kissed Grace's cheek like a brother. "You deserve one as much as anyone else." Standing, he looked again for Lou but the crowd had swelled and he could no longer see her.

"May I have this dance?" Liam appeared at Grace's shoulder. "Hello, David. Congratulations."

Distracted, he shook Liam's hand, but then the crowd parted and he saw her, weaving her way toward him. "Excuse me, y'all. I've got to go dance with my wife."

Never would he get tired of that expression.

He caught her on the dance floor and pulled her close, his hand splayed across the small of her back, hers tucked around his shoulder. "I missed you."

"I was gone ten minutes."

"Fifteen at least."

"Well, Charlotte does like to talk."

She set her cheek against his and he breathed deep again. Her perfume, the salty breeze off the creek, the sweetness of a day well lived settling over them all.

"What did you talk about?"

"My mother." Lou leaned her head back. "Did you know she was valedictorian of her high school?"

"Why would I have known that?"

Sighing, she dropped her chin. "So many things I didn't know."

"We'll find them out. You've got a house full of boxes with secrets." He thought of the shoebox of letters she'd only recently begun to share with him.

Dear Mama, one he'd read last night ran. *David is so kind and funny. There's no way I could deserve someone as easygoing as him.*

Cheers erupted all around. Tennessee had dipped Cora Anne for a kiss that delighted their friends but made her father look away.

Lou laughed. "Guess you don't want to see too much of that."

"Not at all. Can't watch them when I'm kissing you." He pressed his lips to hers, savoring how she softened and responded.

Cheers again. And gags from the triplets. But the music played and the song's words rang true.

Some things are meant to be.

Dear Reader,

Edisto Island, South Carolina is a very real destination for those seeking a slower pace of life, and I'm proud to have family roots—and three stories—set in this magical place. To learn more about Edisto (and plan your own vacation) check out ExploreEdisto.com.

If you enjoyed this story, might I suggest you'll also enjoy *Magnolia Mistletoe*? This Christmas novella featuring Hannah and Ben is FREE when you sign up for my newsletter.

And what's in that newsletter? It's full of things I only want my subscribers to know—early book news, my favorite monthly reads, and how I really feel about turning 40 and trading my teaching career for a writing one.

If you missed *Still Waters*, my award-winning debut, I hope you'll choose Cora Anne's journey to forgiveness as your next read.

Want to connect in real life or online? Check out my website at lindseypbrackett.com for author events or follow me on Facebook or Instagram: @lindseypbrackett.

Please—tell me what you'll be reading next!

Lindsey